The House by the Cemetery

Also by Lisa Childs

The Bane Island Novels

THE RUNAWAY
THE HUNTED
THE MISSING
THE BURIED

The House by the Cemetery

LISA CHILDS

KENSINGTON
PUBLISHING CORP.
www.kensingtonbooks.com

This book is for the real-life "grave digger" I knew when I was teenager.
He passed away long ago, but he had an impact on my life and my imagination.

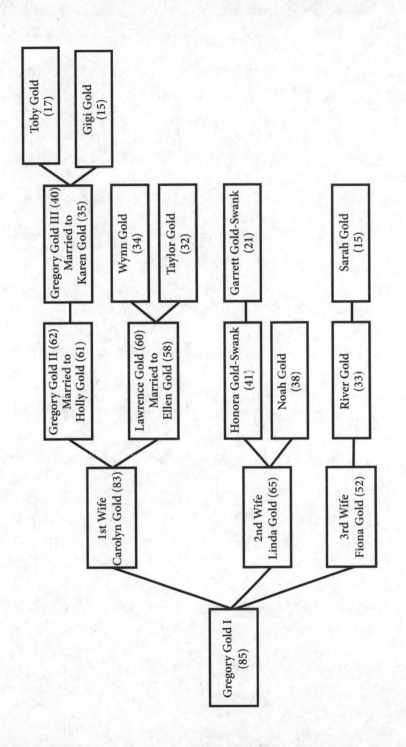

Chapter 1

He was dying. Despite everything Gregory Gold had done to put it off, to look younger and feel younger, to try to defy death, it was coming for him. And he was powerless to stop it. He couldn't move. He was literally frozen like one of the memorial statues in the cemetery outside his bedroom window. He would have suspected he was having a stroke, but there had been no warning. No headache. No blurred vision.

He could clearly see his own image reflecting back at him from the mirror above his vanity. He sat stiffly in front of it next to the open window where the evening breeze teased the curtains. His face was pale but nearly unlined despite his age, and his hair was thick and dark. But he was drooling now, like the old man he'd fought so hard to never become. He tried to close his eyes, to shut out that image, but he couldn't even blink.

He'd been sitting in his private dressing room, studying his reflection for any sign of his age when the paralysis had hit. His arms locked, and he was unable to lift his hands. His feet were stuck to the ground, too heavy for his legs to pry from the carpet. And while his mouth had dropped open slightly, it wasn't lower on one side or the other. He hadn't had a stroke. He just couldn't move. He could barely even draw a breath anymore, his lungs as numb as his body.

But his mind continued to move as nimbly as it always had, and he quickly drew the only possible conclusion. He'd been poisoned. He knew it. And he knew that it had to be one of *them*: one of the people who were supposed to love him or at least respect and maybe even fear him. His family . . . or employees . . . but so many of them were one and the same and had complete access to him.

One of them had to have slipped the poison into something he ate or drank. But he was always so careful, avoiding alcohol, eating only organic foods . . . doing everything he could to stay healthy. To stay vital. To stay relevant.

The irony wasn't lost on him that the man who'd made his fortune off death was afraid of dying. He worked out, ate well, took vitamins, and as he'd aged despite his efforts, he'd even sought medical intervention. Surgery. Botox. Hair plugs. He'd also removed the people from his life who aged him, like his first wife and his second and now . . .

He'd taken every action so that the man staring back at him from the mirror looked young and vital. His body fit, his face perfect despite his slightly open mouth and blank expression. The only thing that moved on him was the look in his dark eyes as it turned to one of terror. Because nothing that he'd spent most of his eighty-five years doing mattered at all.

Maybe it had even caused this . . .

Death.

And through that open window, he glimpsed the wavering light of a lantern moving through the cemetery. Then, moments later, the faint scrape of metal against stone rang out. This was the urban legend that teenagers, after they'd trespassed in Gold Memorial Gardens, had spread around town for more than three decades; they claimed to have seen the ghost of the grave digger. Before the business had had the money to invest in specialized equipment like the small backhoe, a man dug, by hand, most of the graves in the cemetery. Even many years after the machinery had been purchased and the business had flourished, the man had insisted on continuing to dig the graves by hand, making them perfect for the caskets that would be lowered into them the next day.

That man, Lyle McGinty, had died more than thirty years ago, but those teenagers swore they saw that lantern light moving through the cemetery at night and that they could hear him digging graves, the blade of his shovel hitting rocks and stones.

So when Gregory saw that light and heard that scraping sound, he knew those kids hadn't been lying. And he knew what it meant . . .

The grave digger was digging *his* grave.

"You need to come home."

Ever since River Gold ran away sixteen years ago, her mother told her this every time they spoke either over the phone or on the rare occasions when Fiona Gold had pried herself away from Gold Memorial Gardens and Funeral Services. But River couldn't ignore the statement like she usually did because there was something new in her mother's voice, as it cracked through the cell speaker with an urgency she'd never heard before. Then the tears came. While her mother had pleaded and cajoled in the past, she had never cried like this before.

"Mom! What's wrong?" River asked, her own voice cracking a bit to hear her always optimistic mother so upset. "Are you okay?"

"It's not me," Fiona said. "I'm fine. But your . . ."

"My what?"

Everyone else River cared about was in the house with her. This house was nothing like the one where River had grown up; this one was bright and full of light with white walls and whitewashed floors and even the vaulted wood ceiling was painted white. But that brightness wasn't everywhere. And that was where the other people she loved were. Her daughter was in her room, with its black walls, probably brooding over something, and her grandmother was in her room, with its burgundy walls, probably brooding over something. Neither of them was anything like River's mother, who was always upbeat and happy even when she shouldn't be.

Until now . . .

"Mom," River prompted Fiona, "tell me what's going on." *And stop crying.* The sobs were making River's eyes tear up and had a heaviness weighing on her heart. "Please . . ."

"Your father." Fiona finally got out the words like she was gasping them between sobs. "He's dead, my darling. I'm so sorry . . ."

"My father . . ." River whispered. She had never been certain who her father was, but she knew the man her mother claimed was her father. Gregory Gold I. She'd just never felt any particular emotional connection with him even though, for the first seventeen years of her life, she and her mother had lived with him in his house by the cemetery. But once River ran away she'd vowed to never go back to that creepy place.

Gold Memorial Gardens and Funeral Services, specifically its first location in Gold Creek, Michigan, a wealthy enclave of vast estates just minutes from the Lake Michigan shoreline, was where River had grown up. But there was no view of the crystal-blue lake or the sandy shore and dunes at that huge mausoleum of a "home." The brick and stone building had parlors, showing rooms, and offices on the main level, its living quarters on the second and third floors, and, in the basement, the embalming rooms and crematorium. And the only view, if the heavy drapes were pulled open over the many windows, was of the memorial "gardens" that surrounded it. While there were flowers and trees, there were also all those headstones and monuments and statues, mausoleums and fountains. The cemetery wasn't a garden any more than the funeral parlor was a home. It was a house of death.

But the one person River had never expected to die was Gregory Gold I. In the seventeen years she had lived with him, he'd almost seemed to be aging in reverse like he'd made some pact to retain his youth. She suspected he'd traded his soul and his personality in exchange for looking a little younger.

But still . . .

He was gone. While she didn't necessarily feel a sense of loss, a pang of sadness struck her. River had never been close to the man, but he had given her both her names. His last and even her first. When he'd brought his pregnant bride home to Gold Creek, Fiona had made a comment about how the creek was so wide and deep with rushing currents that it should have been called a river instead. And he'd said that was what they should call their daughter. Or at least that was the story that Fiona told whenever someone had asked about her daughter's unusual first name.

"I'm sorry, Mom," she said.

Fiona Gold had been totally devoted to her much older husband and not for the reason his ex-wives and other family had claimed. She hadn't cared a bit about his money. He'd offered her something else she'd wanted so much more: security. And not through his money but through the career of her own she'd developed with his guidance. Even though Fiona probably didn't need him anymore, she stayed with him out of devotion and gratitude as well.

"I don't know when the funeral is going to be . . ." Fiona muttered, and she sounded flustered and confused. "I don't know what's going on . . ."

"You're his wife," River said. "You're the one who should be planning his funeral."

But she could imagine the others taking over, pushing Fiona aside now that Gregory Gold I wasn't there to protect her. But River would; she had to, her mother wasn't strong enough to deal with the Golds even when she wasn't grieving.

"I'll get on the next plane to Michigan," she promised. "I'll be there for you as soon as I can get there."

"You should be here for *him*," Fiona said, her voice cracking with her grief. "He was your father."

That wasn't what anyone else had believed, probably not even him, although he'd been too proud to ever admit that anyone could or would try to trick him. River felt a pang of guilt for doubting her mother because she knew all too well how painful it was to have one's integrity questioned. Which was another reason she'd vowed to never return to Gold Creek, Michigan, where that original location of Gold Memorial Gardens and Funeral Services was located. There were franchises all over, probably one in every state by now. Gregory Gold I had expanded his family's original one-location business into a vast empire of death, and now, with his death, that empire would be up for grabs.

River suspected that all of them were probably fighting over it already, fighting to keep it away from her mother especially. They wouldn't want her to inherit anything. River didn't care about the money herself and she cared even less about the morbid business.

But she cared a lot about her mother. She didn't want her to get hurt.

Knowing how vicious his family could be meant that going back to Gold Creek and to that horrible house by the cemetery was going to be dangerous. For many reasons . . .

What had she done?

Fiona clicked off her cell and dropped it onto the bed next to her, atop all the crumpled, damp tissues.

River was really coming home. That was a good thing. Maybe...

No. That was a good thing. The child never should have left, especially not the way and for the reason that she had. Every day she'd been gone, Fiona had missed her, had felt this empty ache inside her. She pressed her hand against her heart, which pounded so hard inside her chest that she could feel it on the outside of the robe she wore over her nightgown.

No. It was good that her daughter was coming home. But Fiona couldn't help but fear that with River's return, the truth would come out.

Chapter 2

The house by the cemetery . . .

Everyone had been calling the Golds' home that for years, probably long before Sheriff Luke Sebastian was even born. But that brick and stone mausoleum was much more than a house. Right now it was possibly a crime scene.

At least that was why Luke was presently driving through the ornate wrought iron gates . . . because he'd been called here in his official capacity as the newly elected sheriff of Gold Creek. Surprisingly, despite all the years he'd been gone, he'd drawn a lot of support from the locals, including the Golds, during the election. But that was probably more because Luke's father was a popular albeit retired Gold Creek minister than because of anything to do with him personally. Despite that support, Luke was still a little stunned he'd won and even more stunned he'd actually run for the position. Hell, he was stunned he'd even returned to Gold Creek.

But after everything that had happened . . .

Gold Creek had seemed like the safest place to be, and Luke

had run for sheriff so that he could keep it that way. But if the dispatcher was right, and someone had been murdered . . .

Then Luke had been wrong. And he'd failed.

Again.

He pulled his SUV into one of the open parking spots in the large lot at the side of the house. On the other side of the house stretched the "gardens" with all the memorial statues and head-stones. When he pushed open the driver's door and stepped out, he could hear the gurgle of water from one of the foun-tains. Like a golf course, the grass was lush and green, shaded by the trees that towered over the lawn. While some of the trees were as green as the grass, with moss hanging from the limbs, other trees had leaves that had begun to turn into colors nearly as vibrant as some of the yellow, orange, and red flowers planted in beds and around the headstones.

As beautiful as the place was, revulsion gripped Luke, but that wasn't just because of the cemetery. Death wasn't the only loss this place represented for him.

He lifted one hand, which shook a little, to his head to shove his overly long brown hair back. He needed to get it cut. But there was never enough time. Being sheriff wasn't the easy job he'd figured it would be. And coming out here was just one more complication in his already complicated life. He drew in a steadying breath and headed toward the long portico that led to the double front doors at the entry to the "house." Those doors opened onto a large lobby where Dr. Jeffries waited for him.

"Thank God, you're here, Sheriff," the doctor said. The man was in his mid-sixties with white hair and finely lined skin; he probably could have retired years ago but kept working. Maybe he loved what he did; he was obviously devoted to his patients because he was one of the few doctors who still made house calls.

But this was Gold Creek, and a lot of people here had the

kind of money and influence that entitled them to special treat-
ment. Or so they thought.

While some of them were insufferable, nobody else acted as
entitled as the Gold family. That was probably because the
damn town had been named after them, which was one reason
why Luke hadn't intended to ever move back after he'd left for
boot camp.

But circumstances had changed.

"So you actually think there's been a murder here?" Luke
asked for clarification. The dispatcher had been breathless with
excitement when she'd called him, so breathless that she'd been
a little hard to understand.

Dr. Jeffries grabbed his arm and tugged him back outside. In
a whisper, he said, "Gregory told me if anything happened to
him that it would probably be murder."

Luke hadn't had to be back long for the gossips to confirm
to him that Gregory Gold I hadn't changed; the old man still
believed he could live forever. Apparently, he'd been proven
wrong. But that didn't mean that he hadn't died of natural
causes.

"You want there to be an autopsy?" Luke asked.

The older man nodded. "Gregory insisted that I make sure
one was performed on him."

Luke nodded. "Well then, we'll make sure that there is one.
Unless . . ." There was a crematorium on-site, in the basement.
"They haven't already disposed of his body, have they?"

The doctor shook his head. "No. They waited for me to sign
the death certificate."

"And then what did they do?"

"I haven't signed it yet," he replied. "And I won't until I
know what he died from."

"You really don't believe old age?" Luke wondered aloud.
The guy had to be in his eighties.

Dr. Jeffries shook his head again. "I don't think that's the case."

Moments later when Luke stepped into the old man's dressing room, he had to agree. Sitting stiffly upright in the chair, Gregory Gold I didn't look old. With his eyes wide open and staring back at Luke from that mirror, he didn't even look dead. But he did look scared.

Luke understood that feeling all too well. There had been so many times he'd thought he was going to die. But he'd survived. Gregory Gold hadn't. Had he been murdered, though?

"There are no obvious signs of trauma," Luke pointed out. No blood. No bruises, though there were jars of cream and something that looked like theatrical makeup on the vanity table in front of him. Had that been used to cover up something besides wrinkles and age spots?

"No, I didn't see any obvious injuries," the doctor agreed, his voice a low whisper. He stood behind Luke in the doorway as if he was reluctant to enter.

The doctor had probably already entered the room earlier, to confirm that his patient was dead, so it wasn't as if he was disrupting the crime scene now. Hell, a lot of people had probably been in and out of this dressing room checking on Gregory I, so the scene was already contaminated. If this was a crime, it was going to be a tough one to solve, especially for Luke.

As an MP, military police in the Marine Corps, he had experience in law enforcement but that hadn't included premeditated murders despite the explosions and gunfire. None of the dead he'd seen had been personally targeted; it was just because of their uniforms that someone had killed them. Or they'd died in tragic accidents. Or random acts of violence.

This hadn't been random or an accident. If someone had murdered Gregory Gold I, it had damn well been intentional. When Luke glanced down and noticed the syringe inside the wastebasket next to the dressing table, he couldn't help but wonder if that was the weapon of choice.

He knew better than to touch it. He needed the crime scene techs to photograph the scene and collect evidence of whatever happened here.

"Was your patient on a lot of medications?" Luke asked. In addition to the creams, there were prescription bottles and a few vials of something and packets of different colored pills that were probably vitamins.

The doctor sighed. "Let's just say that Gregory would do anything or take anything to retain his youth and his vitality."

"So could he have accidentally overdosed?" Luke asked.

The doctor shook his head. "No. He knew what he was doing and exactly how much to take without consequences. In fact, that was why he preferred to administer it himself because he was the only person he truly trusted. I think that he probably knew what he was talking about as well . . ."

"When he told you that if he died, to make sure it wasn't a murder?" Luke asked.

Dr. Jeffries glanced around again, too, but through the open door to the hall as if making sure that they were really alone. Then he whispered, "Gregory said that if he was murdered, one of his ungrateful family members did it."

Where was all that family now?

"She's my daughter, so I need to be here for her," Mabel Hawthorne insisted. "Just like you need to be here for her."

Except Fiona hadn't asked River to bring her mother to Gold Creek. And River hadn't wanted to bring her daughter, but with Mabel coming along, she couldn't leave Sarah home alone. She was only fifteen years old. But River had vowed to never bring her daughter to this place. Ever.

But now her grandmother, Mabel Hawthorne, shuffled down

the jetway in front of River while her daughter, Sarah Gold, shuffled along behind her. Mabel's hair was long and silver and flowed around her thin shoulders as she walked stiffly, probably from her arthritic joints stiffening up during the long flight.

River felt a little stiff herself, but that was mostly with tension. With dread.

She pushed her hair back as she turned to look at Sarah again, making sure she was keeping up with them. River's hair was long, too, and dark blond except for the lighter streaks from the sun.

Sarah's hair was a deep, glossy black and cut in a chin-length bob. Sarah was the last one off the plane, but that was less the teenager's fault than Mabel's. Mabel had wanted to wait until everyone else was out of her way; she hadn't wanted to be jostled or shoved.

And Sarah just didn't like being that close to people.

Any people.

What had happened to the cuddly, happy little girl she'd once been? The one who'd preferred River's lap to any other seat in the house and who'd snuck into River's bed every night.

Teenage hormones must have happened.

But, thankfully, they weren't the kind of teenage hormones River had had, the ones to blame for her becoming a mother at seventeen. Right now Sarah just had the moody, surly, snarky kind of hormones. And that snarkiness was only if she deigned to speak at all. And usually she didn't . . . unless she was prodded into it with threats of losing electronics.

Surprisingly, River hadn't had to threaten her at all to get her packed and on the airplane with them. And she'd been so certain that Sarah would insist on staying home, swearing that she would be fine on her own. She probably would have been; even at fifteen, she didn't seem to need anyone. Certainly not River.

She didn't seem to need or want any friends, either. At least not friends her own age. Her only friend was probably Mabel.

River could relate to that; sometimes she felt that *her* only real friend was her grandmother. And she wondered if Mabel had insisted on coming along for Fiona or for River.

Grandma had kept watching her on the plane, like she expected her to break down sobbing at any moment. But River had yet to shed a tear over Gregory Gold's death, and she probably wouldn't.

At least she hadn't done what her grandmother had when she'd told her: cackled with glee.

"Are you here for Mom?" River asked. "Or are you here to dance on his grave?"

Mabel chuckled. "I might have packed my tap shoes . . ."

River pressed her lips together to keep them from curving up into a smile. If she showed her grandmother any encouragement, Mabel was likely to bust out some dance moves at the service. Though that would be fun to watch, it would upset Fiona. River really shouldn't have let her grandmother come along; even if Mabel didn't dance, her presence was bound to upset her only child.

River was Fiona's only child and Sarah was hers. Unfortunately, her relationship with Sarah had begun to mirror her mother and grandmother's relationship in that they couldn't seem to understand each other anymore. Like they spoke different languages, cared about different things, or maybe didn't care at all.

She glanced back over her shoulder at Sarah who, for once, wasn't preoccupied with her cell but was watching them. Was she worried that River was going to break down, too? But she didn't seem concerned, just curious. And maybe that was why she hadn't fought coming along; she was curious about the place her mother hated so much.

About the people, too.

She hadn't hated the people, though. The people had hated her. The kids in school had taunted her for being one of the "Ghoul" family and had mercilessly bullied her except for one person. But probably the people who'd hated her the most were the ones who were supposed to be family. They'd insisted that she wasn't one of them, that her mother, whom they'd called a gold digger, had passed off another man's child as his in order to trap Gregory Gold I into marriage.

A knot tightened in her stomach with the realization that she should have prepared Sarah better for this experience. That she should have warned her even before they landed in Grand Rapids. There was only a private airport in Gold Creek, so they would have to rent a vehicle for the trip to the house of death. So at least she had time on the drive to warn Sarah about how she might be treated, just like River had once been treated. Badly.

She suspected Sarah had already suffered some bullying herself and that was why she'd chosen to keep schooling online even post-pandemic when schools returned to in-person instruction. Even though Sarah hadn't admitted to the bullying, probably because she hadn't wanted River to get involved, River had approved the homeschooling. It was better than dealing with it like River had, by running away. If only homeschooling had been an option for River when she was in school . . .

But she'd had a protector . . . for a while. There had been just one person he hadn't been able to protect her from.

"Remember that I checked my bag," Mabel said over her shoulder as she headed through the terminal now.

"Of course I remember . . ." River had wanted carry-ons only because she'd wanted to just fly in for the funeral and fly back out again with her mother with them. She had no intention of leaving Fiona alone in the house of death with the ghouls and gargoyles that were that family. But her grandmother had insisted on having more outfit options; she'd probably packed a party dress with her tap shoes.

Maybe River would accidentally open that suitcase when she grabbed it from the luggage carousel. She didn't need to check Sarah's carry-on, though. Her daughter only ever wore black, so she was already dressed for the funeral in her black leggings and long black sweater.

River didn't even own anything black, so she would have to borrow something from her mother and hope it was loose-fitting enough for her to squeeze into it. Or maybe, depending on when the funeral was, she would have some time to go shopping for something appropriate for her and maybe for Mabel, too.

She looked at the monitors above each carousel until she found the one for their flight from LAX, which had been just a short drive from their home in Santa Monica. Should she wait for the luggage to arrive or get in line for a rental car? The lines were already beginning to form. As she studied one of them, trying to determine which was the shortest, a man stepped into her field of vision. And she nearly screamed in shock.

He was supposed to be dead. What the hell was Gregory Gold I doing here?

Had her mother lied? Was this all some sick joke to get her back to Gold Creek? But then she realized that Gregory Gold would never have put himself out like this, driving to Grand Rapids to pick her up from an airport. He would have thought that was beneath him. Just like he'd thought everyone and everything but making money was beneath him.

No. This wasn't a dead man but one of his sons or grandsons who looked eerily like him. So eerie that when Mabel followed her gaze she didn't hold in her scream but released it at a volume that had everyone staring at them with the same shock River felt. Clearly, her grandmother thought she was staring at a dead man.

*   *   *

If they'd been back in Santa Monica, Sarah would have wanted to crawl into a hole and hide with everyone staring at them. But here . . . she didn't care. Nobody knew her here.

That was why she hadn't fought her mother about coming along for the funeral. For one, she'd never gone to a funeral before, and she was curious, and for another she'd never met any of these people that Mom refused to talk about even when Grandma Fiona came to visit.

Whatever her mother had left behind in Gold Creek she hadn't wanted to ever see again. But here they were . . .

Mom's face had drained of all color, leaving her pale and shaky, while GG Mabel was flushed with her mouth hanging open as that bloodcurdling scream she'd just let rip still echoed around the baggage claim area. If life were a graphic novel, there would have been a big bubble hanging over all of them with that scream trapped inside it. Sometimes Sarah wished life were a graphic novel, one with no colors, that was only grayscale. But she knew life wasn't like that; it was much more black than white.

Her mom saw everything exactly the opposite. She found the good in everyone, even the homeless guy GG Mabel had caught rummaging through their trash a few weeks ago. Instead of being offended at what could have been an attempted identity theft or at least an invasion of privacy, like GG thought, Mom made the guy a sandwich. But she didn't see things just as white, though. River wanted all the colors like the face paint she put on those brides and social media models and high school graduates, trying to make them something that most people really weren't.

Trying to make them beautiful when so many people were just so ugly inside.

But now, with the way Mom was staring at this guy, it was clear that River Gold knew more about ugliness than Sarah had realized. And maybe that was why Mom worked so hard to try to hide it . . . and her past.

River wouldn't be able to hide it now, when they were walking right into it, and maybe Sarah would finally get answers to all the questions she had about her mom, her family, and Sarah's own dad.

Chapter 3

River's heart was beating fast and hard. But this wasn't the ghost of Gregory Gold I greeting them at the airport. While this man had the same black hair and dark eyes and the sharp, almost hawklike features as the one who her mother claimed was her father, it couldn't be . . .

"River, you haven't changed a bit," he said.

His voice even sounded like his, and that sounded like something Gregory Gold I would have said, praising her for retaining her youth. That was what had mattered most to him. More even than his beloved business and his not so beloved family.

"You look so much like your mother," this man told River.

"And you look like the devil," Mabel remarked.

He chuckled. "I guess I do look like my namesake, even more than my father does. I'm Gregory Gold the third," he said, and he held out his hand to Mabel. "You must be Mrs. Hawthorne?"

"Yes," she said with a sniff. But she ignored his outstretched hand.

His smile slipped a bit and he turned his attention to Sarah, who'd walked up on the other side of Mabel, with her great-grandmother's bag in her hand. His breath escaped in a slight gasp, and he looked as if he'd seen a ghost, probably like how River and her grandmother had looked when they'd seen him. "She looks like a Gold," he murmured as if he was surprised.

River had no doubt why he was shocked—because he hadn't believed that River was a Gold.

"I am Sarah Gold," the teenager introduced herself, and she dropped Mabel's bag to shake his hand. "Are you my uncle?"

Gregory chuckled. "I'm not your mom's brother. I'm her nephew. So you and I are cousins, Sarah, even though my son Toby is older than you are. My daughter, Gigi, is about your age, and man . . ." He expelled a shaky sigh. ". . . you two could be twins."

Sarah tensed and pulled her hand away. She probably would have preferred that all her cousins were Gregory III's age. She didn't have much interest in kids her own age. Maybe that was River's fault for not giving her any other sibling besides Mabel. Mabel, even though she was seventy-three, was more like River's child than her grandmother. River's mother was also more like her child than her parent. They probably both needed her more than Sarah did.

Fiona definitely needed her now, even more than River had originally thought she would. Because there was some reason Gregory III had shown up at the airport . . .

"Is this just a coincidence that you're here?" she asked even though she was well aware that it wasn't. Even if Gregory had just arrived from one of the many other Gold Memorial Gardens and Funeral Services locations, he would have used the company jet and flown into the private airport in Gold Creek. But she wasn't good with confrontation, especially not with the Golds, or she would have already asked what the hell he was doing here.

Gregory grinned. "No. The minute your mother mentioned

to my father that you were on your way, he asked me to pick you up."

"And dump us off somewhere far away so we can't make our way back like an unwanted animal?" Mabel asked. She had no problem with confrontation. Verbal or physical.

River had to pull her off the man they'd caught in their garbage cans a few weeks back. She wasn't even sure why Mabel had gotten so possessive and upset. They wouldn't have thrown something out if they'd needed it anymore. But that poor man had . . .

Gregory chuckled again, but it sounded a little strained now. Mabel was probably wearing on his nerves. But he couldn't deny how often he and his family had made River feel like the unwanted animal her grandmother had just described.

"Of course I'm bringing you all home," he said.

River would have preferred the place Mabel had described, the one too far away for her to find her way back from; she'd thought Santa Monica was that place. Until her mother had called just hours ago.

"I'm so sorry about . . . your grandfather," River said with a jab of guilt that she hadn't offered her condolences yet.

He closed his eyes for a moment, but she doubted it was to hold back tears. He nodded and sighed. When he opened his eyes again, he looked immediately at Sarah before turning back to her. "I'm sorry, too, River. He was your father . . ." And he said it like he believed it.

River didn't. Or maybe she just didn't want to believe it. She didn't want that taunt from school to be true; she didn't want to be one of the "Ghoul" family. Tears rushed to her eyes, but they were self-pitying . . . probably more because of the past than because a man had died. And that jab of guilt struck harder now, making her suck in a breath.

"Mom?" Sarah asked, her voice a little shaky.

River forced a smile for everyone. "Gregory, it really wasn't necessary for you to pick us up," she said. "I planned on renting a vehicle. I really should in case I have to go somewhere while we're here." Somewhere being anywhere but where they were going.

"You don't need to rent one. There are several vehicles that you can use whenever you need," Gregory III assured her.

"A hearse?" Sarah asked, and now her voice rose with excitement.

Gregory chuckled again. "You even sound like Gigi."

Sarah stiffened. In Santa Monica, with her total disregard for social media and popularity, she was an anomaly, and while River had worried that bothered her daughter and was the reason why she'd chosen online schooling, now she wondered if Sarah actually preferred to be a loner.

To be unique.

Just as River should have warned her daughter about the Gold family, she should have also warned her that being unique made someone more of a target than being like others. Not that River ever wanted to be like the rest of the Golds.

She didn't want to be a ghoul in that house by the cemetery. But she had no choice now. She had to stay for the funeral, but once it was over, she wasn't ever coming back.

Was *she* coming back? And if she did, would she be alone? Or . . .

But those weren't questions Sheriff Luke Sebastian could ask in the course of his investigation of . . . whatever happened to Gregory Gold I. Was it a murder or just a natural death?

That syringe could have been for anything. Dr. Jeffries hadn't specifically listed the old man's meds, but in order to look the way he did at his age, it was probably a long list. The crime scene unit was going over the room now, photographing and collecting everything pertinent, like that syringe.

While Luke should have been focused on the old man's

death, his mind kept wandering to her, wondering if she was coming back. And would she be alone? And where they lived. What they did . . .

He wanted to ask those questions, though, so very badly of anyone who would answer him. It had been too long . . .

And so much had happened since . . . to him. He'd been gone for a very long time before he'd come back to the States. He'd spent his military career signing up for tour after tour with the intention of staying in the service until he was entitled to full retirement as a colonel or a general.

But life . . . and deaths . . . had had other plans for him and for Jackson, too. The result of one of those plans was the move to Luke's hometown or at least the home where he'd spent most of his childhood. He'd once felt safe here, and he'd wanted Jackson to feel safe, too.

In town at least. But here at Gold Memorial Gardens and Funeral Services, Luke had never felt safe. This place, and the people, had always creeped him out. He stood now in the doorway to one of the conference rooms on the main floor. With boxes of tissues on every available surface along with cof-fee table–sized books of caskets and flowers, this must have been one of the rooms where survivors came to plan their de-ceased loved ones' funerals.

But of the people gathered around that table, nobody was reaching for a tissue or flipping through any of those books. They hadn't gathered here to mourn or plan a celebration of life for Gregory Gold I. They'd gathered here because Luke had one of his deputies knock on every door and bring every person in the house to this room, to him, just as he'd had Greg-ory Gold I's body brought to the morgue for that autopsy the family patriarch had wanted to have.

The deputy had rounded up all the family and the staff on the premises. Most of the staff were family members, though. Some of them were actually ex-family members like Gregory

Gold I's first and second wives. While the first wife was retired, she still had a room in one of the wings of the house in the same way that the second wife also had a room, and even the third and current wife had a room of her own. She hadn't shared the primary suite with her husband. Luke had figured that out by finding only men's clothes and toiletries in the dressing room and bathroom. There had been no indication that anyone else had been in the room with the man when he'd died; at least there had been no signs of a struggle of any kind. So he probably hadn't been a victim of a crime.

But after what Dr. Jeffries had shared with Luke, he couldn't quite shake his own suspicions now. Why would a man say such a thing unless he believed one of his family might kill him?

"I don't understand why you're taking his body," the first wife, Carolyn Gold, remarked. Her voice quavered a bit, but it wasn't with emotion. Her eyes were dry, but her hands shook with an obvious tremor. Parkinson's? As Gregory Gold's first wife, she was probably close to his age, but unlike him, she showed it with her white hair and heavily lined face.

"We need to determine the cause of death," Luke replied.

The woman pointed one of her shaking hands at Dr. Jeffries, who stood next to him. "That's why he was called here. He knows Gregory's health better than anyone, so he knows what caused his death. Old age, no matter how much Gregory wanted to deny that he was old."

Jeffries shook his head, but he kept his lips tightly pressed together. Obviously, he didn't want to share his or his former patient's suspicion with the rest of the family. That Gregory thought if he'd died one of them had murdered him.

Luke shook his head, too. "We need to perform an autopsy to determine the cause of death."

"But . . . but we have a funeral to plan," the third Mrs. Gold remarked. The blond-haired woman was the only one in the room whose eyes were red and swollen. The only one visibly affected by his death. But why? Because she loved him or she felt guilty . . .

Or . . .

She was the only member of the Gold family Luke had talked to after he'd left Gold Creek. But she'd never told him what he'd wanted to hear. So he didn't mind telling her the same. "We have to do a thorough investigation," he said. "Once the autopsy is concluded, you can have a funeral. But until then, we are taking his body and sealing off his suite of rooms."

"We'll need one of his suits for his funeral," she said, as if hyper-focused on that ceremony.

But then they were all hyper-focused on funerals; that was their business. The dead.

"He has them tailor-made especially for him," she said, her voice rising a bit. "He wouldn't be caught de—" She interrupted herself with a gasp and a widening of her blue eyes.

One of the sons chuckled. Must have been the older one because his hair was already white like the woman who was probably his mother since he looked older than the second and third wives. His father must have dyed his hair because there hadn't been a single strand of gray on the corpse's head. The glossy black hair hadn't looked entirely real either, though. Plugs or a toupee that had been custom-made like his suits?

An autopsy would probably determine that, too. Not that it mattered. All that really mattered was what or who had caused his death.

And if it was one of the people in this room . . .

He glanced around the room again, looking at each of them. The first Mrs. Gold and then her son. As the eldest would he inherit everything? Wasn't that how some wealthy families handled their estates? Everything to the oldest? Wasn't that how Gregory Gold I had taken over the family business when his father died?

Gregory had more than one son. Lawrence Gold sat on the other side of his mother with his wife and his kids next to him. His kids, Wynn and Taylor, were in their thirties like Luke. Since they were alone, maybe they were also still single like Luke.

On the other side of Gregory Gold II from his mother sat his wife. The red-haired woman stared down at the table instead of meeting his or anyone else's gaze. She was probably older than the third Mrs. Gold and maybe even the second, who sat farther down the table sandwiched between both of her kids, a daughter named Honora, who was in her early forties, and Noah Gold, who was Gregory Gold I's third and youngest son but not his youngest child. Both Honora and Noah worked at Gold Memorial Gardens and Funeral Services, too.

Luke knew Noah from school. While he looked like the rest of the biological Golds with his black hair and dark eyes and worked at the family business, he wasn't quite as odd as the rest of them. He was more the outdoorsy type, which was probably why he was in charge of the gardens. Noah and Luke had gone fishing together in the past and even once since Luke's return.

Unlike Fiona Gold, who hadn't given him the answers he'd wanted, Noah hadn't been able to answer anything at all. He didn't know anything about his half-sibling. As far as he'd known, her mother was the only one she kept in touch with.

So she probably wasn't coming back.

"River!" Fiona jumped up from her chair and stared . . . at Luke.

But then he realized she was looking beyond him, and he turned. And there she was standing just behind him in the hallway.

River Gold. Finally one of his questions was answered. Would she come back for the funeral?

Yes. She was here.

But was she alone?

And he looked beyond her, down the hall toward the lobby, and he could see two other people standing near one of his deputies. A silver-haired lady and someone with dark hair and a thin build.

"River!" Fiona exclaimed again as she ran toward the doorway. She shoved Luke partly aside, and then she started screaming hysterically.

"Mom . . ." River closed her arms around her mother, holding her as the woman continued to scream while tears streaked down her face and her body nearly convulsed. "Mom, shh, it's all going to be all right. I'm here."

The two women looked so much alike with the blond hair and delicate features and petite builds. But one was so calm while the other was a mess.

Dr. Jeffries stepped forward and awkwardly patted Fiona's shoulder. "Mrs. Gold, let me give you a sedative—"

"No!" she screamed at him along with all the other incoherent sobs. Then she sucked in a breath and added, "I just need my daughter." And she moved with River farther into the hall.

"I need to conclude my interviews," Luke said in protest.

"Interviews?" River asked the question.

"Luke Sebastian is the sheriff," another man answered her, a man who looked alarmingly like the one the coroner had just taken off to the morgue. Obviously another Gold.

Then that skinny, dark-haired figure rushed down the hall from the lobby. The teenage girl had glossy black hair and pale skin like the Golds. She was a Gold. But as well as some of her mother's delicate features, she had a dimple in her chin and her eyes were deep set like . . .

Was she also . . . a Sebastian?

The aftermath of the murder was all playing out so strangely like the actors of a play had gone off script and were just madly improvising. This wasn't at all like the plan. But the person who'd caused Gregory Gold I's death slipped away to their mind while watching all the drama unfold.

Helping get Luke Sebastian elected as the new sheriff had been a strategic move for a few reasons. One. Sebastian wasn't like the other candidates who all had had degrees in criminology and investigation along with some extensive experience.

While Sebastian, as military police, was used to keeping the peace, he didn't know anything about murder. Let alone how to conduct an investigation of one.

But Sebastian was insisting on an autopsy, so he must have had some idea that something else had happened here. Or maybe that was all Dr. Jeffries. His patient had undoubtedly shared his belief with his longtime physician, who was also one of his few friends, that he could live forever.

He might have, too, if not for the person who'd killed him . . . because they hadn't been willing to take the chance that Gregory Gold I was right. And he might live forever.

He had already lived too long as it was. And if he hadn't been killed when he had, he might have done something that couldn't be undone. So he'd been undone first.

Soon enough, after the autopsy, the sheriff would have confirmation of the suspicion, or perhaps the tip, that he'd had . . . that Gregory Gold I had been murdered.

Chapter 4

River's heart was racing faster than it had been from seeing Gregory III in the airport and thinking he was a dead man. Luke Sebastian wasn't supposed to be dead, or at least not that she'd heard.

But she had certainly never expected or wanted to see him again. But she should have known that coming back here, to Gold Creek, was going to lead to many unwelcome and unexpected confrontations.

Thanks to her mother's histrionics, she had a reason to get Fiona out of there, upstairs to her suite, to calm her down if that was possible. While she was with her mom, her arms wrapped around her trembling body, she'd sent Mabel and Sarah off to get her mother some tea or soda water so she could take the sedatives Dr. Jeffries had given her. While Fiona had claimed she didn't need them, River had taken the prescription bottle from the doctor; he must have had the pills with him because he had suspected how Fiona would handle her husband's dying, how hysterical she would be.

Yet with each step they ascended of the stairwell, her mother's sobs grew a little softer. And when they started down the hall of the second floor, Fiona stopped crying entirely.

Had she been faking?

While she hated to see her mother upset, River was grateful that in that moment—when Luke Sebastian turned toward her—her mother had lost it. Because Fiona had given River the chance to escape without having to say anything to *him*. To answer any of his questions . . .

Because how could she? She knew less about the death than anyone else. She wasn't even sure the dead man had been her father. While she knew who Sarah's father was, she had no idea where he was or what he was doing. Not that she wanted to know. She didn't want to talk to him or his brother again, let alone *about* them.

But once she closed the door to her mother's suite, she said, "You didn't tell me he had moved back." If she'd known she wouldn't have come . . .

And her mother probably knew that and that was why she hadn't told her.

But Fiona blinked eyes that were surprisingly clear now and replied, "Who? Gregory the second or third? While they manage other branches of the business, this is the headquarters, so they're here a lot, probably trying to make sure that Honora doesn't get her wish and somehow become her father's favorite."

River couldn't think about the family right now and how they always jockeyed for their father's favor. Maybe that was why they'd made it so clear to her that she wasn't family, so that she wouldn't enter their sad competition. The only person she'd ever competed against had been Luke, and she'd lost.

"I'm talking about Luke Sebastian and you absolutely know that," River said.

Fiona shrugged her thin shoulders. "No. You never talk about any of them, any of that . . ."

Because River didn't like how it made her feel, like she was feeling now, like she was about to throw up. She drew in a deep breath through her nostrils, so she didn't vomit. Then she murmured, "I wonder where I get that from . . ." Her avoidance of anything unpleasant, of any confrontation.

Even now, after all the drama downstairs, her mother was acting as if nothing had happened, as if she hadn't just had a meltdown. But because she had, River had to push aside her own concerns and focus on her mother. Just in case she hadn't faked that whole scene down there. And if she had, why would she have done it?

It must have been real. And that concerned River. "Are you okay?" she asked.

Despite everything, or maybe because of it, River believed that her mother truly had loved her husband.

Fiona's shoulders moved in a slight shrug as if her feelings didn't matter. "It's all so unreal . . ."

It certainly was. Gregory Gold I dying and Luke Sebastian showing up here . . . as the sheriff. She'd seen the sheriff department vehicles in the lot when Gregory III drove them up to the house. But . . .

"Is Luke Sebastian really investigating this . . . death . . . like it's a crime?" River asked. Hadn't the man done enough damage?

Fiona's shoulders lifted and fell again, and River could see now how bony they were, how thin her mother was. How there were such dark circles beneath her red and swollen eyes.

Those dark circles weren't from waking up early to find her husband dead. Those were from not sleeping at all for more than one night.

River couldn't remember ever sleeping all that well when she lived in this house. Too many times she'd woken up, looked out the window, and saw something . . .

A light.

Just a light.

It could have been anything. But she knew what everyone else thought it was: the grave digger's lantern.

And that sound she'd heard so often . . .

His shovel.

She hadn't believed that nonsense any more than she'd believed she was a "Ghoul" until that last night she'd spent in Gold Creek. Then it hadn't been just a glimpse out her bedroom window.

That last night she'd been in the cemetery . . .

Waiting . . .

For someone who had never showed.

But someone, or *something*, else had.

She shivered and shook her head, shaking that memory away. Maybe she'd dreamt that whole thing.

But she hadn't really slept well until she'd left here. So she'd probably had dark circles like her mother had now. But her mother had never had any trouble sleeping.

Any of the times that River had crept into her room for comfort, Fiona had been soundly asleep. So if the dark circles weren't because she was suddenly having trouble sleeping now, they could have been because Fiona Gold wasn't well.

"Mom, are you okay?" River asked again, concern making her heart rate quicken again.

"I don't know how I am, or even who I am without him," Fiona whispered. "I don't know what to do anymore . . ."

River stepped away from the door and pulled her mother into her arms like she had in the hallway outside the conference room downstairs. "It's okay," she said. "It's all going to be all right." Once she got her mother the hell out of Gold Creek.

But first they had to get through the funeral and whatever crazy investigation Sheriff Luke Sebastian thought he had to conduct. Was he doing that just because it was his job or did he still have the problem with her that he'd had when she was a teenager?

And would she still have the problems in Gold Creek that she'd had when she was a teenager?

Would she see and hear things she didn't want to? And would she be just as impatient to run away now, like she'd been back then, before it was too late? Before the grave digger came for her?

"What the hell was that?" the second oldest son of the late Gregory Gold, Lawrence, asked. He'd been quiet until then, like he usually was, and his older brother glanced at him as if surprised, or upset, that he'd spoken.

Luke was glad the man had voiced the question aloud that had been reverberating through Luke's head along with the echo of Fiona Gold's hysterical screams.

The first Mrs. Gold sniffed and shook her head. "She always loves to put on a show."

The guy who'd walked in with them chuckled now. After they'd walked away Luke realized he was the third Gregory Gold. "I think I know where she gets it. Her mother screamed at me in the airport."

Luke nearly shuddered then. Were River and her daughter like the older women in their family? Dramatic and overly emotional. Then what was *his* life like with them?

"Was there anyone else with them at the airport?" Luke asked the youngest Gregory.

He shook his head. "No. Just the three of them."

His father chimed in then. "Fiona actually thought that only River was coming. She seemed calm when she talked to me earlier, like she was looking forward to seeing her daughter."

"Sometimes that's what triggers a reaction like that," Dr. Jeffries remarked from where he stood just inside the doorway. "She was only holding it together until she saw her daughter."

"Or until she had the audience she wanted," the second Mrs. Gold remarked. "She does well playing *poor me.*"

"She looked like she's been crying," Noah said as if defending his stepmother to his mother.

Luke had noticed that, too. The woman hadn't looked well physically or emotionally.

"She's been crying," the second Mrs. Gold remarked, "for a while now. Ever since she got what's coming to her."

"What is that?" Luke asked. "What are you talking about?" This family and their dynamics were hard enough to keep track of without the drama and the obvious undercurrents and now a possible murder.

The woman smiled then, but it was a malicious sort of smile. "Divorce papers. Gregory was dumping her just the way he dumped me for her, for someone younger—"

"Like he did me for you," the first Mrs. Gold coldly interjected. "So you got what you deserved then, Linda. You were no more a victim then than she is now."

But maybe they were all victims of Gregory Gold I. He was the one who'd been married, the one who shouldn't have cheated. And from the rumors Luke had heard, it wasn't just wives that Gregory Gold had betrayed.

Had he gotten what he deserved, too?

And had someone gotten sick of waiting for him to get his and had helped his death along?

Luke was eager now for that autopsy to get done, for the results to come back, almost as eager as he was to talk to River and to meet her daughter. He had even more questions about her and that girl than he had about the old man's death.

Had he been wrong all those years ago when he'd warned his brother that River was like her mother? Everyone believed Fiona had lied when she'd claimed to be pregnant with Gregory Gold I's child. Nobody in her family or in town had accepted that River was really his child.

That was why Luke had been worried that his teenage brother was going to get trapped in a relationship with a woman who couldn't be trusted. But Michael hadn't wanted to hear or heed Luke's advice all those years ago. Or anytime since . . .

That was the last time Luke had talked to his younger brother. Instead of protecting him, which was all he'd been trying to do, from River Gold, Luke had lost Michael to her. And now Gregory Gold I was lost to everyone . . .

Luke needed to focus on him now and finding out what had really happened to him.

Had Fiona had anything to do with her husband's death? If what Linda Gold had claimed was true, that Gregory was divorcing her, she certainly had a motive.

And what had her daughter known about it? While she might have just flown in from wherever she lived now, she still could have been complicit. Or maybe he just wanted to think that so he could believe he'd been right all those years ago when he'd told his brother he was making a big mistake running away with her, with taking on the responsibility of raising a kid that might not even be his when he was still a kid himself. Luke had urged his brother to give them all a better shot in life, that the best thing he could do for this kid, whether or not it was his, was give the baby up to mature people who could responsibly raise her.

But Michael had been determined to run away with River Gold, with leaving and never coming back. And he hadn't.

At least not as far as Luke knew. But except for a short visit here and there, Luke hadn't come back often, either. Not until he'd become Jackson's guardian. Then he'd wanted to bring that kid somewhere safe like Gold Creek had always seemed safe to Luke. And as sheriff, it was his job to keep it that way.

If Gregory Gold I had been murdered, Luke needed to catch his killer right away before anyone else got hurt.

* * *

"This place is so creepy," Sarah said. Even though with its faded floral carpet runner and papered walls, the long hallway wasn't decorated the same, it reminded her of the hotel in *The Shining*. Because of all those closed doors off it. What was behind each one? She wanted to open them up and explore. Not just the second story but the first and the basement.

Even the kitchen where she'd gone with GG Mabel to make tea for Grandma Fiona was creepy. The cabinets were a dark red stain, like the color of drying blood. And there were stainless-steel countertops and appliances and big, deep stainless-steel sinks. It reminded her more of a morgue than a place where someone made food.

But there was a cook in the kitchen, a stern-faced woman who insisted on personally preparing what they needed and bringing it up to Mrs. Fiona. Grandma was up here somewhere, but Sarah couldn't hear her now like she'd heard her earlier, screaming even louder than GG Mabel screamed in the airport.

Sarah's grandmas were always a little overly dramatic, like the girls she knew from school, but the grans had taken it next level here in Gold Creek.

"I know. I hate this place, too," GG Mabel said.

But Sarah didn't hate it. She loved it. And if she'd grown up here, she wouldn't have been like her mom, who hadn't been able to wait to leave and who never came back. She would have been like the rest of the Gold family and Sarah would have never left.

Grandpa Gold was leaving now, though. Because through the window at the end of the hall, Sarah could see the coroner's van pulling away, driving through those open wrought iron gates of the cemetery. Why were they taking him away?

This was the funeral home; the place where the bodies came after people died. And since they were buried somewhere in the cemetery they never left like that coroner's van and some of the sheriff department vehicles that were leaving, too.

And what were all the sheriff vehicles about?

And the sheriff?

He'd looked at her mom so strangely and at her . . .

And Sarah shivered as a chill rushed over her with a frisson of fear . . . but it wasn't of the place, it was of the people.

Chapter 5

River hadn't seen these people in sixteen years, and she didn't want to see them now, all at once. But she couldn't justify staying up in her room, and since her mother was asleep from the sedatives she'd taken, River couldn't even claim that Fiona needed her . . . like she'd done earlier to escape from the sheriff. Actually, she hadn't even had to voice any excuse to Luke Sebastian; Fiona's screaming had made that unnecessary.

River hesitated outside the door to the formal dining room. The last thing she wanted to do was eat right now with the way nerves were filling and churning up her stomach. She shouldn't have been as nervous as she'd always felt around these people. She wasn't a kid anymore, and it wasn't as if it was just her and her mother like it had been all those years ago. Mabel was on one side of her and Sarah was on the other. Usually Sarah, being an introvert, would have been hiding behind her, but she actually stepped forward now to push open the pocket doors wide enough for them to enter.

The conversation, which had sounded like the low buzz of a hornet's nest, ceased the moment Sarah pushed open the doors.

And everyone turned to stare at them. They were all here now; the cook had confirmed that when she'd brought Mom her tea earlier. That all the Golds were expected for dinner.

All of them but one.

Luke Sebastian had had his body taken away earlier. For an autopsy. For what reason?

Despite how hard he'd tried to fight it, Gregory Gold I had gotten old and died. His oldest son even looked like an old man now with his white hair and heavily lined face; he looked older than he probably was. His wife, Holly, with her red hair and pale skin, hadn't aged as much as he had. She'd always been as eager to please her father-in-law as his children had been, and while she hadn't shared his interest in the business, she had shared it in retaining youth. Then there was Gregory III, who had picked them up from the airport. His wife and children hadn't been in the conference room earlier, but they sat around him now, his wife, Karen, on one side and his kids on the other. The teenage boy, Toby, and the dark-haired girl, Gigi. Gigi did look startlingly similar to Sarah.

And Sarah must have seen it, too, because she sucked in a breath. For so long she'd been such a loner and so different from River and Mabel and even from the other kids in their neighborhood and at her former school. Was she happy or disappointed to look like someone else?

There were more Golds. The second son, Lawrence, who looked like a more washed-out version of his father, like a shadow of him, or maybe that was because he always seemed to disappear into the shadows around his dad and older brother. Next to him sat his dark-haired wife and their grown children. Wynn and Taylor were close to River's age, but that was all that was close about them, to her or even to each other. Wynn had never been cruel like the kids from school, but he'd always been focused on his studies. Despite the odds being against it since she was one of the "Ghoul" family, too, Taylor had been one of the popular kids. River had not been anything but a target.

Then there was the old man's second wife, Linda, and her kids. Honora was a decade or so older than River and had never had time for her despite their supposedly being half sisters and the only two daughters of Gregory I. Honora had spent most of her time trying to get their father's attention and his favor, and when she'd failed, she'd spent her time trying to get the attention of any man who would show an interest in her. She'd been married and divorced at least three times. River wasn't even sure who the father of her son was. The boy was probably in his twenties now and sat next to Honora. And on the other side of her son was her full brother, Noah.

Noah was in his late-thirties, like Luke Sebastian probably was now. While Wynn had been focused on his studies and Honora on their father and on boys, Noah had been focused on the outdoors, spending as much time in it as possible.

River would have preferred the outdoors, too, if it hadn't been a cemetery. She'd actually felt safer in the house than she had out there . . . where the grave digger, several decades after his death, was rumored to still walk the grounds, swinging his shovel, holding his lantern . . . looking for the next person to dig that grave for . . .

He had a grave to dig now. For Gregory Gold I.

Of course, that wasn't his job anymore. According to her mother, Noah was now in charge of the memorial gardens. And for years they had specialized equipment that dug the graves. But she didn't want to think about his death. She still couldn't believe that he was dead, that he hadn't gotten his way this time like he had in the past. Like all his wives, ex and current, living under the same roof. While he'd had no problem moving on from one relationship to the next, he hadn't wanted any of his exes to move on or move out. And so they were still all awkwardly and dysfunctionally living together and now they were all staring at her.

"Uh, hello," she said. Then she drew in a deep breath. They weren't going to intimidate or scare her anymore. She wasn't a child now. She was a woman with a child of her own to protect. "This is my daughter, Sarah, and my grandmother, Mabel Hawthorne."

"I've met most of them, years ago," Mabel remarked, disgust in her voice.

Nobody had been pleased when her daughter married the much older Gregory Gold I. Probably Mabel least of all. She'd thought her beautiful daughter could do better like Mabel had done better when she'd married a movie star. Unfortunately, he'd died young, broke, and of a drug overdose. And Mabel had had to go back to doing the makeup of the stars to support her young daughter. That was probably why Fiona had been so determined to marry for security above all else because she'd never really had it before Gregory.

Out of respect for that and for her mother and for him, River didn't want this experience to be unpleasant, especially not for her daughter, who was meeting these people for the first time.

"Sarah doesn't know much about . . . the family . . . or this place," she said, hoping to appeal to their better natures, so that they wouldn't be as cruel to her child as they'd once been to her.

But they all just stared at Sarah, like Gregory III had stared at the teenager when they'd met in the airport. And maybe her black hair and dark eyes had them all accepting Sarah as a Gold because some of them, like Noah and Wynn and Taylor, smiled and greeted her warmly.

"It's nice to meet you, Sarah," Noah said. "I saw you earlier but just for a moment . . ." But he looked from her to Gregory III's daughter and back.

"I told you," Gregory III said to his wife, Karen. "She looks so much like our Gigi."

Gigi smiled. "All Golds look alike . . . well, except for . . ." Then she glanced at River, and color rushed to her pale face. "Sorry . . ."

River definitely looked like her mother and not a Gold, which hadn't helped her mother's credibility. Sarah looked like a Gold, but she also looked like her father. But not many of the Golds had actually met Michael Sebastian. So they didn't know how dark his hair had been nor how dark his eyes.

He hadn't looked much like his older brother, who had lighter brown hair and green eyes. But then she wasn't sure they were actually related since they were both foster kids of Pastor Sebastian and his wife, Mary. They had certainly been nothing alike in personality. Or so River had thought until Michael had let her down just like everyone else.

"Please, take your seats," Gregory Gold II said from the seat he had taken at the head of the table, the seat that had been his father's. "Dinner will be starting soon."

Three open chairs had been left for them. One next to Gigi, but Sarah claimed the one next to Noah, Mabel took the one in the middle, leaving River to sit next to the girl. Gigi did look eerily like her daughter, with that same blunt bob of a haircut with overly long bangs that fell into her dark eyes. And River found her heart warming toward her, especially when Gigi smiled shyly at River and said, "You're lucky you don't look like the rest of us. You look like Grandma Fiona. She's so beautiful."

"That's just smoke and mirrors," the first Mrs. Gold remarked from where she sat across the table from them, right next to her son. "All makeup and magic potions."

Implying her mother was a witch. River's warmth now turned to anger. But before she could say anything, Gigi defended her, "No. The girls at school wear a lot of makeup. Grandma Fiona doesn't—"

"She's not even your grandmother," her actual grandmother interjected angrily.

The boy spoke up then, "Great-Grandfather said that we—"

"He's gone," his grandmother snapped at him as well. "And soon she will be, too."

And River realized that she'd done the right thing coming here. Without Gregory Gold I to protect Fiona, the rest of his family was already taking over and turning on her. Not that he'd been much protection, at least not for River.

"You are beautiful," Gigi whispered at her now. "And I don't think you even have any makeup on now."

"Concealer and mascara," River confessed.

"She always has makeup on," Sarah said softly. She hadn't seemed shy with the older Golds but she was with the younger ones.

And River, who tended to be shy with the older ones, squared her shoulders now and stared hard at the first Mrs. Gold. "And what makes you think my mother is going anywhere?" She couldn't know that River wanted to get Fiona the hell out of here and back home with her in Santa Monica.

The woman's thin lips curved into a malicious smile. "If the sheriff doesn't arrest her for murder, she's still unlikely to inherit anything."

"What are you talking about?" Mabel asked now. "What murder? That bastard just dropped dead of old age."

"I guess Sheriff Sebastian will figure out if that's true or not," Carolyn Gold replied in the condescending tone River remembered so well.

"That's why the coroner's van took him?" River asked. "Why all the sheriff department vehicles were here?"

"Your mother didn't tell you?" Carolyn Gold asked, her thin lips curving into a tight smile.

River shook her head. "We really haven't had a chance to talk since we got here. She's so upset." Too upset for River to ask her all the things she wanted to ask. But she leaned forward, so that she could see Noah around Mabel and Sarah and asked her half brother, "When did Luke Sebastian move back?"

Noah shrugged. "Just a few months ago."

"And he's already been elected sheriff?"

"The outgoing sheriff had health issues, so there was a special election," Noah said. "And we all supported Luke."

Noah's support she could understand since they had been friendly back then because they'd gone to school together. But *everybody* else?

"All?" she asked, her voice cracking slightly. "What do you mean by *all*?"

"Our father said that we should support him," Gregory II replied. "He wanted us to show a united front behind the hometown hero."

She had to swallow down the lump of disgust stuck in the back of her throat before asking, "Hero?"

"He just recently requested a discharge from the military," Noah said. "They honored his request because of all the commendations and medals he'd been awarded during his years of service."

Why had he left the military? What or who had brought him back to Gold Creek?

"But sheriff . . ." she murmured.

"Even your mother supported him," the first Mrs. Gold replied with her annoying smugness. "Didn't she tell you that, either?"

The sense of betrayal overwhelmed River. No matter what a hero Luke Sebastian might have been in other countries, or even for his own country, he hadn't been a hometown hero. He certainly had not been hers, not like his brother had once been.

And her mother knew that.

Most of the Gold family knew that Luke hadn't wanted his brother involved with her. So how could any of them have supported him? But she shouldn't have been surprised, not after all the broken promises and betrayals she'd already suffered.

The tension eased from Luke the minute he stepped into the warmth of the kitchen. His mom and Jackson stood hip to hip at the stove, stirring something in a pot while his father poured water into the glasses already sitting on the table. The kitchen was old with white beadboard cabinets and backsplash and butcher-block countertops. Instead of an island, like most modern kitchens had now, it had that big old oak table that so many kids had sat around over the last decades.

"I think we're going to need this water," Dad warned Luke. "Those two are spicing up the chili."

"Chili's gotta be spicy," Jackson remarked with a wide grin.

And a pang struck Luke's heart over how much he looked like his father, Luke's best friend. If only . . .

But Jack was gone. And now so was Jackson's mother. Luke and this sixteen-year-old boy were really all each other had. Except for the Sebastians.

They'd always been there for Luke, first fostering and then adopting him and later his half brother, Michael, too. He'd known without even having to ask that they would wholeheartedly embrace Jackson, too.

"It's so good to have some young energy in the house again," Mary Sebastian said, and she reached up to wrap her arm around Jackson's shoulders, the boy nearly a foot taller than her. She seemed even smaller now than she used to be, like she was shrinking. The Sebastians were getting older, in their seventies now, so they no longer fostered kids. "I'm so happy you're home, Luke, and that you didn't come alone."

They worried about him. He knew that, that they'd worried for years about his choice of a career in the military. They'd known that even as sheriff of Gold Creek he would be safer home than anywhere else he'd been. He'd wanted that security for Jackson more than for himself, though.

Jackson probably wished Luke had come without him, and that Jackson was back home with both his parents. But that wasn't an option anymore, unfortunately.

"Somebody else came back home today," Luke remarked. "And she wasn't alone, either."

Mom spun around and focused on him, her eyes wide now. "When I was in town earlier today, I heard that Gregory Gold passed away. Has his youngest daughter come home?"

Luke nodded.

"And Michael?" she asked, her voice cracking slightly.

He shrugged. "I don't know. I didn't see him. Just her and her daughter . . ." Emotion rushed up on him, choking him. "She looks like him, Mom."

"Who's Michael?" Jackson asked. "And what about Gregory Gold? And which one, aren't there a bunch of them?"

"The oldest Gregory Gold passed away this morning," Luke said. "And Michael . . ." That emotion choked him so much now that he nearly reached for one of the water glasses. But he cleared his throat and said, "Michael is my brother."

Jackson grinned. "You have a bunch of brothers and sisters and nieces and nephews." His grin faded a bit and he enviously added, "You're lucky."

"I am," Luke acknowledged, and he wrapped his arm around his mother now.

She leaned against him, as if she needed his support to hold her up, and she asked, "So her child is Michael's child?"

Luke sighed. "I don't know. Maybe she just looks like a Gold, but she doesn't look like her mother." While her daughter was cute, River was even more beautiful than she'd been as a teenager. Not that he'd seen her much since he'd left for boot camp before she'd started high school. And then he'd only come home when he'd had leave. But he had seen her in the pictures Michael had sent him of the two of them. Luke's younger brother had been so crazy about her. Luke hadn't understood why Michael was getting so serious at his age; he'd been too damn young.

But now, after seeing her in person, Luke could almost understand how she could get someone so completely besotted with her that he would turn his back on everyone else who loved him.

"You've really never heard from him since he left with her?" Luke asked his parents, looking from one to the other, studying them like he would have a suspect.

Tears rushed to Mom's eyes and she just shook her head.

"We're always happy when kids stay in contact, like you did, Luke," Dad said. "But so many times foster kids, even ones we've adopted, don't want to be reminded of the past. Or if they've reunited with their biological families again, they feel like it's a betrayal of them to stay in contact with us."

"We have no bio family left to reunite with," Luke reminded them.

His and Michael's mom's addictions finally caught up with her; that was how Michael had finally been found and reunited with Luke seventeen years ago. And neither of them knew who their father was, just that it wasn't the same man. He and Michael hadn't really even looked much like brothers, and, until their mother died, they hadn't lived together since Michael was a baby. Child Protective Services took Luke away from her after he'd been hurt in a car accident she'd caused driving drunk. CPS had placed Luke in the Sebastians' foster home while she'd disappeared with Luke's baby brother who, thanks to a car seat, hadn't been injured in the crash. She'd fought hard to keep Michael, moving around, hiding, making sure that CPS couldn't take her baby, too.

"Sometimes, if they haven't reunited with those bio families, then it feels like even more of a betrayal to them," Dad said.

"And he was so crazy about that girl," Mom remarked. "I think he felt protective of her, like he did your mother."

"Bio mother," Luke automatically corrected. "You're my mother." And he tightened his arm around her.

Jackson studied them all, and there was that envy in his dark eyes again, that Luke had family and he didn't. How could he make the kid realize that it wasn't just DNA that made a family? Love was enough.

Love and security.

Luke had to make sure that he could provide that, that he could keep the kid safe. He'd failed Jackson's family. He hadn't protected Jack and Adele. He hadn't even protected his own family, his mother or Michael, although he'd tried.

Where was his brother? Had he come back?

"Have they asked you to do the service for Gregory Gold?" Luke asked his father.

Pastor Sebastian shook his head. "I am retired," he said.

"That hasn't stopped other people from asking and from you doing it," Luke pointed out. "As well as all the sermons you give at church yet . . ." He'd only been back a few days when he realized his "retired" parents were not very retired.

"Gregory and I didn't always see eye to eye on things," Dad said. Instead of trying to fight his age, like the oldest Gold, Dad had let his hair go gray years ago. And all the lines in his face and the stoop to his shoulders just showed how hard he'd worked, how much he'd cared about everyone, all those kids he'd fostered, especially the ones they hadn't been able to save . . .

Who'd run away like Michael had.

Luke was going to be at that funeral for certain. Especially since the coroner's preliminary exam had already determined that the old man's death might not have been natural. Or at least that was what the text he'd sent had suggested: **Sending off samples to toxicology** . . .

So had the old man been poisoned?

To investigate more, Luke had a reason to return to Gold Memorial Gardens even before the funeral. And hopefully, when he did, he would catch a killer and maybe catch up with his brother, too.

Chapter 6

Fiona lay in the dark, listening. Wondering . . .

Would River creep into her room like she used to when she was a young girl? Scared from some vivid dream, too scared to be alone, needing her mother . . .

Fiona had never been there for her as much as she should have been, certainly not when it had mattered most to River. But Gregory had always needed so much from Fiona, so much of her time and her attention and her talents.

Talents that she'd found here, where she'd found *herself*, in Gold Creek. Within the funeral services, Fiona had discovered and honed a service she could provide. A way to make survivors remember their departed loved one in a better light, in a more flattering way.

So that they could forget the suffering, or the tragedy, or the age that had taken away their loved one. Fiona was still needed for that, for the business, but for the last couple of years Gregory hadn't needed her in the same way that he once had.

And she knew why, because when Fiona looked in the mirror she could see what he had.

Her age.

But instead of fearing and fighting the progression of time in the way that Gregory had, Fiona wanted to embrace the lines and even the few fine silver hairs mixed in with her thick blond tresses. She'd actually been looking forward to aging because she'd hoped that with age would come more wisdom. So that now, after a little more than five decades of life, if she was faced with the same situations she'd faced in the past, she would make better decisions, less selfish and fearful ones. Smarter ones.

Because even though Fiona had known how much her child had needed her, she hadn't been there for River like she should have been. And River had run away, leaving Fiona all alone and aching from missing her daughter. But now that River was back, Fiona was the one who was scared.

She was terrified that the plan she'd set into motion was going to be discovered and that the truth was going to come out. And her biggest fear was that she was going to lose her daughter all over again.

And this time for good . . .

River stood outside her mother's door, torn between checking on her and confronting her. How could she have supported Luke Sebastian after what he'd done to her?

To Sarah.

But her mother had been through so much already today that River didn't have the heart to ask her all the questions she needed to have the answers for . . .

What was the deal with Luke? And why was the first Mrs. Gold so convinced that Fiona was going to be gone soon, too?

But instead of pushing open the door to her mother's room, River drew in a breath and continued down the hall, past the door with the crime scene tape stretched across it. The door to Gregory Gold I's suite. Was it really a crime scene, or was Luke trying to make it something it wasn't? Just as he'd tried to make her truth into a lie all those years ago.

But why bother now?

He'd gotten what he wanted. And in the end so had she.

Two more doors down, she opened the one to the guest room she was sharing with Mabel and her daughter. It was the one she'd used when she'd lived here, but it had never felt like hers. She'd always felt like a guest in what was supposed to be her home.

She still felt like a guest despite how her mother had decorated the place for her with blush-colored walls and white carpet and drapes. It was girly and inviting and totally unlike every other room in the house. It also had two queen beds for all the sleepovers River was supposed to have had with childhood friends. But she really hadn't had any friends until Michael moved to Gold Creek.

After stepping inside the room, she closed the door behind her and leaned against it. Even though she'd only stopped behind Sarah and Mabel for a minute outside her mother's door, each of them had already claimed a bed, leaving her to either choose to squeeze in next to one of them or to take the couch. It was a daybed type; again for all those sleepovers she'd never had. It would have been comfortable but somehow, being here in this house again, she wanted to share a bed like she had so often shared her mother's.

While Sarah was engrossed in her phone, her grandmother stared at her with concern in her blue eyes.

"How is Fiona doing?" Mabel asked.

"She's sleeping," she said although she really had no idea. "I didn't want to disturb her."

"Her or you?" Mabel asked with her usual insight. And River realized that concern in her grandmother's eyes wasn't just for Fiona but for her, too.

"I'm okay," River said, and forced a smile. "You know that I never had much of a relationship with Gregory."

"But he was still your father."

River sighed and shrugged. "You're not any more certain of that than I am."

Sarah glanced up then from her phone. "What do you mean? Do you think Grandma Fiona lied about who your dad is?"

River shrugged again. "A lot of people think she did." That Fiona had already been pregnant when she'd met Gregory Gold, who had been attending a conference in Santa Monica, and that she'd passed that baby off as his in order to trap him into a marriage.

"But wouldn't she tell you the truth? You're her daughter . . ." Sarah murmured, and she focused intently on River's face. "Is that why you always say you'll never lie to me?"

Feeling that old connection with her daughter, she crossed over to her bed and settled onto the mattress next to her. She would have reached out and put her arm around her, but every time she tried to touch Sarah lately, the teenager pulled away from her. "I say that because I love you and I respect you, so I will always be honest with you."

Sarah pursed her lips and narrowed her eyes. "But you tell me that I'm beautiful."

"You are," River said.

Sarah snorted. "Not like you and Grandma Fiona."

Had what Gigi said affected her? Teenagers were so sensitive, apparently even Sarah, who sometimes acted like she didn't care about anything. "Like Carolyn Gold said, it's all smoke and mirrors."

Sarah shook her head. "No, it's not. I know the difference."

River didn't know whether to be flattered or concerned.

"What I don't know is anything about this place," Sarah pointed out, "or about these people because you never want to talk about it."

"No, I don't like to talk about it," River admitted. "But I have answered your questions." Not that Sarah had asked her all that many about her life, fortunately. She hadn't seemed all that interested in her boring mother. "I told you that I grew up in a house next to a cemetery and that my family doesn't really like me much or even consider me family."

"What about the sheriff?" Sarah asked, and she was studying River's face intently now.

River tensed. "What about the sheriff?"

"You've never mentioned him, but it's pretty obvious that you and him must have had a thing at some time."

River shuddered at the thought. "The sheriff and I do not have a thing."

"Well, not anymore," Sarah agreed. "But you must've . . ."

"He's your father's brother," River said.

And Sarah sucked in a breath. "I thought he was looking at me weird today, but I just thought . . ."

"What?"

Sarah shrugged.

"I promised to always be honest with you," River said, "and I expect you to always be honest with me." But Sarah was a teenager, a moody, secretive teenager, so River didn't expect that to be a promise that she could keep. River had been a moody, secretive teenager herself once; she knew . . .

And that was why she was so damn afraid for Sarah. She really shouldn't have brought her here. Especially if Luke Sebastian was looking at her strangely . . .

"I thought that he was just wondering how I could be *your* daughter when I don't look anything like you," Sarah said. "But you never even introduced me to him."

"I don't like him," River admitted.

"Why not?"

"Because he convinced your father that I was lying about

you," she said. "That I was just like my mother . . . who every-body thinks lied about me being a Gold."

Sarah snorted. "Then how the hell do I look so much like them?"

"Sarah," River admonished her for the swearing.

"They were wrong about Grandma Fiona lying about who your dad is," Sarah said.

But River still wondered . . .

"And about my dad," Sarah continued, and her voice cracked a bit, "you said that he didn't believe he was my dad, but I didn't know why, that it was somebody else's fault, his brother's fault, that *he* was the one who didn't believe you."

River sighed and leaned against the headboard. "It didn't matter who told Michael what, he should have known me bet-ter than that," she said, her voice breaking. "I thought he was my best friend. And he just bailed on me. On us."

Sarah was the one who reached out then, wrapping her arm around River's shoulders. "It's okay, Mom. We've never needed him. And we never will."

"No, you both got me," Mabel chimed in. "I'm way better than any stupid man."

But Michael hadn't been stupid. He'd been sweet and funny and special. And River couldn't believe how badly he'd let her down when he hadn't showed up that night.

But Michael had adored and worshiped his older brother even more than he had her, so River really shouldn't have been surprised. He'd even admitted to her that Luke was probably right, not about Sarah's paternity, but that it would probably be best for the baby to be adopted into a loving home with older parents instead of being raised by kids like she and Michael had been at seventeen and eighteen.

So maybe Luke had been right about them being too young. And not thinking clearly.

River had been so desperate to get away from Gold Creek

that she'd considered running away so many times long before she'd gotten pregnant. And Michael had done his running another way, through substances.

So maybe they hadn't been equipped to be parents back then. But even then River couldn't imagine giving up her child, just as she couldn't imagine losing her now. She wrapped both her arms around Sarah, hanging on tightly.

And predictably Sarah squirmed away from her with a protest. "Mom, you're squeezing me . . ."

She had been because she was so afraid of losing her. And she could already feel her slipping away from her. Maybe being here would bond them, though.

But Sarah didn't just pull away, she jumped out of the bed and rushed over to the window. "There's a light out there, moving through the trees . . ." Her voice quivered with excitement. "Who's out there?"

Mabel grumbled. "It better just be a night watchman. Surely, they got security around this place."

"I hope that's what it is," River murmured, but she shivered.

"What else would it be?" Sarah asked.

River had promised to always be honest with her, so she sighed, then replied, "According to the local legend, that would be the grave digger . . ."

"The what? The who?" Sarah asked, and she turned away from the window to look at River.

"The ghost," River murmured. "Of the man who used to dig the graves the night before the funerals. Sometimes even before the people died . . ."

Sarah's dark eyes widened, but instead of looking afraid, she looked excited. "That's so cool."

"No, it's not," Mabel said before River could get out the words. "This place is so damn creepy. I can't understand why your mother ever wanted to move here, let alone why she stayed, especially after you left."

Sarah was good at tuning out her great-grandmother. "I want to go out there," Sarah said, "and try to catch him!"

"No," River said, a little sharply. "It's dark and dangerous." Way too dangerous for a teenage girl to be out in the cemetery. While Michael had never showed up that night they were supposed to meet out there, a few other teenagers were rumored to have disappeared from the cemetery over the past thirty years or so. The local authorities had written them off as runaways, like she'd once been. But River wasn't as convinced, not after what she'd seen herself that night she'd been waiting for Michael.

And she didn't want her daughter to be the next one who disappeared.

This was the usual reason Luke was called out to Gold Memorial Gardens and Funeral Services. Not to investigate a murder but to chase off the teenagers who were conducting their own investigation into the ghost of the grave digger.

The truth was they were just out here partying and potentially causing damage. And Luke usually sent one of his deputies to handle it because he hated that the Golds used the local sheriff's department like their personal security company. But given the money they'd contributed to his campaign, maybe they felt like he was their personal watchdog.

That wasn't why he'd answered this call tonight, though. It was because he'd already been awake, thinking of Michael and of murder.

The coroner had texted him an update: **Will finish up autopsy tomorrow. Toxicology will take longer for results to come back.**

Toxicology. While the medical examiner was checking Gregory Gold I's body for poison, the crime lab was checking that syringe, figuring out what had been in it and whose prints were on it.

Maybe one of his heirs had gotten sick of waiting for him to die to take over the family business, which ironically was death.

Death was literally all around him now as he walked the grounds of the cemetery. Every tombstone marked a grave where a dead body lay. And the mausoleums contained many bodies and ashes of bodies.

If Dr. Jeffries hadn't called him when he had, would the family have already cremated Gregory Gold I's body? Would they have tried to destroy whatever evidence might have been left on it or in the house?

Gregory's suite had been processed, too, the techs taking pictures and collecting prints and other samples of DNA. But what would it all prove? Would there be enough evidence of anything? If the old man had actually been poisoned or . . .

Luke swung his flashlight around the grounds, the beam glancing off those marble mausoleums and gravestones. But nothing else.

There was no evidence here that any teenagers had been partying on the grounds this time. Other times he'd found beer cans and liquor bottles and drug paraphernalia. And he'd wondered and worried that Gold Creek wasn't as safe as he'd hoped it would be for Jackson.

But it had been safer than where he'd been because there had not been bullet shells nor any dead bodies . . .

Until today.

He glanced up toward the house. In one of the windows was the silhouette of a woman. Was it her?

And was she watching him? Or had she seen the light and was worried that he was the grave digger?

Chapter 7

With GG Mabel snoring, Sarah thought she would never fall asleep. And that noise was all that was keeping her up. Not the story that Mom had told her. The legend of the grave digger.

Stuff like that didn't scare Sarah. It excited her. She loved scary movies, loved being scared. And she would have loved going out into the cemetery to find the ghost if her mom hadn't gotten so freaked out about it. She hadn't wanted to push it tonight, knowing that Mom's dad had just died and that being back here seemed to scare River Gold even more than seeing a ghost.

So Sarah had agreed to go to bed early, really early if you considered that they were still on West Coast instead of Midwest time. She must have dozed off a little bit because a soft knock at the door startled her fully awake. She wasn't scared, though, but she was surprised she heard the knock over GG Mabel's snoring.

Mom wasn't snoring. Maybe she wasn't even sleeping yet. While she'd told Sarah to go to bed, she'd stayed standing at the window, staring out of it for the longest time. Even after Sarah had given up on trying to see the ghost from this far away.

But maybe there were other ghosts closer than the cemetery. Because if ghosts really existed, wouldn't they be here? In this house?

Maybe that was what she heard now. One of those ghosts softly knocking at the door.

"Sarah . . ."

The whisper sent a chill rushing over her, and she realized she hadn't even undressed or pulled up the covers. And Mom hadn't covered her up, either, like she usually did.

"Sarah . . ." that disembodied voice called out again.

A thrill of excitement, more than fear, shot through Sarah. She smiled in the dark. This place was great. She slid off the bed and headed over to the door. There was a shadow under it, blocking out part of the light from the hall. Did ghosts cast shadows? Wouldn't the light go right through them?

"Sarah . . ."

She reached for the doorknob, and it turned easily beneath her hand. She'd thought Mom had locked it earlier when she'd first joined her and GG Mabel. Clearly, her mom might believe in ghosts since River had stayed even longer at that window looking for the grave digger. But if she'd been worried about a ghost getting inside, she must have known that a locked door wouldn't keep one out anyway.

If ghosts were real . . .

Curiosity compelled Sarah to pull open that door. And when she did, it was nearly like looking into a mirror as her cousin or niece, or whatever the hell Gigi was to her, stared back at her. The sensation was strange, looking like people for once after years of looking like no one she knew.

Not that she knew these people at all even though she was related to them. And after knowing how they'd treated her mom, she wasn't sure she wanted to get to know them.

"Hey," Gigi said, as she studied Sarah intently.

"Hey . . ." she whispered back, at a loss as to what else to say.

"I didn't get to talk to you at dinner," she said.

That was because Sarah hadn't wanted to talk to her. And she'd figured that Gigi probably felt the same since the girls at Sarah's school had rarely wanted to talk to her. Just about her.

"It's late," Sarah pointed out.

"Aren't you on West Coast time?" Gigi asked.

She was, but she went to bed early at home and woke up early . . . like her mom did. Mabel usually slept in even though she went to bed early, too. She was getting older. And Sarah tensed with fear that someday they might be having her funeral. Hopefully, not anytime soon.

Not knowing what to say to this new relative, Sarah murmured, "It's just been a long day, you know, flying and all . . ."

"And meeting all of us for the first time," Gigi finished for her. "That must have freaked you out, huh?"

She shook her head. "My mom . . ."

"Warned you," Gigi finished for her again.

But she really hadn't warned Sarah. "It's more like how she doesn't talk about you all, about any of you."

"She ran away before I was born. But from what I've heard, everybody was pretty dicky to her," Gigi admitted.

And Sarah wondered if the girl intended to continue that family tradition and treat her the same shitty way. So she narrowed her eyes and glared at her reflection.

Gigi held up her hands. "Like I said, I wasn't even alive when all that happened. I had nothing to do with it. I'm really not a shit person like the rest of them."

"The rest of them?"

Gigi sighed. "A few of them are kind of cool, like Uncle Noah and Taylor and Wynn, but even my own dad can be a prick—"

"He was nice at the airport," Sarah defended him.

Gigi chuckled. "Yeah, he can do that, just like Great-Grandfather, turn on the Gold charm when he wants to." She shivered then as if that charm left her cold. "You should have seen the old man charm all the funeral groupies into drooling over him."

"Funeral groupies?"

"Yeah, there's this group of old ladies with nothing else to do. They show up at every funeral to get some free food mostly, I think, at the luncheons after the interments. Or maybe they crash the services because they're crushing on Great-Grandfather."

"He was good-looking?"

Gigi nodded. "Yeah, you'll see at the funeral. He looks like my dad's age. It was creepy. Like Benjamin Button or something . . ."

Sarah couldn't wait for the funeral. "I've never been to one before," she admitted.

"One what?"

"Funeral."

"Really? Nobody you knew ever died?"

Sarah shrugged. "A couple of friends of my grandma's, but my mom didn't want me to go to their funerals."

"You were too young?"

Maybe that had been the case with the first one, but the last one was just a few months ago. Sarah shook her head. "I think she just hates all this a lot."

"Probably all of us, too," Gigi said. "Do you?"

"I don't know you," Sarah pointed out. "But I'm not really thrilled that people treated my mom like shit, you know?"

Mom wouldn't have liked that if she'd known about the people who'd treated Sarah that way. But instead of confronting them and insulting them, like Sarah wanted to do, Mom would have invited them over to talk it out and bake them cookies or do their makeup or something to make them friends. That was why Sarah hadn't told her about the problems.

"Yeah, I get that," Gigi said. "But again, I had nothing to do with that. I'm actually really nice."

Or was she just turning on the charm like she said her dad and great-grandfather had?

Sarah had had that happen before, people pretending to be her friend when they were just setting her up to be humiliated. After that had happened a couple of times, Sarah had changed, so that it wouldn't get to her anymore. She'd stopped caring.

"I'm not very nice," she admitted.

Gigi chuckled. "At least you're honest. Why aren't you very nice?"

She sighed. "I don't know . . ." Was it because of those people who'd hurt her in the past and she didn't want to get hurt again?

"Your mom is nice," Gigi said with a certain wistfulness.

Everybody liked Sarah's mom. Even those girls who'd been mean to Sarah had liked River. And that was why some of them had been nice to her, to get close to the woman who could make anybody beautiful . . . except her own daughter.

At least that was what they'd said.

Sarah glanced over her shoulder into the dark room. GG Mabel was still snoring, but she heard nothing yet from her mom. She hadn't been in bed with Sarah, so she must have taken the couch. Was she awake? Was she listening to this?

"Yeah, she is," Sarah agreed. "Sometimes too nice . . ." That homeless guy GG had caught digging through their trash could have hurt her when she'd made him a sandwich. And if she kept doing stuff like that, trying to help people, she would probably end up getting hurt.

Again.

Obviously, she'd been hurt in the past. By her family and by Sarah's father and her uncle, the sheriff.

At the thought of her mom suffering, anger surged through Sarah. She didn't have time for people who'd treated her mom badly. "Yeah, I better get back to bed," she said, and she started to close the door on her near-mirror-image.

"You don't want to explore?" Gigi asked.

Sarah studied her for a moment, wondering what the catch was and if she could trust her. Like Gigi had said, she hadn't been alive yet when everybody had treated her mom so badly.

"Explore what?" she asked. "The cemetery?"

Gigi shuddered. "Nah, I don't want to go out there and run into the grave digger."

"Mom just told me about him after we saw a light out there," Sarah said, her voice getting a little too loud with excitement.

Gigi shuddered again. "Yeah, you know that kids have disappeared out there before."

"So you're scared of ghosts?" Sarah asked with surprise. How could anybody live here and be scared of them?

"I'm scared of my family. My dad and grandfather would kill me if they caught me going out there after dark. But we can explore this place, the house and the business," Gigi said. "I can show you around . . . unless you're scared?"

For the first time, Sarah smiled at the girl. "No, I'm not scared."

Not yet but she wanted to be.

Instead of closing the door on her cousin, or whatever Gigi was, and shutting her out, Sarah stepped into the hallway with her. Then she slowly closed the door behind her, careful not to shut it too loudly, and she waited for her mom to call out. But there was no sound except her great-grandmother's snoring.

And she wondered . . . was her mother even in there, in the dark? Or had she already snuck out of the room before Sarah?

River did not believe in ghosts. Or at least she hadn't until that night. But who the hell really knew what she'd seen then, so many years ago? She'd been young, scared, pregnant . . .

hormonal and heartbroken. Even then she hadn't known for sure what she'd seen.

But tonight she had no doubt that someone was out here. Not a ghost but a person carrying a flashlight, not an old oil lantern. And for some reason, if only to prove to herself that the intruder was human . . . or not . . . she felt compelled to seek out that person.

Maybe it was because she was edgy and restless, so she'd known there was no way she was going to sleep. Being here again brought back so many feelings, so many bad feelings.

She was also still on West Coast time, so she wasn't tired. While Mabel and Sarah had fallen asleep pretty quickly, River had slipped away. Out of the room and out of the house . . .

And now into the cemetery.

The minute she stepped outside, the breeze swept over and through her. As cold and sharp as a knife blade. She'd forgotten how low the temperature dropped at night in Michigan in the fall, especially this close to the big lake. She regretted now that she hadn't grabbed a jacket before she'd slipped out of the bedroom. But she wasn't sure she'd even packed one.

It all seemed so surreal now. The entire day starting with that phone call from her mother to the flight bringing her back to Michigan then Gregory driving them back to Gold Creek. And now River was here . . .

Where she'd been supposed to meet Michael all those years ago . . . in the cemetery, not just anywhere, but specifically at the grave of the grave digger. Lyle McGinty. That was where all the teenagers hung out, trying to catch a glimpse of the ghost when he returned to his grave after digging fresh ones for the newly dead, people he killed.

That was the legend. But the only person River knew who had ever died here was the man her mother claimed was her father. And that had just happened . . .

Today.

And that was so surreal, too, like a dream, and maybe that was why she wasn't scared. That coming out here, walking among the gravestones and the ghosts, just seemed like a dream, like it wasn't really happening. Like none of it was really happening.

She continued down one of the paved lanes toward where Lyle McGinty's grave was located near the back of the cemetery, where it bordered swampy woods, in one of the cheaper plots. As she walked, she wrapped her arms around herself for warmth. But that brisk wind still cut through her as it swept fallen leaves across the asphalt and through the grass.

While the maples were losing their leaves, the willows just swayed, their limbs and the moss hanging from them dancing all around her, as if taunting her. Like it had seemed that *he* had taunted her that night . . . when he'd showed up when she was waiting for another.

For her lover . . .

She drew in a shaky breath as she stepped out of the light, cast from the house and from the landscaping lights, and into the darkness. But it wasn't completely dark out here, the clouds kept shifting with the wind, letting the moon shine through onto patches of the cemetery. She had to be near the grave, but she didn't see it.

She saw only the man standing over it. The moonlight cast him in silhouette but she would know his face anywhere. The sharp cheekbones, the slightly hooked nose, and the chin with the dip in the middle.

"Michael?"

She'd come out here to confront one ghost from her past, and she'd found another . . .

Lyle McGinty, 1899–1990.
This was the grave digger's headstone: his grave, the place

where the teenagers usually hung out. But just like everywhere else on the grounds, there was no one here tonight. No beer cans or used vapes, either.

And no person until she stepped out of the moonlight, her blond hair shimmered with it, shining like gold. Like a Gold. She was the only one of them who actually looked like the name, like something shiny and bright . . . instead of like the rest of them who were all so dark and gloomy.

"Michael . . ." she whispered, and then she launched herself at him, closing her arms around him and holding him tight as her body trembled against his. "Oh, Michael . . ."

His body tensed with shock and with something else, something he didn't want to feel. He jerked back. "What the hell . . ."

She stumbled, and he automatically reached out and grasped her arms to hold her steady. She kept shaking, though. "You're not Michael . . ."

"No. Is he here? Were you meeting him here?" he asked. And his heart beat fast with hope that he might see his brother again. He'd spent most of his childhood hoping that same hope, that he would reunite with his baby brother, and it had finally been realized after his mother died. Maybe another death would bring another realization of a dream for him. He peered around, into the shadows.

"I was meeting him here," she said, and she pulled away from his grasp. "Sixteen years ago. But thanks to you, he never showed up."

Luke's head pounded with confusion. "What? What are you talking about?"

"I know what you told him," she said. "That you didn't think my kid was even his. That even if it was, we had no business trying to raise her. That I should . . ." Her voice cracked. ". . . give her up."

"But you didn't," he said. "That teenage girl with you, she's Michael's daughter." He'd been wrong about her paternity.

And maybe he'd been wrong about the rest of it, too. But they'd been so damn young.

And Michael . . .

Despite how fast he'd had to grow up, he had so many issues with maturity. With judgment.

But that was their mother's fault. She'd never been a good role model. Like Michael, she'd thrown herself into every relationship like she was Juliet to someone's Romeo. Michael had thought he'd found his Juliet in River Gold, and so it had not surprised Luke when he'd decided to run away with her just like their mother had run away and taken Michael with her, leaving Luke behind in that hospital bed, broken more than physically. He'd missed them both so much despite how his mother had been or maybe because of how she'd been, and he'd been so worried about Michael. When finally, Michael had come to live with him again, he'd thought everything would be good at long last, but then *she* had come along. And he'd lost his brother all over again.

"She's *my* daughter," River said, and there was no crack in her voice now but a sudden hardness.

"Where's Michael?" he asked.

"You tell me," she said. "I haven't seen him in sixteen years." She glanced around then, as if she was searching the shadows for him now.

He chuckled but without any humor. "Bullshit."

"What?" she asked.

"Your mother told me how happy you two are. Every time I tried to get her to give me Michael's contact information, she said her son-in-law wanted nothing to do with me. He didn't want me trying to ruin the perfect life he had with you."

She laughed now but without any humor, too. "Are you on drugs?" she asked. "Where the hell did you get that?"

"I just told you," he pointed out. "Your mother."

She sucked in a breath and shook her head. "I don't know why she would tell you that . . ."

"So you're saying it's not true?" he asked, and his head pounded harder with confusion.

"God, no," she said as if the thought horrified her now.

Luke studied her through narrowed eyes. "Why would your mother lie about that . . . and for all these years?"

"All these years?" she repeated, her voice a hollow echo in the night. "I thought you just came back."

"Just moved back, but I've visited my family over the years." All family but one of them. "And every time I came home, I talked to your mother about Michael."

His visits admittedly hadn't been often, but he had reached out to her, trying to get her to give him Michael's contact information. He'd even searched for him a few times himself, but he'd figured that Michael must have dropped Sebastian as a last name especially since he'd taken off before his adoption had been official.

"River?" he prodded her, and he reached for her again, touching her arms, trying to compel her to answer him. Her skin was cold against his palms.

And she shivered. "I don't know which one of you is really lying," she said.

"You think I'm lying?" he asked. "But why?"

She shrugged. "To protect Michael from having to pay child support for one, or— "

"He hasn't been paying you?" he asked. "He really hasn't been with you this whole time?"

She shook her head. "No. We are not married. He never showed up that night, so I ran away alone."

The thought of a teenage girl, a pregnant teenage girl, running away on her own jabbed at Luke's chest. She would have been just a little older than Jackson. "I can't believe . . ." Hell, he shouldn't have believed Fiona Gold. But why had she lied?

Or was River lying?

He had no idea which one of them to trust.

Then a scream rang out . . . coming from a distance. Probably from inside the house. "Is that your mother again?" he asked.

River shook her head as she started running toward the building. "No, that's my daughter."

Michael's daughter.

Screaming . . .

Chapter 8

River shouldn't have left Sarah inside the house with only an old lady for protection. Was Mabel all right? She would have tried to defend her great-granddaughter, and if she couldn't, then something must have already happened to her.

River ran as fast as she could across the cemetery. Instead of following the winding paved paths, she took a direct route across flat tombstones, around monuments, until she came to the back door she'd left open. But before she could pass through it, Luke was there, easing her aside, so that he stepped inside first, with his hand on his gun, holding it against his side.

The sight of the weapon chilled her even more than that brisk, autumn wind.

He held up his other hand, the one not on the gun, and whispered to her, "Stay out here."

But once he turned around and started down the hall toward the lobby, she followed him inside; she wasn't going to wait, not when her daughter needed her. Sarah wasn't screaming now, though. Now there was no sound at all but for the gurgle of the fountains outside the door River left open.

Luke started across the lobby area toward one of the showing rooms while she headed for the staircase. That was where she'd left Sarah and Mabel, asleep in her old room. But then another sound, a thud, a groan, and another muffled cry drifted into the lobby. Luke threw open the doors to one of the showing rooms. Then he pulled out a flashlight, along with his gun. He swung that beam around the room like he swung the barrel of the gun.

And the beam and the gun pointed at a girl lying on the ground. Only her silky black hair was visible beneath the body of a man in a suit that covered her.

"Oh, my God!" River exclaimed, trying to get past Luke to get to her daughter, to get that man off her. But then she realized that the man wasn't alive. His eyes closed, his skin pale and waxy and his body stiff, he was a corpse.

"Get him off!" the girl shrieked.

River recognized that voice: it wasn't her daughter lying on the ground but Gigi. Her great-niece.

A giggle slipped out of someone else in the room and then another deeper chuckle followed it. Luke's flashlight beam passed over Sarah and the boy who stood beside her. Gigi's brother, Toby.

River fumbled around on the wall until she found a switch and the room glowed with soft ambient lighting. "What's going on?" she asked her daughter. "Was that you I heard screaming?"

Sarah shook her head. "No. It was Gigi." She stepped forward now, as if to move the body off her cousin.

But Luke was already there, pulling the corpse aside to lean it against the casket that had toppled over. Once the body was off her, Gigi jumped up from the floor just as other people rushed into the room. They must have heard the scream as well despite all the insulation in the ceiling between the first and second stories. But Mabel, with her bad hearing, and Fiona, who was probably knocked out from the sedative yet, weren't among the group.

Some of the people were dressed in their street clothes, like they'd just walked in from somewhere else. Like Gregory II, Noah, and Wynn. While others were in their robes, like Gigi and Toby's parents, Gregory III and Karen. But even though they were the kids' parents, they stayed back behind Gregory II, who strode up to where Luke and River stood by the teenagers.

"What the hell's going on?" he demanded to know.

Gigi began, "Grandfather, we were just—"

"You kids know better than to mess around in here!" he bellowed. "This is our business, not a fun house!"

River could have told him that there was nothing fun about this place. But yet . . . her daughter's face was flushed and her eyes bright as if she was excited. And she acted now as if she was trying to hold in another laugh, like she and Toby had laughed just moments ago.

"You're supposed to be in bed like everyone else was," Karen told the kids. She was wearing a robe like her husband, but she glanced around at the others and her eyes widened as she must have realized not everyone else had been asleep.

"And you know this area is off-limits," Gregory III admonished his children. "You had no business being in here!"

"It was my fault," Sarah said. "I asked Gigi to show me around because I've never been in a funeral home before. We didn't want to turn on the lights and bother anyone—"

"There shouldn't have been anyone to bother in here," Gregory II said as he stared at the corpse and the caskets.

"That's irrelevant right now," Noah said. "Why did someone scream? Is anyone hurt?" Which was the question the others should have asked first.

River smiled at him with appreciation. While he was an introvert like Sarah was, he had always been the nicest to her. Unlike Honora, who glowered next to him, her robe cinched tightly around her waist. She glared at River, clearly blaming her for this for some reason.

"We tripped and fell into the casket," Sarah said.

There were two caskets. The one on the ground and another lying open and empty, making River suspect much more had gone on than her daughter was admitting. But all she cared about was that her child was all right. Sarah had never been in a place like this; River hadn't let her attend funerals. So she'd never seen a dead body . . . until tonight.

River shuddered at the sight of that man in his suit with makeup caked on his face. She didn't know how her mother did it, how she catered to the dead like she did. She easily recognized her mother's handiwork in the man's expression, in how his mouth was curved into just the slightest hint of a grin and how one of his eyebrows appeared to be slightly arched, like he was about to tell a joke. And maybe he had since Sarah and Toby had laughed.

"Are you all right?" River asked her daughter.

Sarah nodded. "Yeah, I'm fine, Mom." And she seemed fine but still, River wanted her out of there, away from the dead body, away from her cousins and most especially away from her uncle . . . Luke.

The girl was lying. Maybe that was all her family did: lie. Luke wanted to question her more and he had even more questions for her mother and grandmother. But after her explanation, her family all headed back upstairs but for Gregory Gold II.

"I didn't realize you had come out here again, Sheriff," the older man said.

"I got a call that there were lights moving around the cemetery," Luke reminded him.

Gregory shrugged and then reached up to smooth down his white hair. "I didn't make that call."

"The dispatcher told me it was a Gold that reported seeing the lights and was worried about vandals," Luke said. If Gregory II suspected Luke had just been looking for an excuse to come back out here, he wasn't wrong.

"I called the sheriff's department non-emergency line," Lawrence Gold said.

Luke jumped a bit and touched his holster. He hadn't seen him, lurking in the shadows. That seemed to be the way undertakers worked, always standing on the edge, watching, waiting . . .

"I saw the lights," Lawrence said. "And I called Noah first to see if it was him, but he didn't pick up." Which was strange since he was one of the few who hadn't been in his pajamas.

"Why didn't you wake *me*?" Gregory asked his brother, his tone full of irritation. But Gregory wasn't in his robe and pajamas like Lawrence was. He was still wearing his suit with just his tie undone. Unless that was how he slept . . .

Or maybe hanging upside down . . . or in a casket . . .

Luke glanced from Lawrence to the two caskets that were still in the showing room.

"I didn't know *you* were in charge now," Lawrence said to his brother, his usually mild voice just as sharp with irritation.

"Someone's going to have to step in," Gregory said. "Now that Father's gone. Look at this . . ." He gestured a shaking hand around the showing room. "Those kids messing around—"

"Your grandkids," Lawrence interjected.

"They said the body was already here," Gregory said. "Someone left him out. That is unacceptable."

Lawrence shook his head, almost as if he pitied his older brother. "You really think someone left him out?"

"What are you suggesting? Are you blaming my grandchildren?" Gregory II stuck out his chest then, posturing like his father had, trying to be intimidating.

But he was really a poor imitation of the old man. Lawrence, though, was an even poorer one. He sighed and said, "Given how chaotic the day was, that could have happened . . ." But he sounded doubtful. He must not have believed the kids any more than Luke had. Then he shrugged and said, "I'll take care of him."

Gregory grasped Luke's arm and led him into the lobby. "Do you have any idea what's going on, Sheriff?"

"Kids messing around like your brother said," he deduced.

"I mean about the lights out in the cemetery."

"Kids messing around," Luke said again with a smile. But he hadn't found any evidence of that. He hadn't found any evidence of anyone else in that cemetery until River had found him.

"And what about my father?" Gregory Gold asked. "What do you think really happened to him?"

He thought of what the coroner had texted, of the toxicology report he'd ordered. "I think that he might not have died of natural causes," he admitted. "But that's for the medical examiner to confirm."

"How long will that take?" Gregory asked. "We need to plan his funeral. Settle his estate so that nothing happens to threaten our business or our reputation."

And he clearly thought that as the oldest son, he was going to receive it all. No wonder he was in a hurry. In too much of a hurry to wait until his elderly father died of natural causes?

If Gregory Gold I had been murdered, there were a whole lot of suspects in this house. And Luke was going to have a hell of a time trying to figure out which one of them was responsible for the old man's death. But that was not the only mystery he had to solve now.

Now he had to find out what the hell had happened to his brother, too.

Chapter 9

"I didn't expect you to do that last night," Gigi said as she dropped into the chair next to Sarah at the breakfast table.

There was so much food it looked like the Mother's Day buffet Sarah's mom took GG Mabel to every year and sometimes Grandma Fiona if she was in town that weekend. Neither of Sarah's grans nor her mom sat around this table yet. Mom wasn't in their room, just like she must not have been in it when Sarah left to go "exploring" with Gigi last night. Had Mom been with the sheriff? And why?

"Did you hear me?" Gigi prodded her.

"What?" Sarah asked. "You didn't expect me to shove you into a casket after you had your brother jump out of one to try to scare me?"

Gigi rubbed her shoulder. "Yeah, that, too. But I didn't expect you to cover for us. You really saved us from Grandfather's lecture."

Sarah shrugged. "No big deal."

"The whole thing really wasn't a big deal to you," Toby said as he dropped into the chair on the other side of her. "You didn't scream as loudly as Gigi did." He chuckled. "And she should be used to dead bodies by now."

Sarah had let out a squeak of surprise when Toby had jumped up so suddenly from the casket he'd been lying inside, which had been next to that other one. His sudden movement had startled her. Even though Sarah wasn't used to being around dead bodies, she wasn't scared of them, either. They were dead. They couldn't hurt her, not like living people could.

"That wasn't part of the plan," Gigi said, and leaned in front of Sarah to glare at her brother.

A pang of regret struck Sarah's heart. Even though she'd suspected last night had been a setup to humiliate her, she was still disappointed. She'd thought it might be different here. That they might be different since they were family.

"I guess it doesn't matter whether you're rich Michigan kids or rich Santa Monica kids," she said, "you're all assholes."

Toby chuckled again. "Tell us how you really feel."

"It was a joke," Gigi said.

"I didn't hear you laughing," Sarah reminded her.

"It was an initiation," Toby said. "Garrett did the whole jumping out of a casket thing to us when were just little kids."

"Garrett?"

Gigi pointed across the table at a guy in his early twenties. "Our cousin. Second cousin . . ." She shrugged again. "Whatever . . ."

The guy looked like a Gold except that his pale skin was a little more flushed, at least around his eyes, which looked swollen and bloodshot like he'd either been crying or he'd gotten like GG Mabel sometimes did when she and her "book club" cronies opened a couple more bottles of wine than they usually did. He was hungover.

"Was he close to your great-grandpa?" Sarah asked.

Toby snorted. "No. If anybody actually offed the old man, it was probably Garrett."

The guy glanced up and focused on them, his swollen eyes narrowed. "What are you losers talking about?"

"We're not the losers. You're the one who couldn't even hang on to your girlfriend—"

Garrett jumped up from the table so fast that it came up with him, knocking dishes, glasses, and bowls around the surface, while his chair flipped over onto the ground.

"What's going on?" a woman asked as she rushed to Garrett's side. She was older than him but looked a lot like him. Honora. Wasn't that her name?

Sarah had met so many people the day before that she couldn't keep them all straight.

"Those kids are being assholes again," Garrett said. "Mom, I can't stay here. I can't—" As he started from the dining room, his mother grabbed his arm. But instead of stopping him, she rushed out with him.

"What's going on with them?" Sarah asked. "Why would Garrett kill his own grandfather?"

"You never met your grandfather or you might understand," Gigi said with a soft sigh. "Your mom probably does."

Toby chuckled again. "Yeah, but Great-Grandfather never stole her girlfriend like he did Garrett's."

Sarah's stomach churned at the thought of someone who probably wasn't much older than her hooking up with some old man. "Ew, gross."

He hadn't done that to her mom. He wasn't even the one who'd convinced Sarah's father to abandon them. According to her mom, it was the sheriff who'd done that. So why had she been outside with him last night?

Unless it had just been a coincidence that they'd both heard the screaming at the same time and they hadn't actually been together. But Sarah really couldn't be sure of anything anymore, not with how strangely her mom was acting.

River really hated it here.

But Sarah didn't. Not even after last night . . .

"You lied to the sheriff," River said to her mother.

"When?" Fiona asked, her startled gaze meeting River's in the mirror of her dressing table. "What are you talking about?"

"Have you lied to him more than once?" River asked.

And she couldn't help but wonder how many times her mother had lied to her. About her father? Or were there more lies than that? And which was the lie and which the truth? Did her mother even know?

Fiona drew in a breath and averted her gaze from River's. She seemed more focused on her face. River was relieved that her mother looked better today; the dark circles were nearly gone. Her eyes were no longer swollen like they'd been yesterday.

River was the one with the dark circles now; she hadn't slept well last night after she and Sarah had gone back to their room. And it wasn't just because of Mabel's snoring. Fortunately, the commotion in the showing room hadn't awakened her at all. Or apparently Fiona, either, since she looked so well rested.

Even Sarah had dropped off to sleep relatively quickly after they'd settled back into her room. So maybe her daughter had been telling the truth at least when she'd said that seeing the dead body hadn't bothered her.

It had bothered River. But not as much as learning what she had from Luke Sebastian last night.

"Mom . . ."

Fiona sniffled as if she was about to cry despite her dry eyes. "I don't know what you're talking about . . ."

"According to Luke, you've been saying that Michael and I are together, that we're happily married," River said, her voice raspy as the thought of that overwhelmed her, of being with him all these years instead of raising their daughter alone.

Well, with Mabel. But sometimes that had felt more like raising two children than one.

Fiona uttered a heavy sigh, as if she were long-suffering. "I just couldn't stand how Luke Sebastian treated you all those years ago, how he acted like *his* brother was too good for you." She tensed then, and her face flushed with sudden fury. "Like he and his brother weren't just more of the Sebastians' sad charity cases, kids of an addict. And you could tell that Michael was already heading that way, drinking too much, smoking. He certainly wasn't better than you, my gorgeous girl. He wasn't good enough for you."

River sucked in a breath, feeling like her mother had struck her. "I never knew—"

"You had to see the drinking," Fiona interjected a bit impatiently. "The smoking. I was worried that he was going to lead you down that same dead-end path."

River shook her head. She'd always had to be the one to keep her wits about her, with her mother, with the Golds, so she'd never been tempted to numb the pain the way that Michael had. But with his childhood, he'd definitely had his reasons. "I never knew you felt that way about him or about me . . ." That she'd been worried about her.

Fiona shrugged and released a shaky sigh this time. "While his brother couldn't admit it, at least Michael knew who and what he was. That's probably why he didn't show up that night. But his sanctimonious brother . . ." She stiffened again. "The things he said about you and about Sarah, I didn't want him to think he was right."

River sucked in another sharp breath. "Ouch."

"He wasn't right," Fiona said. "You were. You were right to keep your daughter. You've done a wonderful job raising her, River."

"I'm not done yet," River said. "And it feels like I have a long way to go."

"The teenage years are long," Fiona said with a smile as she met River's gaze in that mirror again.

"I'm sorry, Mom, for what I put you through," River said. If Sarah ever took off like she had . . .

Fiona jumped up from her chair and hugged her so tightly that River lost her breath for a moment. How could her mother be so petite and yet so strong?

"I'm sorry, too, baby," Fiona said, her voice thick with tears. "I'm so sorry . . ."

And all River's doubts about her mother's truthfulness rushed back. What exactly was she apologizing for?

Lying to Luke?

Or for something else she'd done?

Something much worse . . .

Luke waited for the dread that always gripped him when he drove through the gates of Gold Memorial Gardens. But today he felt nothing but anticipation. Maybe today he would finally get some answers.

Not about Gregory Gold's death; he was still waiting for the toxicology report on the body and syringe he'd found. He wanted answers about his brother, too. River had to have some idea of where Michael was. Unless she was telling the truth and her mother was the one who'd lied . . .

And what about River's daughter? What did she know, if anything, about her father? Luke wanted to talk to her even more than he wanted to talk to her mother or grandmother. But he didn't even know her name so that he could ask to see her. All he could do was what he was doing now, lingering in the lobby in the hopes of catching her on her way somewhere.

"Sheriff, do you have news for us?" Gregory Gold II asked.

"Or at least a damn body so we can have a funeral and settle his estate," his mother grumbled as she held tightly to her son's arm. Carolyn Gold was showing her age in ways that her former husband hadn't. Even in death, Gregory Gold I looked more vital than she was. Had she gotten sick of waiting for her ex to get what was coming to him? Or for her to get what was coming to her?

Would his former wives be in Gregory's will?

"You should be able to speak with his lawyer, and get the process of settling his estate started," Luke suggested. He'd like to know what was in that will, too. If this was a murder, he would have to know even if he had to get a warrant to find out.

Gregory shook his head. "No. Because if someone caused his death, that person will not be able to profit from it."

Luke wasn't sure if the man knew what was in his father's will, or if he just knew that was a Michigan law. The slayer statute.

"And we all know who killed him if he was murdered," the first Mrs. Gold remarked.

"And who is that?" he asked. He knew they'd been throwing River's mother at him as a suspect. But they all had a motive: money. Her son the most *if* as the oldest male he inherited everything like his father had from his father.

"Isn't it obvious?" Mrs. Gold asked.

Not to him, not with so many possibilities just in this house. And in town . . .

Gregory Gold I wasn't as revered as Luke's father was. The nicest thing Luke had ever heard anyone call Gregory Gold I was a bloodsucking ghoul. He'd heard that a lot among other names that had been used for the man. The biggest complaint about him was that he overcharged for his funeral services and burial plots because he had a monopoly on death in Gold Creek and in the surrounding areas. And that he used the money of the dead and the bereaved to try to outlive everyone else.

So really anyone could have been provoked into making sure that didn't happen. Into murdering him.

There were plenty of motives for killing Gregory Gold I. Revenge. Jealousy. Greed.

And as for means . . .

Luke hadn't found a locked door yet at the house. So pretty much anyone would have had access to him.

"Who is your prime suspect?" Luke prodded the Golds when they both just stood there, staring at him.

"His next ex-wife," the first Mrs. Gold replied. "The flaky Fiona isn't quite as flaky as she acts."

Luke had already wondered about that, suspecting that Fiona's whole grieving widow hysteria might have just been an act to hide her guilt. She was definitely already one of Luke's prime suspects if the old man had really been murdered. But he just shrugged again. "Well, we won't have confirmation that a crime has been committed until some reports come back."

But he did know that Fiona Gold had been lying about Michael. If he believed her daughter . . .

He wasn't sure what to believe right now, though.

"If you don't have confirmation yet, why are you here again, Sheriff?" Gregory Gold II asked.

Luke drew in a deep breath as he tried to come up with a reason that wasn't personal to him. That wasn't about his brother and his brother's daughter.

"Sheriff?" a soft voice called out his title.

And he turned to find *her* standing behind him. A pang struck his heart over how much she looked like Michael and like Michael and Luke's mother. She had that same slight dimple in the middle of her pointy chin, and her eyes were deep-set like Michael's and Laura's had been. Even the shape of her eyebrows looked like theirs, thick with a slight arch to them.

"Yes," he said with a nod. "I'm Sheriff Sebastian. What's your name?"

"Sarah . . ." She stared at him, her dark eyes hard. "Sarah Gold."

"Sarah!" another voice called out. "Sarah!" River ran down the staircase from the second story, obviously determined to keep her daughter away from him.

Or him away from her daughter?

Had she done the same thing with Michael? Taken him away from his daughter? Just like she'd taken him away from Luke, or so he'd thought. But if Michael really hadn't left with her, where had he gone? And why hadn't he contacted Luke or the Sebastians at least once over the past sixteen years? Something had to have happened to him.

Maybe Dr. Jeffries and the Golds had planted too many suspicions in Luke's mind. Or maybe it was just that Luke had seen too many times how vicious people could be to each other.

Because now he was worrying about what the hell she might have done with Michael. The same thing her mother might have done to her husband? Gotten rid of him permanently?

Chapter 10

"What did you want with the sheriff?" River asked her daughter, her heart thumping fast and hard with the panic she'd felt when she'd seen them together in the lobby. Sarah looked more like Luke Sebastian's daughter than she did hers; she usually acted more like him, too, now that River thought about it. Grumpy. Suspicious. Judgmental.

Were personalities as genetic as physical features?

Sarah stared after Luke as he walked out of the double doors of the lobby, his cell pressed to his ear. If it hadn't started ringing, River wasn't sure that she would have gotten her daughter away from him. Even now, on the double stairwell, Sarah had only ascended a few of the steps up from the lobby. The teenager turned back toward River, and the look in her dark eyes was so hard, so angry. "I want to ask him about my dead-beat dad," Sarah replied. "And I want to tell him what a jerk he is for treating you like trash when you were just a teenager."

River hadn't been wrong to panic the minute she'd seen them together, but yet she couldn't help pride in her child swelling her heart for a moment. Sarah had never been protective of her before. But that wasn't her job. River didn't want her daughter to have to become the responsible adult in their relationship like River had had to become, when she was much too young, with her own mother and grandmother.

"Well, remember he is the sheriff," she cautioned her child. Something she was going to have to keep reminding herself so that she wouldn't be as blunt with him as she'd like to be. She couldn't tell him to stay the hell away if he was truly investigating a crime.

But what crime? An old man's death of natural causes? Or was he just looking for an excuse to come after their family? After her?

Distrust of him, fear of him, was what made her want to protect her daughter from him. River would not let him hurt Sarah; she wouldn't let him close enough for that. They needed to get this funeral over with, so they could go back to Santa Monica. All of them.

"Your grandma Fiona wants to see you," River said. "She didn't get the chance last night. And GG Mabel is in there with her, so you need to referee while I get breakfast."

But with the way her stomach was jumping around, she had no intention of putting any food in it. When Sarah passed her to head up the stairs, River touched just her daughter's shoulder even though she really wanted to close her arms around her and protect her . . . the way River had needed someone to protect her all those years ago. Before Sarah could shrug off her affection, like she often did since she hit thirteen, River pulled her hand away and started down the stairs.

"Mom, the family dining room is up here," Sarah reminded her. There was another area on the main level, the massive formal dining room, where meals were served, but that was for the funeral brunches, luncheons, or refreshments after interments. They'd used it last night because they'd all been eating at the same time but there was a smaller dining room on the second level. The big commercial kitchen on the main level serviced all the dining areas.

River forced a smile and nodded in acknowledgment that her daughter was right. Gigi and Toby must have given her quite the tour the night before. "I just need to speak to Gregory a moment."

Sarah hesitated, but then she must have heard what reached River's ears. A high-pitched scream of frustration and then the hurled words, "You never should have come here. I don't want you here!" And a door slammed.

"Oh, God . . ." River murmured.

Sarah started running up the rest of the way, taking on the role of referee that River had hoped her daughter would never have to be. But River should have known . . .

Mabel and Fiona acted more like teenage sisters than mother and daughter. Whenever they were together, the drama started. She didn't rush up after Sarah, though, because the slamming door suggested one of them had separated herself from the situation already. Another door slammed. And now so had the other . . .

Or whoever slammed that door just hadn't wanted to be outdone by the other. They wanted to be the outdoer.

"I never truly appreciated you, River," Gregory II remarked.

"What?" she asked.

"You were always so quiet and shy," he said. "Nothing at all like your mother."

She wasn't certain if he was complimenting her or not. After the way he'd always treated her . . .

"She got pregnant to trap a man," Carolyn Gold remarked. "She's exactly like her mother."

God. Had her mother lied to everyone about Michael? Did they all believe she'd forced him to marry her?

"I raised my daughter on my own," River said, her voice

hard now. Because she really couldn't consider Mabel much help, at least not at the moment, and because she had had to do all the hard stuff without much support.

Carolyn sniffed. "Then I guess you aren't like your mother."

"I need to bring my daughter back home as soon as possible," River said, ignoring the old biddy's comment, "to not disrupt her schooling." Which was online so it wasn't any disruption at all. Maybe River was like her mother, a liar when she wanted to be. "When will the funeral be held?"

"Ask our newly elected sheriff," Gregory said. "He's holding our father hostage."

"You just paid the ransom," Luke remarked as he slid his cell back into his shirt pocket, the one with the star embroidered on it. "By getting the governor and the attorney general to call the mayor."

Gregory arched his white brows in probably feigned innocence. "Did they do that? I had no idea."

Luke snorted. "As I told them, we can't rush the lab results, and if something gets missed, we might have to exhume his body. You can't cremate him."

"Father didn't want to be cremated," Gregory said.

"He prearranged his funeral?" River asked with surprise. She'd always thought he'd convinced himself, as well as everyone else, that he could live forever.

"It was something he said often," Lawrence remarked.

His sudden appearance made River jump with surprise. Where the hell had he come from? One of the showing rooms?

"Any time we fired up the cremation oven," Lawrence continued, "Father would get especially anxious, shudder, and exclaim how it was a little too much like hell . . ."

"I guess he knows for sure what hell feels like now," Carolyn said, her thin lips curving into a smug smile.

To River, this place was hell. Not just the cremation oven

but the whole building, the whole town, and she just wanted to get her daughter, mother, and grandmother out of here before they all burned up.

Anger burned inside Luke. The former sheriff had warned him about the politics of the job. Naively he'd thought he could stay out of all the political games. But as the mayor had just pointed out to him over the phone, he could be recalled. And if he resisted doing what the mayor wanted him to, then the governor would personally and directly call him with the same order. Maybe even the president or the vice president might extend themselves to make the request.

Apparently, the damn Golds knew them all. Growing up in Gold Creek, Luke had been well aware that the Gold family was rich and powerful, but until his phone had blown up with all those threatening phone calls from the mayor and the attorney general and even a local news station, he hadn't realized exactly how rich and powerful they were.

Enough to elude justice?

Was that the reason they were trying to rush the funeral? Because one of them, or maybe all of them, was trying to get away with murder? He was going to make damn sure that didn't happen. He wanted to go over that body himself before the coroner released it. So he turned on his heel and headed back out the double doors.

Just as he was about to step out from under the covered portico and into the parking lot, someone caught his sleeve and jerked him to a stop. He turned around to see what Gold had stopped him and nearly smiled when he saw that it was the Gold nobody had considered a Gold. But he could see it now in the way that she was glaring at him. She wasn't nearly as intimidating as her relatives, though.

And he'd wanted to see her again, to talk to her.

"Stay away from my daughter," she said, her voice a low hiss like a cat protecting its kittens.

He shrugged off her hand on his arm and shook his head. "She's *my* niece."

"You wanted me to give her up," she reminded him. "You never wanted a relationship with her, so you're not going to have one now."

"What about my brother?" he asked. "Are you going to keep denying me a relationship with him, too?"

"I have no idea where Michael is," River replied with an even more intense glare. "And I don't want to know."

"I do," he said. "I've already missed so much of his life."

Except for those eighteen months he'd lived with the Sebastians, but Luke hadn't been around much then, either, because he'd already joined the military. Maybe if he hadn't left so soon, he wouldn't have lost his brother again.

"I need to find him, River," he implored her, letting the emotion churning inside him make his voice gruff. "You swear you have no idea where he is?"

A slight grimace twisted her mouth for just a second before she shook her head. "No idea."

He reached for her then, clasping her arms in his hands. "I can tell that you know something."

She shrugged and wriggled out of his grasp, stepping back, away from him. "I don't know where he is now. But I'm not surprised he took off."

He sucked in a breath.

"Running away from his problems, hiding from them," she said, "that was all he knew . . ."

Because of their mother.

Luke released the breath he'd drawn in as a ragged sigh. "I wasn't surprised that he took off because of those same reasons," he admitted. "But I am surprised that he took off without you."

"It was too much pressure," she said. "The pregnancy, the baby coming. He was dealing with it with drinking and . . ."

"Drugs?" Luke felt like she'd punched him again. How had he had no idea what had been going on with his brother? Because he hadn't wanted to see it . . .

He'd wanted instead to blame it all on River Gold. But she'd been just a kid then.

"I don't know what all he was taking," she said. "I just know that he self-medicated a lot."

Like their mother had.

Luke jerked his head in a quick nod. "Thanks for telling me. Now I might have some idea where to look for him." But he was afraid that now it would be too late to save Michael just like it had been too late for their mother.

"I'm sorry my mother didn't tell you the truth," she said, her voice and her face soft now with regret and sympathy.

She probably knew what he did, that it was too late to help Michael now, even if he could find him. He forced thoughts of his brother from his mind, though, to focus on his case now. "Do you know what else your mother is lying about?" he asked.

She stiffened, and the hardness came back in his eyes. "I don't know what you mean . . ."

"Could she have done something to your father?"

She shook her head. "She loved him. He didn't deserve her love, but she loved him."

"Did he deserve to get murdered?"

"You don't know that he was."

But he could see the doubt on her face . . . about her father's death and her mother's guilt?

Fiona stared at the naked body lying on the table in the preparation room. Crude staples held the skin together over the hollow cavity where his organs had been.

"Mrs. Gold," Warner Thoms said as he stepped through the door of the cool room. "You shouldn't be in here."

"We have to get him ready," she said. "There will be a showing first thing in the morning for an hour before the funeral."

"I can do this," Warner assured her. "You shouldn't have to see him like this."

Oh, no. She needed to see him like this, exactly like this . . . dead, the perfect corpse he'd wanted to leave behind desecrated. His flesh cut, his organs gone . . .

She wondered if they'd even found a heart in him. Or maybe there had been some kind of computer instead that had pumped the blood through his body.

"He would want me to take care of him," she said. "To make him look his best." That was true. The one thing he had appreciated about her was her ability to make him look good.

Warner studied her for a moment and nodded. "You are the best, Mrs. Gold. I've never seen anyone work the magic you do with the dead."

And he'd worked at a few other places before coming to Gold Memorial Gardens and Funeral Services. But Fiona didn't know if he was telling her the truth or just trying to charm her. Maybe he thought she was going to become his new boss.

Was she?

Or had this all happened too late for that?

What had Gregory done?

She would know soon enough. After the funeral, the lawyer would read Gregory's will. Colson Howard had shared things with her about the will and about Gregory, but she couldn't be sure that she could trust him. That Gregory hadn't told Colson what to tell her.

Her husband had enjoyed playing games. Manipulating his family had been one of his favorite pastimes. And they were all so easily manipulated except for her.

"I've got this," she told Warner. "I'll take care of every-thing."

"But he needs to be embalmed and . . ."

"I know how to do it," she assured him. And more than that, she wanted to do it. She also wanted to be alone with her hus-band one last time.

As if he'd finally sensed and respected that, Warner nodded and stepped back through that door. He closed it behind him-self and left her alone in that cold, brightly lit space.

She could see everything so clearly here.

Every line on Gregory's face. On his body . . .

The wrinkles and the scars from where he'd tried to have those wrinkles removed. He'd fought so hard against aging. No. He'd fought so hard against this . . .

"You thought you could beat it," she whispered close to her husband's ear. "You thought you could escape death, but now you know, nobody lives forever, my darling Gregory, not even you . . ."

Chapter 11

Sarah didn't have much time. The funeral stuff was going to be starting soon, which was the only way she'd managed to convince Mom to let her go to town for a minute. Mom was so busy with the grans that she hadn't realized Sarah was up to something.

"Thanks for driving me here," she said to Toby.

Supposedly, he was driving her to town to pick up some black tights to go with the dress Mom thought was going to be too short for GG Mabel. Sarah had claimed she hadn't packed an extra pair, but she had one back in her bag to loan to GG Mabel.

Gigi had an extra pair too, but before she'd been able to offer them, Sarah had shaken her head and shushed her with a look. Gigi and Toby both owed her for not ratting them out over the disruption they'd caused the other night, so they'd been happy to drive her. They were also nosy, too, and wondered what the hell she was up to.

So after Toby turned the van into the driveway next to the

mailbox marked *Sebastian*, he shut off the ignition and turned to her while Gigi leaned over the console from the back seat.

"You really want to see the sheriff?" Gigi asked.

Toby snorted. "What are you going to confess? Did you off Great-Grandfather?"

She felt a pang of regret that she would never officially meet the man, but at least she would be able to see him pretty soon. "The sheriff needs to confess," Sarah said, "and tell me where the hell my deadbeat dad is."

Toby's mouth fell open, and Gigi whispered, "Oh . . ." as her face flushed. Then she stammered, "Sorry . . ."

"You guys are lucky," she said. "You grew up here in Gold Creek with all your family."

Gigi shook her head. "I think you got the better deal with your mom and great-grandma. Your mom is sweet, and your great-gran is a riot."

They were, so maybe she was right about Sarah getting the better deal.

"I still want to know where my dad is," she said. And if anyone knew, it would be the guy who talked him out of leaving with her mom.

"You have to hurry," Gigi said. "Or our dad and grandfather will kill *us* if we're late to Great-Grandfather's funeral."

Sarah pushed open the passenger door and jumped down onto the asphalt driveway. Her legs threatened to buckle, but she quickly locked her knees so she wouldn't fall.

The side door of the van slid open and Gigi dangled half her body out. "You want me to go with you?"

Toby leaned over the console inside the front. "I can go with—"

"No," she said. "Then your dad and granddad might find out you were here with me and talked to the sheriff without your lawyer present." The rich kids at her old school had always refused to talk to anyone without their lawyer present, not the principal, the guidance counselor, and especially not the police who had occasionally searched lockers and cars in the parking lot.

"*We* don't have a lawyer," Gigi said with a smile as she hopped out.

"What do you call Colson Howard?" Toby asked his sister. "He's the family lawyer."

Gigi giggled. "Yeah, but it's pretty obvious that he likes some of the family more than others."

Her cousin seemed to love gossip as much as GG Mabel and her card-playing friends did.

"Anyways, Sarah's right," Toby continued as if his sister hadn't spoken. "Dad and Granddad would pop a blood vessel if we talked to the sheriff without Howard. We'll stay here but, Sarah, stay out on the porch. Don't go inside. That way if you need us . . ."

A sudden warmth chased away the chill of the autumn wind that scattered fallen leaves across the driveway. Sarah smiled, touched that they cared.

"Then we can call someone else to help you," Toby finished with a wicked grin.

She laughed. "Asshole."

Gigi called, "Shotgun," and hopped into the passenger seat Sarah had just vacated. "And hurry up!"

Sarah drew in a deep breath, bracing herself, before she walked stiffly up the driveway, past the Gold Creek Sheriff SUV, to the steps of the front porch that wrapped around the entire first level of the two-story farmhouse. Before she made it up the stairs, the door opened, and a kid leaned against the jamb. He was Black and tall and skinny. He had a little bit of hair on his chin and his upper lip, so maybe he was her age or older.

Sarah knew her dad had lived in a foster home here in Gold Creek with the Sebastians. Mom had told her that once when

Sarah had asked her how they'd met. Her dad had moved into this foster home and started going to River's school.

Why was the sheriff staying here now that he was back, though? He was a little old to still be a foster kid; a little old to not have a place of his own.

She cleared her throat and said, "I need to talk to Sheriff Sebastian."

"Then you probably should have gone to the sheriff's office instead of here," the kid replied. His voice was deep like his dark eyes.

"That would have been a waste of my time since he's here," she said, pointing behind her to the SUV parked in the driveway.

The kid's mouth curved into a slight grin, and he turned and called into the house, "Luke!"

"Jackson!" the man yelled back, chuckling as he walked up beside him. He was messing with a tie that he wore with a dark suit, not his uniform. When he saw her, the smile slid off his mouth. He sucked in a breath and asked, "Does your mother know you're here?"

She snorted. "Like you care about my mother . . ." Like anyone cared about Mom except her and GG Mabel. She wasn't even sure how much Grandma Fiona cared about her own daughter because she'd just let her leave as a teenager and raise a child on her own. Mom never would have let Sarah do that on her own; she would have been there for her. Not that Sarah would ever get into *that* kind of trouble.

"She'll be upset that you're here," Luke pointed out.

A jab of guilt made Sarah flinch, and the kid, Jackson, stepped a little closer to her. She could have asked him to leave them alone, but she was kind of glad that he was sticking around. Maybe she shouldn't have insisted on coming up to confront the sheriff on her own.

"Yeah, she would be pissed," she admitted. "But I also have

a right to know about my dad. Where is he? What happened to him?"

The sheriff flinched now, and Jackson stepped a little closer to him, as if to protect him. "I wish I knew, Sarah."

She glared at him. "Like you don't . . ."

He shook his head. "I really thought he was with you and your mom this whole time."

She snorted again. "Yeah, right . . ."

"Your grandma Fiona told me that he was, and that he didn't want to talk to me," Luke said.

"Why would she do that?" Sarah asked.

"Pride?" He shrugged. "I don't know." He hesitated. "You've really never seen him?"

The intensity of his questions had her stepping back, and she might have tumbled down the stairs if that kid hadn't shot out his arm and grabbed hers. "Hey, careful . . ." Jackson's deep voice rumbled with concern.

Heat rushed to Sarah's face and to her arm where he was holding it. She tugged free of his grasp. "I have to go. The funeral is starting soon." And she turned and ran down those steps and back to the van. Gigi had left the side door open, and Sarah jumped inside it.

Gigi leaned around the front seat and stared at her. "You okay?"

Sarah jerked her head in a quick nod. "Yeah, he didn't tell me anything."

Because he didn't know?

"He's a dick," Toby said. "Did you meet the kid that lives with him? I've seen him around school. What's his name?"

Sarah shrugged. "He didn't introduce himself." And that shouldn't have mattered to her. She doubted that she would ever see him again. It wasn't like she was going to stay in Gold Creek and go to school here with her cousins. "The sheriff called him Jackson."

She didn't want to see the sheriff again, either, because he might rat her out. Hell, Toby and Gigi might rat her out, too. She'd been stupid to trust them after the crap they'd pulled with the casket.

But she hoped like hell they didn't tell her mom. She didn't want her to know that she had come here. Enough people had already betrayed her mom; Sarah didn't want to be another one.

"That was smooth, man," Jackson remarked. "You scared her."

That fear coursed through Luke now as she rode off in that speeding van with the other Gold teenagers. She would be okay. She had to be, but clearly he'd rattled her. "I didn't mean to . . ." That was the last thing he'd wanted to do. "I just wanted . . ."

"You interrogated her like a suspect," Jackson said. "She didn't do anything wrong. She just wants to know where her dad is."

"So do I," Luke said, his voice cracking slightly.

Jackson grabbed his arm like he had hers, and he squeezed it slightly. "Yeah, I know. You just got a little too intense with her, though. Remind me to never wind up in an interrogation room with you."

"Never do anything that will put you there," Luke advised with a slight grin. Jackson was a good kid. "Now I better get going." He reached up to adjust his tie. Instead of his uniform, he was wearing a suit for the funeral. Out of respect . . .

He wasn't sure to whom he was giving the respect, though. Gregory Gold I or his family or the other important people who were likely to be there. His dad was giving the sermon, and his mother was probably there to fend off the old ladies like she had to at church. Everybody loved his father a little too much.

"I want to go to this funeral, too," Jackson said.

"At the risk of interrogating you," Luke teased. "Why? You never met Gregory Gold. And you hate funerals."

"I hate funerals for people I know," Jackson said. "Like you said, I don't know this guy."

"Then why go?"

"I wanna see Pastor Sebastian in action," Jackson replied.

"He's invited you to the church services he's held," Luke reminded him.

"He's invited you, too, but I haven't seen you heading off to church with them," Jackson said. "You know I don't believe in God. And you know why, probably for the same reasons you don't."

Luke flinched. They'd both lost a lot over the years. "I never said that I didn't . . ." He just wasn't sure what the hell he believed anymore, especially after the conflicting stories from Fiona and River. But Sarah hadn't seemed to be lying; she wanted to find her dad nearly as badly as Luke did.

Jackson grinned. "You haven't said anything because you're scared of your mama Mary."

Luke nodded. "Dad would handle that better than she would," he heartily agreed.

"I just . . . I want to go to a funeral," Jackson said. "Like get closure or something, you know . . ."

Luke narrowed his eyes and studied the suddenly fidgeting teenager. "Or do you want to see the pretty girl again?"

Jackson's grin widened.

"She's my niece," Luke reminded him.

Jackson shrugged. "So. We're not related."

But because Luke was solely responsible for him now, Jackson was beginning to feel like Luke's son, at least to Luke. "I'm not sure that you going to a funeral is a good idea . . ."

"I'll be fine, Luke, stop worrying," he said with all the annoyance of a typical teenager. But he wasn't a typical teenager. Not anymore.

All Luke wanted for Jackson was for him to be okay after everything he'd been through, everyone he'd lost. Sometimes he seemed all right but then he'd have an anxiety attack or a mini meltdown. Just like a soldier who'd been in war, Jackson had some PTSD.

He was working with someone to get through that and everything else. And the therapist had advised Luke to listen to the kid, to let him do things that he wanted to . . . to let Jackson set his own pace.

So if the kid wanted to go to the funeral for that closure, Luke wasn't going to deny him. "I am worried that if you show up like that, we'll both be in trouble with Mama Mary," Luke said, gesturing at Jackson's basketball shorts and stretched-out T-shirt.

"I'll change into something else," Jackson said, and he started up the steps toward the second story. Then he leaned back down and said, "Don't leave without me." There was a note in his voice, just a soft break . . .

And Luke felt his fear, that fear of being abandoned or left behind like Jackson's parents had left him behind. But unlike with Luke's mom, it hadn't been their choice.

"I'll be here," Luke said. "But hurry . . ."

Jackson's big feet pounded on the steps as he ran up the rest of the stairs.

"I'll always be here . . ." Luke murmured, but he wasn't sure that was a promise he could keep. Like Jackson, Luke had lost a lot of people he cared about, too.

Like his best friend Jack, his bio mom, and his brother . . .

Where the hell was Michael?

Sarah lied to her . . .

River couldn't stop the thought from gnawing at her, or maybe she'd latched onto it as a distraction during this spectacle. Gregory Gold I's wake was a standing-room-only event that everyone must have thought they needed to attend before the funeral that would follow.

Or maybe they just wanted to make sure that he was dead. He didn't look that way. He didn't even look real. He had been in his mid-eighties but he looked at least half of that.

Was that from plastic surgery or her mom's handiwork, though? River didn't want to get close enough to that casket to try to figure it out. Instead she just wanted to focus on her daughter, who stood beside her, standing on tiptoe, trying to peer over the others to see inside that casket.

Thanks to the other night, this wasn't the first dead body her daughter was seeing. But it was the first time she would see her grandfather.

Had this been the first time Sarah had lied to River? Or were there other times? And why did it hurt so much to realize she had when River had been able to let go of her anger over all the times her mother had lied to her?

She had no doubt Sarah had lied because the tights she'd loaned Mabel weren't new. She hadn't gone into town to buy anything. So where had she and her cousins gone? What were they up to?

They kept shooting each other furtive glances across the crowded room. The divider between two showing rooms had been removed, so that there was enough space for all the mourners and the flowers. Flowers were everywhere, elaborate displays of roses and carnations as well as the greens of peace lilies and ivy plants.

Toby and Gigi stood with their parents in the official receiving line. River had been invited to join the line, but she would have felt like a hypocrite receiving condolences for the loss of a man who'd never really been that much a part of her life. After she ran away to California, to her grandmother, he'd never visited her like her mother had. He hadn't even spoken to her on the phone.

If she'd truly been his kid, wouldn't he have wanted to maintain some contact with her? He hadn't even let his ex-wives leave his family; why would he have let an actual daughter go as easily as he had River?

"Mom, I want to see him," Sarah said, and she tugged on the sleeve of the black sweater River had borrowed from her mother. River wore the cardigan over the cream-colored dress she'd packed because all her clothes were much more summery in nature than anything anyone wore in Gold Creek even in the summer. But it was fall now.

River's stomach moved, shifting inside her with nausea and dread. "Are you sure?"

"Mom, you have to go up there because you need to referee the grans before they start throwing down right next to the casket."

Mabel had taken River's spot next to Fiona in the receiving line, and they were whispering to each other, not loud enough for anyone to hear the words but the tone was waspish. They were sniping at each other again.

And River felt a pang of guilt. She'd come here for her mother, to support her, but instead she'd found herself wanting to avoid her. Did Sarah want to avoid River? Was that why she'd manufactured an excuse to slip out earlier?

Just like River wanted to avoid all the other mourners and the sympathy they kept coming up to offer her despite her not being in that line. One of the men from Gibson Brothers Grave Vaulting Services approached her. Like Gold Memorial Gardens, their business was a family one. Their father and uncles had started it years ago, and there were rumors that Gregory Gold I had helped them start it and had a stake in it, like he had a stake in everything in Gold Creek, apparently even in the local sheriff.

"Nice to see you again, Miss River," the man said to her. "Of course not under these horrible circumstances . . ."

"Hi, Jerome." Although he was older now, with more lines in his face and some silver threading through his sandy hair, she remembered his lanky build and big grin. He was always cracking jokes to her when she was young. Dad jokes he'd called them, but her father had certainly never cracked a joke in his life.

"Like I told the rest of your family, let me know if you need anything," he said.

She smiled and nodded.

"Like I always told you, I will be the last to let you down," Jerome said, and emitted a hearty chuckle that had heads turning toward them.

Sarah's brow furrowed; obviously, she didn't get the joke like River hadn't the first time he'd told her, either.

"I'm a grave vaulter, honey," he explained to her. "The one who puts the casket in the concrete before we lower it into the open grave."

River shuddered, as she always did when she thought of the cemetery or death. But Sarah laughed now in appreciation of the ghoulish humor. But then her laughter slipped away, and she tensed next to River.

As Jerome slipped away into the crowd, Sarah clasped River's hand in hers. She wasn't trying to get away from her now. "Mom . . ." Her gaze was focused on the back of the room instead of the front where the casket took center stage.

River's stomach jumped around even more as she noticed Luke Sebastian walking into the room. He wore a dark suit, and his brown hair was clipped short like he was still in the military. He stood that way, too, with that perfect posture of a man in uniform. And he surveyed the room the way a military man probably had to, in order to assess the situation for threats.

He was the threat to River, to her peace of mind. Not that she had much of that here in Gold Creek. He needed to close this investigation, so that she could go home. The clients she'd had to pawn off on her apprentice were not happy with her.

She was bound to lose their repeat business and other clients if she didn't get back to Santa Monica soon. There were a lot of makeup artists in California, like her grandmother from whom River had learned so much more than she'd learned from her own mom.

Luke's gaze locked with hers for a moment before Sarah tugged harder on her hand. "Mom!"

She turned toward her daughter, wondering what the situation was. Then she followed Sarah's gaze to the person who was talking with her mother and grandmother. A young woman, probably late teens to early twenties, was flushed and crying. Maybe because of what her mother was saying because Mabel pulled Fiona away from the girl and headed toward River. Before they could make it across the room to them, some older ladies stepped closer to Sarah and River, shifting them toward the front of the room.

"Miss River, that is you," one of the trio of blue-haired ladies said with a smile. "You are even more beautiful than you were as a teenager."

"A true beauty, like her mother," another chimed in.

"Her mother is as talented as she is beautiful," the third said. "What she does to the dead . . ." She trailed off with an envious sigh as if her mother was a chef who made particularly appetizing dishes.

"These people have never looked as good in their lives as they do after they die and your mama gets her hands on them," the second one chimed in again.

The first one chuckled and patted her blue hair. "I think some people are willing to die to look as good as Miss Fiona makes them look."

River was grateful for that sweater as a chill rushed over her now at their words.

"So those are funeral groupies . . ." Sarah whispered.

And River nodded. She couldn't remember their names, or she would have tried to introduce them. Then her mother was there, and while the women praised her, Fiona just gave them a curt smile instead of basking as she usually would have. Then she tugged River and Sarah to the side. "Can you believe she's here?"

"Who?" River asked.

"That hussy . . ." She pointed toward the girl who had continued down the line of Golds.

Garrett shoved her away from him and went running from the room, his mother hot on his heels after she fairly growled, like a mother bear, at the woman. "You have some nerve showing up here! Leave us alone!"

The girl started to sob. Loudly. Nearly as loudly and hysterically as Fiona had sobbed when she'd seen River standing outside the arrangement-making conference room. Then she stumbled and knocked over a display of flowers. When she stepped back, the cardigan sweater she wore opened up down the middle, revealing her swollen belly.

And River felt a pang of sympathy for the girl. She didn't know her, but on some level she could identify with her. With being that young and pregnant.

Hopefully, she was older than River had been, though. "Who is she, Mom?" River asked.

"A homewrecker," Fiona said, her words sounding like a hiss. "She moved on from Garrett to his grandfather."

Now River's stomach churned with revulsion.

The girl wailed, "No! No!" and launched herself onto the casket as if trying to crawl into it with Gregory Gold I. Then the girl's body shuddered, either with sobs or maybe even a seizure. After that she went suddenly quiet and still as she continued to lie across the open half of the casket on top of Gregory Gold I's corpse.

"Look at her . . ." Fiona murmured, shaking her head with disgust. Her voice was the only one in the room as everyone else had fallen silent after the flowers crashed to the floor. They were all obviously in shock because no one moved toward the girl, who was so strangely still and quiet now.

That chill rushed over River again, and she found herself edging closer to the girl and the casket.

Sarah moved ahead of her until she stood next to it, next to them. Then she turned back and said, "Mom, look at her. I think she's dead."

Chapter 12

"I think she's dead . . ."

Sarah's words echoed throughout the eerily silent room. Luke figured the eeriest thing was that that many people had gone so quiet so quickly after the flower arrangement fell over, scattering dirt across the plush carpeting. It was like the aftermath of an explosion . . . when everything went deathly quiet after the blast. Like the world had stopped turning for a moment.

And Luke almost slipped back . . . into that moment that Jackson's dad died. Jackson. He glanced at him to find him staring where everyone else was, at the front of the room. Then remembering what Sarah had said, Luke rushed forward, shoving aside people to get to the girl. Dr. Jeffries moved, too, pushing through the crowd to join him at the casket.

But the corpse in the casket didn't look as dead as the young girl who'd collapsed across his chest. Her eyes were open and staring as if she was looking right through Luke. The expression in her eyes was the same as the one Luke had seen in Gregory Gold's the day his body had been found: fear.

"Can I touch her?" Dr. Jeffries asked as he held back for a moment as if afraid that she was a sculpture that might break.

Luke nodded. "God, yes, try to save her." She was so young. Too young to die.

He helped the older doctor ease the woman down onto the floor. But her body was already stiff, nearly as stiff as the one in the casket. And her belly was swollen but not very much. How far along was she?

Someone, maybe the teenage boy, brought the doctor's bag and dropped it next to him. But Luke was already on the phone, already ordering an ambulance and backup.

Dr. Jeffries pulled a stethoscope from his bag and listened to her heart and to her lungs. But then he shook his head and murmured, "She's gone . . ."

"What about the baby?" Luke asked in a hushed voice as everyone stayed so silent, watching them.

Dr. Jeffries moved his stethoscope over the mound of her belly and shook his head again. "I don't hear a heartbeat, and she doesn't look far enough along for the fetus to survive on its own."

"What about a defibrillator? Do you have one? Could you bring her back?"

Dr. Jeffries shook his head. "I don't have one."

"The ambulance is on its way," Luke said. "They'll have one. Maybe they can bring her back. Do CPR, try to save her . . ." Or at least act that way for their audience.

The doctor moved his hand over her neck, tipping it back to try to get an airway. As he brushed her long blond hair aside, Luke noticed a mark on her pale skin. He leaned a little closer to get a better look. "Is that a needle mark?" he asked, pitching his voice low to the doctor because everyone stood around them, wide-eyed and listening.

Dr. Jeffries nodded.

And Luke was reminded of that syringe he'd seen in Greg-

ory Gold I's trash. The crime techs had promised him the results today, just as the coroner had promised his preliminary
report would be done soon, too.

While Luke had been waiting around for the evidence to
come back of murder, another murder had just been committed
and this one right in front of his damn face. Not that he could
see much with the crowd all gathered around him. Kneeling on
the floor as he was, he could only see all the black of their
clothes, of their funeral garments. He drew in a deep breath
that was thick with the floral odors from all the flower arrangements.

He'd already called for an ambulance and backup. But now
he called in the crime scene techs and every available deputy.
He had a crime scene to secure and a suspect pool that was already edging toward the double doors to the lobby. In the silence of the room, they'd had to overhear what he'd ordered,
and now they were either afraid that they might be next or . . .
that he might catch them.

He should have already caught the killer before they'd killed
again.

It was too late for this woman, but he had to make certain
that he protected everyone else.

"Everybody needs to remain where they are," he said, raising his voice. "We need to secure the scene and take statements."

But instead of freezing everyone in place like Gregory Gold
had seemed frozen in the chair in front of his vanity and this
girl had frozen over his casket, other people acted as if he'd released them. And they rushed out of the room . . .

Like his prime suspect . . .

"Mom!" River exclaimed as her mother tried to shove past
her and flee the room. And that was how it felt, like Fiona was
running away. From the sheriff or from her?

The sheriff hurried past everyone and ran toward the double doors that led outside. "I said nobody is leaving! You are all required to stay here."

"On whose authority?" someone asked, someone who looked vaguely familiar and acted as though he was important.

Instead of being intimidated as the speaker might have intended, Luke's lips curved into a slight grin. "On my authority."

"I need to use the bathroom," Fiona murmured, her voice faint. "I'm about to pass out."

River slid her arm around her mom whose body was trembling against hers. "Hang on to me."

"Nobody's leaving this place or even this area until they're searched," the sheriff proclaimed with a hard glare at Fiona . . . like he suspected her.

Of killing that young woman in front of everyone?

River shook her head. "She's not well."

Mabel rushed up with a chair and wedged it under her daughter. "Here . . . sit down . . ."

Instead of looking appreciative, a frown of annoyance pulled down Fiona's mouth. River dropped to her knees next to her mother. "Do you want me to get you some water? Something?"

Sirens wailed outside; it hadn't taken long for the reinforcements to arrive that the sheriff had called in. He really intended to keep all the mourners there to what . . . interrogate them all like murder suspects?

Surely nobody had killed her just as nobody had killed Gregory Gold I. He must have died from old age. And the girl . . .

Maybe she'd been on drugs or had purposely taken something to end her life. It couldn't be murder. River wouldn't let herself think that, that there was so much evil in the world that someone had purposely killed a young woman with her whole life ahead of her. And another life inside her that would never have a chance now.

As for Gregory Gold . . .

River tried to push thoughts of him from her mind, too. Because if he was her father, she'd lost the opportunity to ever get to know him. But then he'd never wanted to know her, either. Back then she'd thought it was because she wasn't really his daughter. But looking into the past, she realized he hadn't given any attention to Honora, either, who had been his daughter and had desperately tried to get his attention and earn his respect. She'd always told him, "Daddy, I want to run the business with you." Even after she'd left for college and had a child, she still had called him Daddy.

Why had Honora and Garrett been so upset with that girl?

Had she really been with Garrett first like her mother had claimed?

"Who is that girl?" River asked her mother again. Besides the homewrecker that Fiona had called her. "What's her name?"

"Justine something . . ." Fiona murmured, then shrugged. "It doesn't matter. *She* doesn't matter. Not anymore . . ."

That sudden chill rushed over River again, like icy fingers sliding down her spine. And she wanted to ask a question of her own: *Mother, what have you done?*

Maybe Sarah should have been freaked out like everybody else was acting. She'd touched a dead body. Again.

At least it looked like that girl was dead or the doctor would have kept working on her instead of shaking his head. Then the sheriff made his announcement and everybody started running around like he'd said "Stampede" instead of stay put.

And the person who ran the fastest was the kid who'd been at the Sebastian house. Sarah could move quickly, too, so she followed him out the back door he'd slipped through while everybody else had headed to the front, probably to where their cars were parked. They'd intended to speed off on four wheels. He was just running on two extremely long legs.

"Hey!" she called after him. He was so much taller than her that she couldn't catch up with his strides. And she was wearing clunky shoes, too. *Sure, it was the shoes . . .*

She nearly snorted at herself. She sounded like the grans, making excuses. Too many excuses . . .

"Hey!" she called out again. "Are you trying to kill me?"

He stopped so abruptly and whirled toward her that she nearly slammed into his chest. The look on his face, the wild-eyed panic, had her heart racing even faster than the run.

"What's wrong?" she asked him. "Are you okay?"

"Do I fucking seem okay to you?" he asked, his voice shaking, and there were tears in his eyes.

"Did you know her?" she asked, sympathy for him gripping her. "Or did you know my grandfather?"

He shuddered and shook his head now. "No, no . . ."

"Then why are you freaking out?" she asked with concern. Because with the way he'd been running and his wild-eyed look, he was definitely freaking out.

"Dead bodies . . ." He shuddered. "All the dead bodies . . ." And he closed his eyes and covered his face with his hands. He dropped down onto the grass. His shoulders shook and tears slipped through his fingers and dripped from his chin, leaving dark tracks on the light blue shirt he wore with a tie, with basketballs on it, and navy-blue dress pants.

Sarah dropped to her knees beside him. Then she held out a hand and gently tapped his shoulder. But when she touched him, he jumped and cringed like she was going to hurt him. "It's okay," she said. "The dead bodies are in there." Then she glanced at the tombstones all around them. No. The dead bodies were out here, too. But at least he couldn't see them.

Unless the ghost showed up. The grave digger. But wasn't it too early for him?

Didn't he dig his graves in the middle of the night? But now he had another grave to dig for that girl who had just died.

"That was weird," she said. "Seeing someone not much older than us . . . just drop like that . . ."

"So many bodies . . ." he muttered again like he was seeing them yet, or maybe he was seeing something that she couldn't see.

She reached for him again, and this time she pulled his hands from his face. "Look at me."

His eyes were shut tight, as if he was squeezing them to keep them closed.

"Look at me!" she said louder.

And his lids popped open but his eyes . . .

They looked like that girl's had, like they were staring right through Sarah and the look in them . . . was pure fear. He was making her a little afraid, too, but she forced her voice to be calm, to stay soft and sympathetic like her mom always sounded. Like how she'd talked to that homeless guy after GG Mabel had nearly taken him out. "We're okay," she told him. "Nobody's going to hurt us."

"She's dead. She's dead."

Sarah released a shaky breath. He must have known that girl. That poor girl. "I don't know. Maybe they can bring her back or something." She didn't want to lie to him, but she also wanted that look off his face, that look of such pain.

"They couldn't." His voice cracked. "They tried. They couldn't bring her back. Her and my dad are never coming back . . ."

He was remembering his own parents, she realized. No wonder he'd been at that foster home.

"I'm sorry," she said. And here she'd been worried about some deadbeat father that she'd never met. She hadn't lost anything that she'd missed. Not like he was missing his parents so much that it was like someone had gutted him. "I'm really sorry." And she was so sorry that tears stung her eyes, too. "When . . . ?"

He drew in a shaky breath, then another and another.

And she was afraid he was going to pass out until he finally released a heavy sigh. Then he flopped onto his back on the grass, his head coming dangerously close to a marble monument.

"Hey! Are you okay?" she asked again. "What happened . . ."

"It just reminded me of the mall," he said, his voice just barely a whisper now and raspy from his sobbing.

"Malls can get pretty crazy in Santa Monica but here . . ."

"Not here," he said. "Where my mom died . . ."

All the bodies. A mall . . .

His mom died in a mall. A few malls, in different cities around the country, had had shootings with mass fatalities recently and in the not so distant past.

"I'm sorry," she said, and she blinked several times to clear away her tears.

"It wasn't *your* fault," he said. "It was mine. I nagged her for those goddamn shoes. It's all my fault . . ." And his body started shaking again, nearly convulsing like that girl had just seconds before she died.

Fear gripped her, thinking of how fast that girl had gone. "Oh, my God," she said as she leaned over him. "I'm going to get the doctor—"

But his hand shot out and grabbed her arm like he had on the porch to keep her from falling. She wasn't the one in danger this time. He was. And she had to do something to help him. "You need a sedative or something. My grandma has some."

"I'll be okay," he said. "I just have to stop thinking about it." He closed his eyes and tears leaked out of the corners and slid down the sides of his face. "It was just seeing her die brought it all back."

"You were with your mom?" she asked, her voice cracking now with horror at the thought of seeing her mom hurt like that. Of being helpless to protect her, to save her . . . her mom who had never hurt anyone, not even an insect.

His head jerked in a nod, rustling against the grass and leaves beneath him.

"And your dad, too?"

"No, he died a few years ago," he said, his voice gruff again. "With Luke . . ."

"What do you mean?" she asked. Luke was obviously very alive.

"He was deployed with Luke. There was an explosion . . ." He shuddered. "I wasn't there, but I used to see it in my head, too. Imagine how it happened. That was what it seemed like in the mall. Like there'd been an explosion, all the blasts and the bodies . . ."

"Jackson," she said, calling him the name Luke had used. "Let me get Luke for you. Or the doctor . . ." He probably really needed a therapist more than a medical doctor.

"I'm okay." But he tightened his grasp on her arm for a second.

And she tried not to flinch.

Then he abruptly released her as he sat up, bringing his face close to hers. "I'm sorry. Are you okay?"

She nodded. "I'm fine. Don't worry about me."

She realized now that she'd been through nothing compared to what he had. She was as shallow and narcissistic as the girls who used to bully her in school, feeling all sorry for herself for having a single mom and no dad. At least she had one parent. One pretty damn amazing parent.

It felt weird that she knew so much about him and he might not even know her name. Luke had never introduced them, like maybe he was ashamed of her. So she introduced herself. "By the way, my name's Sarah."

The second she said her name it was like a black cloud stretched over them, blocking out what little sunlight there had been on this autumn day. If her life was the graphic novel she sometimes imagined it was, that cloud would have a human

form, long arms and legs and a big gap for a mouth that threatened to suck them both up into the sky, into the darkness.

The wind picked up, too, hurling leaves and twigs across the
grass. One stick struck her leg so hard that she winced at the
sting she felt even through her tights.

"We better get back inside," Jackson said, and he stood up
and extended his hands to her, to pull her up.

She hesitated for a moment, but it wasn't because of him. It
was because she heard something. Like something scraping . . .
like metal against rock . . .

"Do you hear that?" she asked. Raindrops spattered her face
as she stared up at him.

"Yeah, thunder," he said. "A storm's coming." And he
reached down farther and slid his hands under her arms, pulling
her up like she was a doll. As skinny as he was, he didn't look
that strong, but he must have been.

"That wasn't thunder," she insisted, as she heard it again.
And she peered around him, studying the cemetery in the dim
light. The monuments and statues and mausoleums cast shadows all around, and some of those shadows . . . looked as if
they were moving.

"We have to get inside," he said again.

Thunder rumbled now, and the raindrops got bigger and fell
harder, stinging her skin. And in those deep shadows there was
a sudden circle of light . . .

Like a flashlight beam . . . Or a lantern . . .

Then another light flashed in a jagged streak starting at that
dark cloud that hovered over them.

"Come on!" Jackson yelled over the rain. He caught one of
her hands in his and started running.

If she didn't move, he would probably drag her, so she trot-
ted along beside him. He ducked his head and shoulders low, as
if trying to escape from that cloud or from the rain falling so
hard on them. She turned back and looked into those shadows.

There was something or somebody out there.

Maybe it was just Gigi and Toby. They'd probably followed them out of the funeral showing room and had been hiding out here, spying on them. That was probably all that she'd seen, that she'd heard.

They were just trying to freak her out like they had tried that night with the casket. They were behind that scrape of the shovel sound.

And that lantern light . . .

She could see it now, glowing behind her in the dark. And around it . . . there seemed to be the silhouette of a tall, skinny . . . man or skeleton . . .

What the hell was there?

She tripped over something and probably would have fallen, but Jackson caught her. "Hey, careful," he said.

She nodded but risked one more glance behind her. But whatever she'd seen . . .

It was gone now.

What had she seen?

Chapter 13

She was gone. The pregnant woman.

The paramedics hadn't been able to save her, just as Luke and Dr. Jeffries had suspected. She'd gone so stiff and cold right away. And that needle mark on her neck . . .

It reminded Luke of the syringe he'd found in Gregory Gold's trash. He had the crime techs searching for another one while he was searching, too. Not for the needle. Or even the killer right now . . .

"Where did Jackson go?" he asked his mom, who stood near his dad on one side of the crowded lobby. His deputies were working the room, getting information and statements from everyone present.

"Jackson was here?" she asked, and she gazed around, too. "Why was he here?"

Luke shrugged. "He wanted to come." But Luke should have said no; he'd known it was a bad idea. And that was even before anyone had been murdered. And the young woman must have been . . .

Unless she'd done something to herself.

And what about Gregory Gold I? Luke still didn't have confirmation that there'd been a murder, which was the only reason he had conceded to letting Jackson tag along to the funeral. If he'd thought there was any risk . . .

But they both knew, better than most, that there were risks everywhere.

"I have to find him," Luke said. "Make sure that he's okay. That this didn't—"

"Luke," his dad interrupted him, gesturing behind him toward the back of the wide lobby.

He turned just as two kids ducked inside the room, drenched from the rain. He'd heard the thunder rumbling and had glimpsed streaks of lightning. He hadn't imagined that Jackson and Sarah had been out in that.

"Can you take him home?" Luke asked his parents.

Mary nodded. "Yes, of course."

"Do you want our statements first?" Dad asked, as determined as ever to do the right thing.

The right thing was to get that fragile teenager out of this house of death. "I can do that later unless you saw something you think I should know now."

His dad shrugged. "There were so many people . . ."

"She caused quite the commotion," Mary remarked. "Garrett Gold and his mother ran out . . ."

They'd nearly run down him and Jackson on their way out earlier. He glanced around for them now, but his gaze kept going back to Jackson, who was approaching them. His clothes and hair wet, the kid shivered with cold. Luke pulled off his jacket and wrapped it around Jackson's shoulders. "Are you okay?" he asked, his heart beating hard and heavy for the poor kid.

Jackson nodded, his lips pressed tightly together as if his teeth were about to chatter.

"Mom and Dad are going to take you back to the house," Luke said, gesturing at the deputy at the door to let them go. As they walked away, a young crime tech, Hannah Patterson, came up to him.

She wore her hair short with no makeup, and she didn't look much older than the girl who'd died. But she was smart and ambitious and they were lucky to have her on the team. "Sheriff," she said. "I have some news . . ."

"You found something?" he asked hopefully.

"Not here, not yet, but the report came back on the syringe that was in Gregory Gold's trash." Hannah led him out of earshot of the people who hadn't already been released from the lobby, and she held out her phone.

"Botulinum A toxin," Luke read off the screen.

Hannah's head bobbed in a quick nod. "And if that was the needle and syringe used, he would have gotten a really high dosage, higher than an ordinary Botox injection. A dose that high would cause botulism poisoning almost immediately."

"Could it have been an accident?" Luke asked.

Hannah shook her head. "Nobody would inject that much for cosmetic purposes."

He wasn't so sure. Gregory Gold I had been notoriously vain.

"And they wouldn't use a needle that big. A dose that high would cause instant complications," she said, "paralysis of the facial features and vocal cords and then the extremities. Then the organs would shut down. He wouldn't be able to breathe and eventually his heart would stop."

Remembering how Gregory had sat frozen in front of the mirror, Luke could believe that was exactly what had happened, how he'd died.

Was that what had happened to the girl, too? Justine Campbell. Hannah was the one who'd found the victim's ID in her purse and told him her name and that she was a student at a college in Northern Michigan. What had she been doing here? How had she gotten involved with the Golds?

Luke had heard the rumors that Gregory was divorcing Fiona; the family had made certain he'd heard. But was it true? And had Justine been the reason?

"What about the prints on the syringe?" Luke asked. "Were there any?" Or had the needle been wiped clean?

Hannah nodded. "Two sets. One was Gregory Gold's, the coroner confirmed that. And the other . . ." She glanced around the room until her gaze settled on Fiona. "The other set had been in the system already but from a long time ago, so it took a while to make the match . . ."

"To whom?" he asked, but he already knew.

"Fiona Hawthorne, now Gold. She was arrested thirty-five years ago, when she was seventeen, for stealing some high-end cosmetics from a counter in a department store in California. That was why her prints were in the system."

Luke had already intended to bring her in for questioning after the service, but he shouldn't have waited.

Justine Campbell might have died because he hadn't gone as hard on the investigation as he should have. But he'd been waiting to make sure he really had something to investigate.

Now he might have two murders on his hands.

Before there were any more, he was going to damn well bring in his prime suspect for questioning. "Thanks, Hannah," Luke said.

The young woman's face flushed with his praise. "I'll keep working the scene, sir, and see if we can find another syringe."

Of course she hadn't missed the mark on the victim's neck. She probably suspected the same thing Luke did: that whoever had killed Gregory Gold had also killed Justine Campbell.

While the tech headed back into the showing room, Luke moved through the crowded lobby. People called out to him, demanding to be released from the scene. "Once you've all given your information to an officer, you will be free to go," he said.

Except for one person.

He wove through the people until he came to her. River Gold knelt on the floor next to her mother's chair while River's grandmother leaned over her daughter, her arm around her shoulders. Like they were supporting her . . .

Or protecting her.

Luke didn't believe she was in danger, though. He believed she was the danger. "I need you to stand, Mrs. Gold," he said to her. "I'm going to read you your rights and take you in for questioning."

"Questioning about what?" she scoffed. "I saw the same thing you did."

He wasn't concerned with what she'd seen. He was concerned with what she'd done.

River jumped up from the floor and nearly fell over from her legs going numb beneath her after all the time she'd been kneeling. While she'd just wanted to be close to her mom, to contain her, as much as to comfort her, she'd also done a little praying.

But the doctor hadn't been able to bring that girl back. And neither had the paramedics who'd left just a short time ago.

She was gone. And her baby as well.

So River's prayers hadn't been answered.

As her numb legs started giving way beneath her weight, she grabbed her mom's shoulder to steady herself and to hold her down. "You are not bringing my mom in for questioning like she's your prime suspect," she told Luke, who stood in front of them.

Had he always been so tall? So intimidating?

Even now that he'd shed his suit jacket . . . for that boy, he still looked intimidating. Or maybe he looked even more so without the jacket since the holster and handcuffs strapped to his belt were clearly visible. Would he put those handcuffs on her mom?

In front of everyone?

Sarah . . .

She glanced around the room, looking for her daughter, who'd come in with that boy and had then disappeared upstairs, probably to change since she'd been soaked.

Guilt and concern simultaneously struck River. How had she lost track of her own daughter during what had happened? One minute Sarah had been saying that the girl was dead . . . and then all hell had broken loose. And somehow Sarah had slipped away . . .

With that boy. What had happened? Who was he?

So many thoughts and fears were flitting through her head that a wave of dizziness rushed over her. And she gripped her mom's shoulder tighter.

Fiona reached up and patted her hand. "It's okay, honey. I have nothing to hide and no reason not to answer the sheriff's questions."

"But he has no reason to ask you any questions," River said even though she wanted to ask her mom some herself. "Nobody even knows what happened to your husband or to that girl."

"I doubt the two of them both died of natural causes," Luke said. "And I also got a report back about Gregory. A report that reveals your mother's fingerprints were found on what could be a murder weapon."

River's stomach flipped with that dread that kept lying so heavily in the bottom of it. Her fingerprints.

Murder weapon.

"And once the techs find what was used to kill Ms. Campbell, we'll check that for fingerprints as well," Luke said as if warning her.

But the hand her mother had placed over River's was wear-

126 Lisa Childs

ing a silky black glove, its partner on her other hand. There would be no fingerprints found on whatever had been used to kill that girl. If her mother was the killer . . .

But she couldn't be. River knew that her mother wasn't always honest. But she wasn't a ruthless murderer. She couldn't be.

River glanced over her mother's head and met her grand-mother's gaze. And there were doubts in her eyes, too. Then Mabel glanced from River to Fiona, and her teeth nipped into her bottom lip, as if she was struggling to hold back a protest. Or a cry . . .

River wasn't the only one who was worried.

"Mom, you shouldn't talk to the sheriff without a lawyer," River insisted. "You are entitled to legal representation."

"I was going to read her the Miranda rights," Luke said softly, "but I was going to wait until we got outside."

Until no one was staring at them, as everyone was now. Heat rushed to River's face with a wave of embarrassment. This family, all the people in this town, had always treated her and her mother like they were trash.

Especially Luke.

He hadn't thought she was good enough for Michael.

"I'm going with you," River said, even though she was torn between the desire to protect her mother and her daughter. Sarah had looked a little shaken when she'd walked inside with that boy. But maybe that was just because of the storm.

It raged outside yet, the thunder rumbled so loudly that it seemed to shake the building. River wanted to check on Sarah first, wanted to find out why she was outside and who that boy was.

But at the moment it felt like her mother needed her more than her daughter did.

"I'm taking her in alone," Luke insisted, his voice gruff as he met River's gaze.

"I'm going with you, Sheriff," a man said, stepping away from the crowd. He'd been standing with the remaining two Gregory Golds and maybe Lawrence was there, too, although he tended to blend into the surroundings instead of standing out like his brother and nephew.

"Colson," Fiona said, and she jumped, knocking River's hand from her shoulder. "That is so sweet of you."

"Colson?" River echoed his name, which sounded vaguely familiar. The man was in his late-forties or maybe early fifties with thick salt-and-pepper hair. He wore a suit, but it was not as dark as the undertakers wore.

"Colson Howard," he said to River. "I'm the family counsel. I'll represent your mother and make sure that the sheriff doesn't overstep his boundaries with his questions."

She wasn't sure if the family lawyer would represent her mother's interest or the family's. What if the two weren't the same? "Mom," she said. "Don't you think you should get your own counsel?"

Fiona smiled at her and then at the lawyer. "I trust Colson, honey."

But her mother had trusted people she shouldn't have before, like Gregory Gold I. Apparently, just as he'd betrayed the wives before her mother, he'd betrayed her mother with that young woman who had just died.

"Mom, I really think—"

"Don't worry," Fiona told her. "Nobody has been murdered, so nobody is going to be arrested. Colson and I will straighten this all out with the sheriff. You'll see . . ."

River saw a lot more than her mother did, like the smug looks the Golds were exchanging with each other. And maybe with the lawyer as well.

Colson Howard cupped her mother's elbow in his hand and escorted her through the crowd of quiet onlookers toward the front doors.

Luke stayed for a moment, his gaze locked with River's, before he turned and followed them through the lobby. As he passed the Gregorys, the older one reached out and patted his shoulder as if giving his approval.

The Gold family had endorsed him to run for sheriff. Was this the reason why? So he would do their bidding?

And their bidding was obviously to get rid of her mother, to make sure that she couldn't take any part of the estate or the business that Gregory Gold I had left behind.

But if River was truly his daughter, then she was bound to inherit something, too. What would they do to make sure that wouldn't happen? Or what would they make Luke do?

Chapter 14

Fiona was used to being underestimated. And she often used that to her advantage. It was better for people to think she was stupid than to realize how smart she was.

She didn't think she could fool the sheriff, though. At least not any more than she already had.

He was trying to intimidate her now in this windowless room with the white concrete block walls and the small metal table at which they sat. A handcuff dangled from a hook on that table. And instead of being afraid of it, like he might have wanted her to be, she toyed with the metal, with the clasp of it, like it was a bracelet . . . like the diamond one that dangled over her gloved hand.

"What did you want to ask me?"

"You don't have to answer any of his questions," Colson cautioned her. "We can leave this interview at any time."

"Until I press charges," Luke said.

"What charges?"

"Murder."

"Do you have proof that there was a murder?" Colson asked.

Luke nodded. "There was a murder weapon . . ."

"What weapon?" Colson asked.

"The syringe," Fiona answered for Luke.

Colson gasped. "Fiona—"

She patted his hand. "Of course he would have found a syringe with my prints on it. I got the fillers Gregory wanted, taught him how and where to administer them himself. He was already good with needles because he administered his own B12 vitamin injections and weight-loss medications."

Colson winced as if the thought of needles frightened him. He wouldn't need them; he wasn't a vain man, at least not with appearance. But like most men he thought he was smarter than he was, smarter than she was.

She wasn't sure what Sheriff Sebastian thought of her, though. Did he really believe she was capable of murder?

"There was a lethal dose of botulinum A toxin in this particular syringe," Luke said.

She gasped. "Oh, no. I wonder if he got his vials messed up. Maybe he administered the botulinum A thinking that it was his B12 or the weight-loss medication he also injected. Or maybe he increased the dosage because he was so concerned about wrinkles."

"So you didn't realize what you were putting in the syringe was stronger, you didn't see the side effects when you administered it?" Luke asked. "It would have immediately affected him, paralyzing him. You didn't notice that?"

"Like I just told you, he administered his own medications and vitamins. I wasn't there," Fiona insisted. "I touched all the syringes at some point. I always help unload the box of them. But that is all I do. Gregory insists . . . insisted on managing everything else himself."

"So your explanation is that *he* must have mixed up his vitamin injection with his Botox and that's why he got too much?" Luke asked. "This man who was insistent on administering his own medications so that he was the one in control?"

Fiona fought her lips from curving into a smile at the thought of Gregory's vanity and controlling nature being the death of him. But she bit her bottom lip and just nodded in response to the sheriff's question.

Colson stood up. "We can leave then," he said. "This was no murder. Just a horrible accident."

"Justine Campbell didn't die by accident," the sheriff said. "She also had a needle mark."

Fiona sighed. "I figured she was a druggie, looking for an easy meal ticket and money to keep her habit going. That was why she latched onto poor Garrett right away in college, probably the minute she learned he was a Gold. And then when he brought her home with him, she figured out who really controlled all the money." As well as all of them.

"You're not denying that she was involved with your husband?" Luke asked. "That he was going to divorce you to be with her?"

She shrugged and glanced up at Colson. "You never served me with divorce papers. Was that what Gregory intended to do?"

Colson held her gaze for a long moment.

"Mr. Howard, why don't you answer that question?" Luke prodded him.

"Client confidentiality—"

"Your client is dead," Luke said.

"I represent his estate, the family," Colson said. He'd inherited the job from his father, who'd served as the Gold counsel before him. Just like the Golds, Colson had been born into his privilege and wealth.

Fiona should have resented that about him, but she used it instead to her advantage.

"Then isn't it a conflict of interest for you to represent Mrs. Gold as well?" Luke asked.

"It would be if he'd been representing my husband against me," Fiona said. She stood now. "But since he wasn't, he's here for me." She was counting on it. "And you really have no case against me or anyone . . . because Gregory wasn't murdered."

"And Justine Campbell?"

She shook her head. "Just a desperate young girl . . ." Fiona felt a twinge of pity and affinity for poor Justine. Fiona had once been a desperate young girl herself.

Luke Sebastian finally stood as well. "You can leave," he said, "the sheriff's office. But I don't want you to leave Gold Creek."

Fiona smiled at him. "I have no intention of going anywhere." And she was going to make that damn clear to her family, too. To the Gold family.

River sat in the dark, staring out at the storm raging over the cemetery. Lightning flashed, illuminating the monuments and statues, while rain slashed across the windows. Her daughter had been out in that.

Why?

She'd wanted to ask her, but Sarah had already been in the shower when she'd finally come upstairs from the lobby, from the chaos of what had happened.

The funeral had been postponed and Gregory Gold I had been moved, in the service elevator, to cold storage in the basement until the crime scene was released. If it was a crime scene . . .

But how else would a young woman have died so suddenly like Justine had?

Unless . . .

There were plenty of sudden deaths. Young people dropping from heart attacks or drug overdoses. Justine could have died from anything and for any reason. And none of them had anything to do with River's mother.

Luke would have to realize and accept that. If only River could, too . . .

A door creaked open, and a small scream squeaked out. "You scared me!" Sarah said, her voice cracking. "I didn't realize it was you sitting there in the dark."

And River hadn't realized the shower had shut off with how hard the rain was falling. She jumped up now and crossed the room to her daughter. Sarah wore pajamas already despite how early it was yet. But with the sky as dark as it was, it felt like night.

"You scared me," River said as she closed her arms around her.

Instead of squirming away like she usually did, Sarah closed her arms around River and hugged her tightly. "I'm sorry, Mom."

River wasn't exactly sure what she was apologizing for. But she patted her daughter's back, which was damp from the water dripping from her wet hair. "I'm the one who's sorry, honey," she said. "I never should have brought you here." She'd vowed never to return when she'd left all those years ago. And she should have kept that promise to herself for her sake as well as her daughter's.

Sarah pulled away then. "It's not this place . . ." But as she said it, she glanced out the windows that overlooked the cemetery and shivered slightly.

She had to be cold. River took off the sweater she'd borrowed from her mother and wrapped it around Sarah's slender shoulders. "Why were you outside?" River asked. "And who is that boy?"

Sarah stiffened and stepped back until River's arms dropped to her sides. "His name is Jackson. I don't know if Luke Sebastian adopted him or if he's just staying with him . . ."

"How do *you* know him?" River asked.

Sarah sighed and released the tension from her body. "That's why I'm sorry. I lied to you earlier. I didn't go to town to get tights for GG Mabel." She glanced around the dimly lit room. "Where is she?"

"She's still downstairs." River had left her in the lobby chatting with the doctor. "You said you didn't go to town." River was glad that her daughter had confirmed what she'd already suspected. "Where did you go?"

"To see Luke Sebastian," Sarah said.

River held back the groan of frustration burning the back of her throat. Instead she asked, "Why?"

"To ask him about my dad," Sarah said.

River closed her eyes as her frustration threatened to turn to tears. Then she drew in a deep breath. "I'm sorry," she said. "That I can't answer all your questions about him."

"Mom, that's not your fault. He let you down."

River cleared her throat again. "Then why do you want to see him?"

Sarah shrugged. "I don't know. The only reason I really want to meet him is to tell him what an asshole he was and that you didn't need him. I wanted to tell Luke the same thing, about what an asshole he was, too. But . . ."

"But what?"

"I don't think he knows where my dad is, either," Sarah said.

And River had a feeling that was true, too.

"And I'm not sure how big an asshole he is now."

"Why?" River asked. Luke must have been nice to her despite how belligerent the teenager could sometimes be, and River was grateful to him for that.

"Jackson," she said. "He's taking care of him because Jackson lost both his parents." Her voice cracked now, and tears filled her eyes.

River gasped over the tears in her daughter's eyes and over that poor kid's loss. "Oh, my God. That's terrible."

"It was really awful," Sarah said, and she shuddered again.

"Like tragic, his dad during an explosion, with Luke, in a war or something . . ."

River touched her own heart as it thudded heavily, thinking of how Luke could have died, too.

"And his mom died during a mall shooting," Sarah continued. "And Jackson was there with her when it happened. That's why he freaked out when that girl died at the funeral. He ran outside . . ."

And Sarah ran out after him, to comfort him even though they'd just met. Pride in her child, for her empathy, rushed through River, and she had to hug her again as tears flooded her eyes.

Like before, instead of pulling away, Sarah hugged back. Hard. "I'm so sorry, Mom. And I'm so lucky and I didn't even know it."

"I'm the lucky one," River insisted.

She couldn't imagine having done what Luke had tried to convince Michael they should do: give her up. Maybe it would have been easier for them both. Maybe Sarah would have been happier in a two-parent home. Maybe she would have had siblings and friends. And River could have finished out her own childhood with school and friends instead of single parenthood. But the only friend she'd actually had in school was Michael, and apparently, he had left town when she had. No, River had no regrets except that she probably had been selfish for not giving her daughter a better life.

"I don't think you are all that lucky, though," River admitted. "You would have had more things and probably an easier time fitting in at school . . ." She suspected Sarah had chosen online over in person classes because she'd been having a hard time with her peers who really weren't her peers; they all had much more money and means than River was able to provide for her. While Mabel had provided them with a place to live, the California cost of living was still high, even with the money

Fiona had sent them from time to time. But River had refused to accept any money from Gregory Gold I; she hadn't liked the conditions attached to it, about staying in this house in Gold Creek. "You might have been happier if I'd . . ."

"Given me up?" Sarah asked.

River couldn't say the words aloud, so she just nodded even as tears flooded her eyes at the thought.

Sarah tightened her arms around her. "It would have been easier for you," she said. "But not for me. I would have always wondered where I came from, who you were . . ." She snorted. "I guess I have still wondered those things . . ."

"And now that we're here . . ."

"I get it," Sarah said. "I understand why you ran away and why you haven't wanted to talk about it."

"We can leave," River said.

Sarah was her priority, even more so than her mother. She had to protect her child at all costs. She just wasn't sure what she needed to protect her from . . .

Luke?

That boy, since Sarah was so drawn to him, like River had been drawn to Sarah's father? She didn't want another generation of her family becoming a mother too young.

Or did she need to protect Sarah from a murderer?

Had Gregory Gold I and Justine and her unborn child really been murdered like Luke suspected?

A knock at the door startled them both this time, and they sprang apart just as the door creaked open. Mabel wouldn't have knocked but River was surprised to see that Fiona had.

"Are you all right?" River asked her mother. "I can't believe you're back home so quickly." She'd been so afraid that Luke intended to do more than question her; that he'd been going to charge her with murder.

Fiona nodded. "Of course. I told you that there was nothing to worry about."

"What was nothing to worry about?" Sarah asked, but she turned toward River to ask the question.

"The sheriff brought your grandmother in for questioning." Mabel was the one who answered as she walked into the room, too.

"Questioning about what?" Sarah asked.

"About murder," Mabel said with a cackle like she found the whole idea diabolically hilarious.

"Two people died as well as an unborn child," River reminded them. "There have been too many deaths." Like Jackson's parents. She shared a look of commiseration with Sarah over the teenager's tragic loss.

"But they weren't murdered," Fiona said. "Gregory was a victim of his vanity."

"What do you mean?" River asked.

She smiled. "Apparently, his cosmetic filler killed him. He must have mixed it up with his B12 injection or something . . ."

That smile had a shiver raising goose bumps on River's skin. It reminded her so much of the smug Gold smile. She'd always thought her mother was an outsider, like River was, but she wondered if her mother was more like the Golds now than like her. Fiona had lived and worked with them for a long time, over thirty years.

"What about the girl?" Sarah asked. "She was young. Did he say what happened to her?"

Sarah had been the first one to go up to her, to check on her, and River felt a pang of pride and concern. She'd tried to get her daughter into counseling before, when she'd gone so quiet and moody in her teens, but Sarah had refused to speak to anyone then. But after what had happened today, River intended to try to get her into therapy again; in fact, River might want to talk to someone herself. Someone who wasn't her mother because she was making her uneasy.

Fiona shrugged. "I have no idea. He blathered on about a needle mark."

"That child didn't need Botox," Mabel said, finally chiming in to the conversation as she studied her daughter with some of the same suspicion that River and the sheriff had studied her.

"She was a druggie," Fiona said dismissively.

And River thought of Michael, of the problems he'd been having. Was that what had happened to him? Had he become the addict he hadn't wanted to be?

"She was pregnant," Sarah said.

"Yes, but not everyone cares about their child like your mother cared about you," Fiona said.

"I never did drugs," River said. Her life had already been too much out of her control living here, in this house by the cemetery.

Fiona nodded. "So of course you don't understand how this girl would keep doing them even though she was pregnant. She was an addict. And maybe she didn't want to actually have the child because then everyone would know it wasn't Gregory's."

"Just like everyone doesn't think I am," River reminded her.

While her mother's face flushed as if she was hot, her blue eyes got cold. "*Everyone* is wrong." She turned that cold stare on her mother Mabel as well before swinging it back toward River. "You are definitely your father's daughter."

"I'm nothing like him," River pointed out. "In looks or anything else . . ."

Fiona smiled again but it was with affection this time instead of smugness. "Everybody got distracted with Gregory's vanity and fear of dying from what he was really about . . ."

"Making money," Mabel remarked.

"Taking care of people, taking care of his family," Fiona said. "Even after he divorced Carolyn and Linda, he continued to take care of them. That's how you are, River, so deeply caring."

"He didn't take care of Mom," Sarah said, her voice hard.

River felt that twinge of guilt now that she hadn't been able to provide for her daughter everything she needed or wanted. They had a roof over their heads and food on the table, but that was more because of Mabel and her social security than the makeup business River worked so hard to do. And now she was probably losing all of her clients to one of her many competitors.

"He would have if she had stayed or even if she would have come back," Fiona said.

Mabel snorted. "Yeah, he wanted to use his money to control her just like he controlled everyone else with it. But *your* mother, Sarah, is a tough and independent woman. She takes care of herself and everyone else."

Tears stung River's eyes. "Thank you, Gran."

Mabel smiled. "She's like me. We don't need men to take care of us."

Fiona grimaced. "You just can't stop criticizing me."

"You are so sensitive," Mabel shot back at her.

"It's been a long day," River pointed out. "It might not be a bad idea to rest awhile."

Mabel shrugged. "I'm fine. I just came up here to touch up my face." And she headed toward the bathroom.

"Let me get my stuff out of your way," Sarah said as she headed after her, leaving River alone with her mother.

"I wouldn't take being like her as a compliment," Fiona said, but she was smiling.

However, her mother couldn't deny that River was more like Mabel than she was like her. And River certainly didn't consider that a bad thing. If only her mother had been more independent . . .

"At least you and I don't fight like she and I do," Fiona continued, her eyes warming as she studied River's face. She cocked her head and asked, "You know that the sheriff is wrong to think that these are murders. But even if they are, you know that I had nothing to do with them dying, right?"

Why would she think River would have any doubts . . .

Unless . . .

Luke could have kept Fiona Gold and her lawyer for a while longer, could have grilled her with more questions. But Colson Howard was right, he didn't have enough to hold her. Not yet . . .

And why waste his time asking her questions, when he couldn't be sure that she answered any of them truthfully. It almost seemed easier for her to lie than to tell the truth. He'd also wanted to get home to Jackson as soon as possible.

And question him.

"Are you okay?" he asked from where he leaned against the open door to Jackson's bedroom.

The kid was already in his pajamas, tucked up in bed with heavy blankets and a cooling cup of cocoa on the table beside his bed. Mama Mary. She couldn't stop herself from fussing over people, especially people she cared about. Jackson didn't seem to mind when she did it, but he didn't want Luke to do any fussing.

"I'm good, really," Jackson insisted with a little impatience sharpening his voice. "Stop worrying about me. Sarah and I just stepped out of that craziness for a minute."

Sarah. Had Sarah helped him? Or just distracted him from whatever had upset him so much? The bodies.

"You stepped out into the middle of a thunderstorm," Luke pointed out. "You could have been hurt."

Jackson shrugged his skinny shoulders. "It wasn't raining when we first went out there. And we headed in as soon as the lightning and thunder started."

"You going to that funeral was a really bad idea," Luke said.

Jackson hadn't just been wet when he and Sarah had come back inside; he'd looked devastated.

Jackson didn't argue with him. He just shrugged, but then he smiled slightly. "Maybe . . ."

"Maybe?"

"I mean it sucked that that girl died, and seeing her die . . ." Jackson shuddered.

God, it must have brought back all those horrible memories for him just as it had brought some back to Luke. "Do you want to talk about that?" Luke asked. Jackson had a therapist, but Luke wasn't sure how much he talked to her. Or if he just told her what he figured she wanted to hear . . .

The same way Luke had done with the therapists the military had assigned him after some of the things he'd suffered through, like losing Jackson's dad. His best friend.

"I talked to Sarah," Jackson said, and that smile curved his lips again.

Luke's niece was the reason for the maybe.

"She's not staying, you know," Luke cautioned him and himself. "They'll head back home after the funeral."

"You stopped the funeral," Jackson said. "How long before they can finish it?"

"Not long," Luke said. The crime scene techs were going over the photographs and evidence they'd collected. While he doubted they'd missed anything, he wanted to see it again himself. But before going there, he wanted to make sure that Jackson was really all right. "They should be able to resume the service in a couple of days."

Jackson frowned, but then the ding of the doorbell transformed him into a smiling teenager again. He jumped out of bed and swept past Luke on his way out the door and down the stairs. Clearly, he thought, or hoped, Sarah was dropping by again.

At a slower pace, Luke started down the steps.

Jackson was already opening the door. "Oh," he muttered, "hey . . ." Then he leaned out as if looking around whoever was at the door to see if someone else had come with them.

So Sarah hadn't rung the bell. Maybe one of her cousins . . .

Luke descended the last tread and joined Jackson at the door. And he was as surprised as the teenager. "Oh, hey . . ." he muttered to himself at the sight of River Gold standing on their front porch. Alone.

"Oh, hey . . ." she echoed their words with a slight smile. She was really beautiful.

"Is . . . Sarah with you?" Jackson asked with another glance out the door to the van parked in the driveway. With the tinted windows, it wasn't possible to see inside.

She shook her head. "No. Nobody's with me."

Jackson nodded, then he turned and hurried back up the stairs. His bedroom door didn't close though, as if he intended to eavesdrop on their conversation. He probably wouldn't like what Luke asked her next.

"You didn't bring a lawyer?"

The killer drew in a deep breath, trying to calm themself as frustration and fear gnawed at them. River should not have come back to Gold Creek. It had been a mistake. For her.

She was just going to get in the killer's way. She was going to mess with the plan and maybe even more . . .

River had to go. But that girl had always been stubborn; she wasn't going to run away this time until she had a reason to run . . .

Chapter 15

"This was a mistake," River said, and she turned away from the open door of the Sebastian home and started back across the porch. She didn't make it to the steps before a big hand caught her arm and stopped her. He wasn't holding her tightly. She could have shaken off his grasp and continued walking down the steps and down the drive toward the van she'd borrowed from the funeral home.

But the same compulsion that had drawn her here had her stopping now. If she only knew what that was . . .

"River? Why are you here?" Luke asked the question she'd been asking herself.

She squared her shoulders and turned back toward him. While she hated confrontation, sometimes one was inevitable. And necessary.

"Without a lawyer?" she asked.

"I'm sorry. That was a stupid remark," he said. "It was just your mother . . ."

"Rightfully had her lawyer with her since you're treating her like a suspect when there hasn't even been a crime," she finished for him.

His lips curved into a slight, maddening grin. "She told you that?"

Her stomach pitched. Had her mother lied to her? "She said that Gregory accidentally used too much filler . . ."

He shook his head. "Nobody would accidentally use that much. And it was too concentrated and too high a dose to simply be filler. And so far it looks like the same thing killed Justine Campbell."

She sucked in a breath. So her mother had lied. "It wasn't drugs?"

He shrugged slightly. "That's what your mother insists it was, but there was no other indication that Justine was a drug user."

"Sometimes people overlook the signs of drug use because we don't want to see them . . ."

"Are we talking about Justine Campbell or Michael now? River, why did you come here?"

"I know Sarah came to see you earlier today, before the funeral," she said. "That she wanted to ask you about her dad."

"I'm glad she told you she came here," he said. "And I'm sorry I couldn't give her any answers. I don't know where he is. But I am going to start a search for him."

"You haven't looked for him before?" she asked.

"I tried to track him down over the years, but I couldn't find anything in his name or even in yours."

Her car and house were in Mabel's name, and her business was an LLC. She wouldn't have been easy to find, and she'd liked it that way. Maybe Michael didn't want to be found, either.

"He and our bio mom were on the run for years," Luke said. "I don't know how many different identities they used. She probably even had fake IDs and birth certificates. She hung out with a lot of shady people."

"And sometimes so did Michael," she admitted.

"I didn't know . . . I thought coming here would get him out of trouble . . ."

"And then he met me," River said, and she let the slight smile curve her lips now.

Luke sighed. "Maybe the responsibility of having a child would have been good for him, would have gotten him to straighten up."

"Instead it overwhelmed him and scared him away." She glanced up now toward that second story of the farmhouse. "What about Jackson? Is he okay?"

He tensed. "What about Jackson?"

"He told Sarah about his parents, and she told me," River said.

Luke let out a ragged sigh. "He never talks to anyone about that . . ."

"He talked to her."

"They just met," Luke said.

River smiled. "I guess my daughter is more empathetic than I realized she was."

Luke released a shuddery breath. "Was it too much for her? That had to be pretty intense."

"I was worried when I saw them come in together, and the look on her face . . ." She lost her breath for a moment when she remembered how she'd looked. "But I didn't know if it was about him or about that pregnant girl, not much older than she is, dying. You really don't think it was an accidental overdose or something . . . like that . . ."

"Like your mother wants me to believe it is," Luke finished for her.

She clearly wanted River to believe that, too. But why? Because it was the truth? Or because . . .

No. River wouldn't even let herself think that; doing so would be a betrayal. Not that she hadn't felt that her mother had betrayed her before. Like when she supported Luke Sebastian running for sheriff.

"She helped you get elected, didn't she?" River asked.

Luke smiled that slight smile again. "You weren't happy to find that out, I take it."

She shook her head. "No. But I know my mother would do whatever her husband told her to do."

He narrowed his eyes as if speculative of her claim. Unlike Michael and Sarah, Luke's eyes weren't dark but a vivid green. "Even divorce him?" he asked.

She sighed now. "I know some of the others were saying that was happening . . ."

"She claims it wasn't, that she never received divorce papers," he said.

She shrugged. "Then I guess that's that."

"Her lawyer didn't really confirm or deny that, and the only other person who could is dead. Your father."

She flinched. Was he really, though?

"So you think that's her motive? That she didn't want to lose him to a divorce so she killed him? She lost him for good that way, so it doesn't make sense," she pointed out.

"Statistics show that a spouse is often murdered during a divorce."

"My mother is not a statistic," she said. "And you know how the Gold family is. Ex-spouses don't go away."

"Your father wouldn't let them go," Luke said. "He used money to control them."

She let a soft gasp slip out. "Ah . . . that's what my grandmother just said . . ."

"She pointed out how controlling your father was," he surmised.

He wasn't wrong, but River wasn't going to admit how right he was.

"Maybe Gregory's killer thought the only way to get away from someone that controlling was to kill them."

"But my mother didn't want to get away from him," River pointed out. "So if he was murdered, you need to look at the others."

"What about Justine Campbell?" he asked.

And now she felt like she was being interrogated like her mother had been. But as she told him, she didn't need a lawyer. "I don't know. Maybe she did kill him, and then she killed herself out of guilt."

He chuckled. "That would tie up everything nicely, wouldn't it?"

"Is there anything to tie up?" she wondered. "Or are you just looking for crimes where there are none?"

"I'm not looking for crimes," he said. "I'm just trying to get the truth. I'm not sure that I did out of your mother."

Neither was River.

And she must have betrayed her doubts because those green eyes narrowed again.

"You're not absolutely certain that your mother had nothing to do with these murders," he said.

"Are you absolutely certain that she has?" she asked without answering his question. "Or are you just trying to pin things on her, things that might have just been accidents, because that's what the rest of the Golds want you to do?"

"You're saying I'm on their payroll?" he asked.

"Don't you think that's why they all supported you?" she asked. "So you would do what they want you to do?"

He shrugged. "I don't know what their reason was, but if that was it, they're going to be disappointed. I am only interested in the truth and justice and making sure that this town is safe." He glanced up, probably in Jackson's direction.

"That's why you brought him here," she surmised, like he'd been making the assumptions about her motives. He hadn't been wrong.

He nodded. "I remember how safe I always felt here, in this house."

River nodded. She'd felt safe here, too, in this house when she'd come by to study with Michael. "Your parents are very sweet people." They had always invited her to dinner even though they'd had a houseful of foster kids to feed as well.

"They're amazing," Luke said, his voice warm with love. "I know I should get a place of my own, but I like that someone's always around for Jackson. That he's not alone."

River suddenly felt as if she was seeing Luke for the first time. Years ago, she hadn't seen much of him beyond the pictures around the Sebastians' house. He'd usually been in his military uniform, and he'd seemed so rigid, cold, and judgmental. Then when she'd first come back here, he'd been in his uniform as the sheriff. And he'd seemed rigid, cold, and judgmental, then, too.

But here . . . talking about his parents and Jackson, she saw another side of him. A warm, loving side. A side that was even harder for her to handle than his rigid, judgmental side. She was used to that; she wasn't used to the warmth, not from Luke Sebastian.

He smiled at her. "I appreciate that Sarah was there for him today. I shouldn't have let him go with me. It was too much . . ."

"You didn't know that someone was going to die," she said.

He sighed. "And I was really hoping that your dad died of natural causes."

"You really don't think that it could have been an accident?" she asked. "That he just injected more than he should have?"

Luke shook his head. "No. Your mother's explanation of it was that he must have mixed up the filler vial with his B12 vial or weight-loss medication, and that's how he injected too much. Dr. Jeffries backed up that Gregory injected himself with all his supplements, but that was because he was the only person he trusted to do it. So how did you mother's prints really get on the syringe?"

This was why she'd come here. On some level she'd trusted Luke to tell her the truth more than her own mother. Tears rushed to her eyes, and she was suddenly overwhelmed . . . with the thought of murder and what her mother might have had to do with it and with all the thoughts of the past.

One minute she was there, standing in front of Luke, looking so beautiful. Then she whirled around toward the steps as if wanting to run away. But her foot slipped on the first stair, and she started to fall. Luke reached out but he could only catch her arm as her legs went out from beneath her. Alarm shot through him and he jumped off the porch to kneel beside her. "Are you all right?" he asked.

She'd landed with her butt on one of the stairs and her legs out in front of her. Nothing looked twisted but maybe her arm from how he'd grabbed it. Tears rolled down her face though, but she put her hands over it.

"I'll get you some ice and drive you to the ER—"

She reached out and grabbed his arm now before he could jump up. "No. I'm fine."

"You just fell—"

"Guess Gold Creek isn't all that safe," she said with a smile even as the tears kept rolling down her face.

He found himself cupping her cheek in his hand. "You're crying, River."

"Cry me a river . . ." she murmured, and hiccupped. "That's what my father used to say. He was the one who named me. Mom said the creek looked more like a river, so he said that was what they would call me. And he would sing a song called that . . ." Her voice cracked, and she dashed away her tears. "I had forgotten all about that . . ."

"I'm sorry," Luke said. "I'm not sure that I ever offered you condolences on your loss."

"A lot of people have," she said, "especially today, and I felt like a hypocrite accepting them. I've been gone so long, and even when I lived with him, we were never close. But now I remember things like that . . . things that I forgot."

"It's easy to remember people differently than how they were," he admitted.

"Like Michael?"

He nodded.

"I did the same thing," she said. "But I probably remember him differently than you did. He let me down when he didn't show up that night. But I realize now how much pressure I was putting on him. And he was just a kid, too. It was too much and he . . ."

". . . ran away," Luke finished for her. "I didn't think he would do that, that he would run away from you and his child. But I remember him as my baby brother, not who he became after all those years of being on the run with our mother."

"I'm glad you're going to look for him," she said.

Was she still in love with his brother? "You came home with just your daughter and your grandmother," he said. "No significant other?" Heat rushed to his face that he'd asked the question because it sounded like he was fishing, like he was flirting. He couldn't remember the last time he'd flirted, though.

"Sarah is my significant other," she said. "I have her and my grandmother to raise. So I'm a little busy to date."

He chuckled. "Yeah, I can see that . . ."

"And you have Jackson."

He nodded. "Yes, he's my total focus, so I understand."

"Bringing him back here was the right thing," she said. Then she shrugged. "Not that you're looking for my opinion . . ."

"I appreciate it," he said, sincerely. "You seem to have done a great job raising Sarah on your own . . ."

"Seem?"

"I'm sorry—" God, he kept putting his foot in his mouth.

She smiled. "I get it. I don't think we ever know anyone's character completely."

"Are you talking about your daughter or your mother?" He suspected she had as many doubts about Fiona's innocence as he had.

She sighed now. "Speaking of them, I better get back to that house . . ." She drew in a deep breath, as if bracing herself for the return. Or maybe she'd braced herself to stand because she flinched as she put her weight on her left foot.

He cupped her elbows, steadying her. "You can't drive like this. Let me take you to the ER."

She shook her head. "It's my left foot, so I don't need it to drive. And it's not broken. I think I just rolled it." She shifted some weight to it and smiled. "See, it's fine."

But the smile looked forced. Beautiful but forced. "I'm sorry you got hurt."

She shook her head. "Not your fault. I'm a klutz."

"I doubt that." She had an innate grace about her and not just in how she moved but in how she treated people. He'd watched her with those old ladies at the funeral home. She'd been so patient with them while other people brushed them off like annoyances. If he hadn't been watching her, maybe he would have noticed what had happened with Justine Campbell and who might have put that needle in her before she died. "Just please be careful," he implored her.

"Gold Creek is safe, remember," she said, but she sounded as if she was being sarcastic.

"Murders aside . . ."

"And the grave digger," she reminded him. "Remember he's out there with his shovel, looking for his next victim to dig a grave for . . ."

Luke snorted at the old legend. "Tell me you don't really believe that old ghost story."

Her smile slipped a little. "There have been some kids who disappeared over the years," she said.

He shook his head. "They ran away ... and usually from this house ..." Like Michael and a few other fosters who hadn't wanted to stay in this backwater town as they'd called it. "Nobody was murdered."

"Ah, then my mother was right—"

"By a ghost," he interjected.

"Don't you believe in ghosts, Sheriff Sebastian?" she asked, and she tilted her head slightly as she studied his face.

A chill suddenly rushed over him, and he realized he was standing outside in his thin dress shirt. He hadn't gotten his jacket back from Jackson yet, and he hadn't taken the time to change, either. He'd been so worried about that kid. But now ...

Standing here, staring at her, he was beginning to worry about himself. He understood now how Michael had fallen so hard and fast for her. "I don't believe in the ghost of the grave digger," he said. But there were other ghosts that haunted him ...

Like Jackson's father and the other service members who hadn't survived that explosion ...

And even Michael ...

But Michael wasn't dead. Luke couldn't imagine him that way, not after all the years he'd spent believing Fiona Gold's lies that Michael was married to River and happily raising their child together. He hadn't minded being wrong, but now he knew what he'd been wrong about was believing anything Fiona Gold told him.

He suspected even her daughter didn't believe her.

"What about you?" he found himself asking. "Do you believe in ghosts, River?"

She shivered now despite the heavy sweater she wore with jeans. "I didn't used to ..." she murmured. Then she shrugged. "But now ... I don't know what I believe."

Then they had more in common than Michael and raising teenagers. Because Luke didn't know what to believe anymore, either.

"Sarah . . ."

The creepy whisper raised goose bumps on Sarah's skin and woke her up from the nap she hadn't realized she was taking. But Mom had tucked her in, like she was a little kid, and suggested she rest for a while so that she didn't get sick from getting soaked in the storm.

"Sarah . . ."

And she suddenly remembered what else she'd seen in the storm . . . that shadow . . .

Or ghost . . .

Of the grave digger.

He sure as hell wasn't calling her name through the door, though. It was undoubtedly the same person who'd called her name a couple of nights ago and set her up. She jumped out of bed and jerked open the door. "What the hell— "

"Hey," Gigi said. "I got a call for you."

Sarah glared at her. "Sure, you do . . ." Nobody ever called her except her mother and GG Mabel and sometimes Grandma Fiona.

Gigi turned her phone around and showed Jackson's face filling her screen. And Gigi gasped and reached up to touch her hair. It was probably sticking out all over the place.

"Hey . . ." Sarah murmured as heat rushed to her face.

"I didn't get your number earlier," Jackson said. "But I know somebody who knew Gigi's."

Gigi wriggled her eyebrows at Sarah. "And I am happy to play matchmaker."

Sarah lowered the phone so Jackson couldn't see her face and mouthed *Fuck you* at her cousin.

Gigi giggled. Then she pushed past Sarah and headed into the bedroom. "You were sleeping already?"

"Yeah . . ." Sarah said, glancing between her cousin and the cell phone screen.

Jackson patted his shirt. "I'm in my pajamas, too. That storm was pretty wild, how quick it came in . . ."

She nodded. "Yeah . . ."

"I'm sorry . . ." he muttered. "I just wanted to call and tell you that. Sorry for laying all that on you."

"No, don't be sorry," she said, and she pressed a hand to her chest, which felt all hollow inside as she thought of how devastated he'd been. None of that was his fault. "It was fine."

He grinned. "Liar."

She shrugged. "Really. It was fine."

"So when are you leaving?" he asked.

She tensed. "Leaving?"

"You know . . . going back home . . ."

Home. That light-filled house in California. It didn't even seem real right now. She shrugged. "I don't know. They didn't bury my grandfather yet . . ."

"Do you think you might stay for a while even after that . . . ?" he asked.

"I don't know. I'll have to ask my mom."

"She's here," he said. Then he moved around and she could see the edges of a window with lights shining on the glass. "Well, she was. She's just leaving now."

"My mom was at your house?" she asked. She glanced over at her cousin, who just shrugged.

"Yeah, she wanted to talk to Luke," Jackson said. "I don't know if it was about your dad or what. They were on the porch and I couldn't hear everything."

She smiled. "But you heard some stuff."

"Just seemed pretty intense. They were talking about her mom and your grandfather's death."

"Murder," Gigi said. "Everybody's saying he was murdered now. And that Garrett's baby-trapping ex was, too."

"Shit . . ." Sarah muttered.

"Yeah," Jackson said. "So much for this place being the safe, quiet little suburb Luke wants to think it is . . ."

A noise rattled out of the speaker on Gigi's phone, like a screeching, crunching metal sound. And the screen shook as Jackson fumbled with the phone.

"Jesus . . ." he said.

"What was that?" Sarah asked. "What the hell just happened?"

He shrugged. "I don't know. It sounded like a crash, but you know there's not much around this place."

Sarah had been out there earlier that morning even though it felt like days ago now. So much had happened since then.

But she thought back and remembered that the two-story house had been in the middle of a lot of wooded land and open fields. There weren't any intersections or anything around.

Jackson was moving, running down his stairs and onto his porch. And Sarah could hear and see other people. That older couple from the funeral home, wondering what that noise was.

And then she heard a car horn in the distance.

Panic rushed over her, squeezing her chest so that she could barely breathe. She could just feel her heart beating, racing like her thoughts. Because now she knew what that sound was.

Her mom had crashed.

Chapter 16

River must have tempted fate or the spirits when she'd made it sound to Luke that she didn't believe in ghosts. Because she didn't know what the hell happened.

She'd just backed out of the driveway, past the mailbox with the wooden sign dangling from it that had *Sebastian* engraved on it, and had put the van into drive when less than a mile down the road everything went black. The headlights went off and the dashboard went dark and when she pressed the brake pedal, it went down all the way to the floor. And the steering wheel was frozen, unable to move.

So she couldn't steer. She couldn't swerve or stop the vehicle. It was like she was suddenly a passenger behind the wheel while someone else had taken control. Someone she couldn't see, she couldn't fight, she couldn't defend herself from this strange attack.

She could only brace herself as the van continued, as blindly as she felt, into the sudden darkness that engulfed it. And then it bounced off the road, scattering gravel from the shoulder, before striking trees. Metal crunched, glass shattered as the limbs of the trees seemed to try to fight back against the van, pushing through the windows . . .

Reaching toward her even as the airbag deployed. But it was too late.

One of those branches caught her like a fist striking a blow. Pain exploded before that darkness enveloped her even more, before it pulled her into unconsciousness.

But then the loud blare of the horn brought her back around as abruptly as a slap. The sound reverberated in the van and inside her head, making her flinch as it felt like her skull was about to shatter like the glass. Blood streaked down the side of her face like the tears she'd shed earlier. She needed to get out of here.

She needed help, but she couldn't see anything in the enveloping darkness. She tried to fumble around for her purse. For her cell phone.

Even with the blaring of the horn, she could hear it vibrating. Someone was trying to call her. Someone would miss her.

Her daughter.

Her grandmother.

Her mother.

They all needed her. She had to be all right. But the blood kept flowing and the pain kept throbbing.

And as she fumbled around, she couldn't feel anything but the deflating airbag and the roughness of the tree branches and the shards of shattered glass. The shards scratched and nipped at her skin, and she jerked and pulled back, afraid to touch anything.

Afraid to move . . .

But then she noticed a beam of light coming toward her through the trees. It swung around unsteadily like the grave digger's lantern.

Was the grave digger coming for her? She'd escaped him once

sixteen years ago, but she wouldn't be able to run from him now. He was going to catch her this time.

Luke paced the hospital corridor, waiting for news on River's condition. When he'd found her she'd been bleeding profusely from a wound on the top of her head. He didn't know what had cut her, the glass or the tree branches. But it was the look on her face that haunted him even more than how injured she was.

She'd looked terrified. Like she'd seen a ghost . . .

"It's me, River. It's Luke," he'd assured her. "I've got you. You're going to be all right."

He'd made that claim before, to other people, and he'd been wrong. They hadn't been all right. He'd lost them anyway. His best friend . . .

Jackson's dad.

Jackson was with him now, but instead of pacing, he was watching the parking lot through the lobby doors. When the doors opened to Sarah running inside with her grandmother and great-grandmother, Luke realized whom Jackson had been waiting for.

But she ran past the teenager to him. "What the hell did you do to her?" she demanded to know, her voice sharp with anger and fear.

"Nothing," Jackson answered before he could.

Luke wasn't sure he would have answered the same way; he'd known she'd gotten hurt when she'd slipped on the porch steps. He shouldn't have let her drive.

But that hadn't sounded like what had caused the crash.

She'd said the vehicle just shut off. She'd kept murmuring that when he'd tried to staunch the bleeding on her head. "Everything went black . . ."

He'd just thought she'd been unconscious, that that was what she was talking about.

But then she'd said it: "The vehicle just shut off."

Jackson was still defending him to Sarah, "He found her where the van had gone off into the woods. And he got her to the hospital right away. He probably saved her life, Sarah."

Did Jackson resent that he'd been able to do that for River but not for his dad?

The girl gasped, though. "Saved her life? It was . . . she was . . ."

"I don't think she's hurt that badly," Luke assured her. "She has a cut on her head, and they're running tests to make sure she's okay." That she didn't have bleeding or swelling on her brain or any broken bones.

Luke had ordered other tests, too. He had his crime techs going over that van, trying to figure out what had caused that crash. Because it had been so strange . . .

As strange as the look on River's face when he'd found her.

That fear . . .

That look was on her daughter's face now. And her grandmother and great-grandmother mirrored those expressions. For once they weren't bickering but were actually holding hands. Well, clutching each other's hands, actually . . . like River had clutched at Luke.

"You have blood on your shirt," Sarah said, her voice just a whisper. "My mother's blood . . ."

River's hands had been bleeding, not as badly as her head, though, and she'd left smudges on his dress shirt.

"There was a lot of broken glass," he said. "She has some cuts and—"

Fiona let out a little squeak of alarm. "Not my beautiful girl!"

"She's not cut badly," he said. But he didn't know that for sure, though head wounds did tend to bleed a lot. And she had obviously had a head wound.

Hopefully, it was a minor one. Once she'd recognized him, that look of horror had left her face, and she'd talked coherently to him. About the van going dark . . .

Like someone had shut it off.

She'd been alone in it, though. So no one else had touched anything. Unless . . .

Had it been done remotely? Some security systems were set up so that a vehicle could be shut off remotely if it was stolen.

"What happened, Sheriff?" Mrs. Hawthorne asked. "What caused the crash?"

"Mom's a good driver," Sarah said. "She's never even had a parking lot accident."

Mrs. Hawthorne nodded. "Not even a fender bender."

This was more than a fender bender. But from how worried they all looked, they knew that.

"This is what you need to be investigating," Fiona said. "Find out how my daughter got hurt instead of wasting your time on things that aren't crimes."

"You don't think this was an accident?" Luke asked her. And he wondered why she would have thought that . . .

She wasn't as close to her daughter as Sarah and Mrs. Hawthorne were. River had probably run away before she'd gotten her driver's license or shortly after she had, so it wasn't as if the woman had a lot of experience riding around with her like the other two women did.

Fiona shrugged her slight shoulders. "I don't know what this was, but it's not my job to know. It's yours. I don't even know what she was doing out there."

"She'd just left my house," he said. "She was talking to me." And he gave her a hard look. If Fiona Gold had known that or had worried that her daughter might have revealed something to him, would she have hurt her? Was Fiona as vicious as some of the other Golds seemed to be? Because she would have to be quite vicious to hurt her own child . . .

"Family of River Gold?" A doctor stood in the doorway between the ER and the waiting room, his back holding that door open.

The women rushed toward him, bombarding him with questions. He held up a hand to quiet them and said, "She's all right. She has some stitches for a cut on her head and a slight concussion. She has some other cuts and bruises and a sprained ankle but no broken bones. She wants to go home, but she's going to need to take it easy."

She wants to go home.

Luke knew where she meant. She wanted to go back to the home she'd made for herself and her daughter that was far away from Gold Creek. She didn't want to go back to the house by the cemetery.

But Fiona was saying, "Of course we will take care of her. We will make sure she rests."

Jackson nudged his arm. "What's wrong, Luke? Do you know what really happened out there?"

He shook his head. "Not yet. But I will find out."

He'd already interviewed River, and now that he knew she was going to be all right, he had no reason to stick around, to see her again. Except to keep her safe.

But the best way to do that was to find out why she was in danger and who had put her there. So after dropping Jackson back at home, he headed into the sheriff's office. He made some calls and pulled in some favors, and it didn't take him long to confirm what River had told him. That the van had just shut off.

And now he knew why.

Someone had called the onboard monitoring system, reported it stolen, and requested that it be immediately disabled. And whoever had called had done it from Gold Memorial Gardens and Funeral Services because they'd had the vehicle identification number of the van as well as the passcode that authorized the monitoring system to disable the vehicle.

"Who was it?" Luke asked. "Did the person identify themselves?"

"Yes, of course," the customer service representative said. "We also get a name along with the passcode and VIN number."

"And so who was it?" he asked. "Who made that call?"

"Gregory Gold the first," the rep replied.

No wonder River had looked like she'd seen a ghost. A dead man was responsible for her crash.

Or at least that was what someone else in that house wanted Luke to believe. But as he'd told River, he didn't believe in ghosts. Someone alive and well had made that call.

Had they intended to hurt River though? Had they known she was driving at the time it had been shut down? Or had they only wanted to inconvenience her by stranding her somewhere? Or had the intent been to frighten her?

Why?

To get her to leave Gold Creek?

Or to get her to stay away from him?

Her mother certainly hadn't wanted her talking to him. And he doubted any of the other Golds would appreciate her talking to him if they suspected that she was trying to get him to look at someone else as a suspect besides her mother.

He had a lot of suspects already. All of the Golds.

And River had gone back to that house where they all lived and worked together. She'd gone back to the house where that call had come from that had put her life in jeopardy.

If that person tried to hurt her again, would she survive the next attempt? Or would Luke have another murder to solve?

Chapter 17

River struggled to remember those moments after everything had gone dark. The crash.

Luke.

He had been there, right?

He was the reason she'd gotten to the hospital? That she'd been numbed, stitched up, and drugged?

Not that she minded the drugs right now. They'd dulled the pounding in her head. If they hadn't, she wouldn't have survived the squabbling going on during the car ride back to Gold Memorial Gardens. Except for some security lighting, the house was dark when they drove up.

It was late. And River didn't want to think about anything right now. She just wanted to sleep. But the squabbling didn't stop when the four of them headed up the stairs.

"Sleep with me, River," Fiona said, "like you used to when you were young and you were scared."

River had been terrified when the van shut off earlier. Even though she'd survived the crash, she was still frightened that something like that could happen again. That she could wind up like her father and that poor Justine: dead.

Or worse yet. Her daughter could. She reached out now to clasp Sarah's hand but realized it was already in hers. She just couldn't feel much through the bandages or maybe because of those painkillers.

But she could still feel that fear. And she had to admit that she was a little scared . . . of her own mother. River wanted to believe her, that nothing nefarious had happened with either death. But Luke had made it clear that neither of them had probably been an accident. That didn't mean her mother was responsible for either of them, though. But still . . .

Fiona stopped outside her door and caught River's arm, pulling her to a stop as well. "Stay with me, like you used to . . ."

"She's staying with me," Sarah insisted a bit coldly.

"With us," Mabel added.

Fiona glared at them both. "You heard the doctor. She needs someone to watch out for her, to make sure that she wakes up easily and has no complications from the concussion."

Had the doctor said that? It was fuzzy to her right now. Just like the details of the crash and the aftermath when Luke had appeared with that flashlight . . .

And she'd thought the grave digger had come for her. She shivered.

"She needs to get in bed now," Fiona continued. "And she needs someone to take care of her."

"You never took care of her before," Sarah said. "She took care of herself. And you never protected her. She got bullied and picked on in this house and in this town, and you did nothing to save her from that."

Tears filled Fiona's eyes.

River felt a twinge of regret and sympathy for her. "Mom, I'm sorry . . ."

"No, she's right," Fiona said. "I never protected you like I should have. Like you would do anything to protect your daughter."

River definitely would. So she needed to get out of here, out of Gold Creek for both their sakes. If someone was responsible for the van shutting off like it had, that was probably the reason they'd done it. They wanted to get rid of her.

So was she playing into their plan by running away again?

Or should she stay and fight this time?

Should she defend herself and her mother and her family? Because despite her doubts about her mother's truthfulness, she couldn't believe that Fiona would have killed anyone, least of all Gregory. She had been so devoted to him. Someone had killed him, though, and maybe that person had used the method they had so that her mother would be implicated.

Then Fiona was the one in danger.

While River knew it was smarter and safer, at least for her and Sarah, to run, she wasn't sure she could leave her mother again. Not if someone was trying to frame her for murder.

She felt as torn between them as she'd been in the hallway when they'd each held on to her.

She'd run away last time for Sarah's sake as much as her own. She'd wanted to protect her baby. But if she left with Sarah and Mabel, her mother would be all alone with nobody to help her.

And if something happened to her, River wasn't sure she would be able to forgive herself.

Luke had to do something to keep her safe. River and his niece as well.

They were both in that house. With those people, one of whom was a killer. He knew it.

Gregory Gold I had been murdered. And Justine Campbell . . . the coroner's preliminary report said she'd also died of botulism poisoning. The same thing that had killed her octogenarian lover if he believed what Fiona had told him. Some of the other Golds had hinted at that affair as well and had indicated it was Fiona's motive to murder her husband. So had his wife killed them both?

But would Fiona have put her own daughter in danger?

"It's late, Luke," the county prosecutor grumbled, but he'd opened the door and let him in. "And I'm not about to wake up a judge for you to go on a wild goose chase."

"I need the voice recording of that customer service call to shut off the van," he said. "I want to know who called for that to be done because we both know that Gregory Gold the first didn't make that call from his casket."

The prosecutor sighed. Donald Borreson had served this county for a long time. Like Dr. Jeffries, he probably could have retired a while ago. But then he probably wasn't as busy as Dr. Jeffries. There wasn't a whole lot of crime in Gold Creek.

"No. Gregory did not," he said as if it needed to be confirmed. But he'd probably known Gregory nearly as well as the doctor did and maybe he'd believed, like Gregory had, that he could live forever. But if he hadn't, then he was murdered.

Luke hadn't taken that claim seriously at first. But now, after another woman died and River had been hurt, he knew he had no time to spare to find the killer. "I need to know who made that call," he persisted.

Donald nodded, and a lock of his thin gray hair fell across his furrowed brow. "I'll ask a judge for the warrant in the morning."

"What else do we need to bring murder charges?"

"Against whom?" the prosecutor asked.

"I questioned Fiona Gold," he said. "I showed you my notes."

"And she had a plausible explanation for why her prints were on that syringe," Donald said. "Even if we could get a grand jury to indict her, we wouldn't get a conviction. No jury of her peers would be able to believe she's capable of murder. A sweet woman like her . . ."

She'd never been sweet to Luke. She certainly had had no problem lying to him and making him believe it, though.

"We need more evidence," Luke said, as much to himself as to the prosecutor.

"Against Fiona Gold?" Donald asked.

"Against whoever is guilty," Luke said. And he was worried that he was in a little over his head. As an MP he'd investigated assaults and thefts and even a manslaughter charge, but it had been easy for him to find the person responsible in those cases. Easy for him to find the evidence he had needed to arrest the guilty party.

But now . . .

"I have to know what it's going to take to ensure a conviction," Luke said.

Donald chuckled. "A confession."

He couldn't get Fiona to tell him the truth about anything, so he doubted she would ever confess. And if she wasn't guilty . . .

Then who was?

"I'm going over to the house again," Luke said. "I'm going to find something."

Donald yawned and nodded. "Just make sure it's not another dead body."

"That's exactly what I don't want to have happen." Especially because he was worried that dead body would belong to someone he cared about . . .

Fiona should have been exhausted after the day she'd had. The funeral. That stupid girl dying . . .

Then the sheriff insisting on questioning her over Gregory's death, like she was an actual suspect. He was never going to get enough to arrest her. And even if he did . . .

She could talk her way into a not guilty verdict just as she'd talked her way into other situations. But River and Sarah and her mother . . .

They hadn't let her talk them into watching over River. And Fiona was alone in her room, staring out the window, while they were all together. Maybe that was good. Maybe they would stay safe that way.

But knowing that her daughter had been hurt was why Fiona couldn't sleep.

Why she paced in front of that window.

The minute River had said she was coming home for the funeral, Fiona had realized it was a mistake. She'd wanted that, more than anything for so long. She'd planned for it. But the reality was that everything was bound to come out if her daughter came back to Gold Creek, and that was going to put River in even more danger.

Chapter 18

Thanks to whatever drugs they'd given her in the ER, River had been able to sleep. But from the dark circles beneath her daughter's and her grandmother's eyes, she wasn't sure that they had slept at all. She'd found Sarah wide awake on the daybed, staring out the window, while Mabel had been tucked in bed next to her, turned toward her and wide awake as if studying her face.

"I'm fine," she assured them despite the pain throbbing at the top of her head, near where those stitches were. It wasn't the stitches that hurt, though. It was the concussion. Maybe that was another reason why she'd been able to sleep despite not having made her decision to leave or to stay. To protect her daughter and abandon her mother.

Her initial plan had been to get her mother to come home with her after the funeral. But she doubted Fiona or Luke Sebastian would agree to her leaving the state.

"You two didn't need to watch over me all night," she told them.

Sarah shrugged. "I took a long nap yesterday, so I wasn't even tired last night. It wasn't a big deal."

River smiled at her daughter. "It was a big deal to me." While she was touched and proud, she was also concerned that her child had been so worried about her that she hadn't been able to sleep.

As a single mom, she'd worked hard to make sure that her daughter had security, that she felt safe and loved.

"Last night, you getting hurt, that was the big deal," Mabel said. She reached out and touched the bandage on River's forehead. "I just kept thinking of how bad it could have gone and I kept seeing that girl, too."

River sighed over the loss of such a young woman. "I know."

Sarah glanced out that window behind her. It was morning now, but the sky was dark as if another storm was coming.

River didn't want her getting caught in it or in the crossfire of whatever was going on in Gold Creek. "I want to talk to you both about what we should do now," she said.

"Breakfast?" Mabel said.

Sarah nodded. "Yes. I didn't eat dinner last night."

River felt a pang of regret that she hadn't made sure her child had eaten. But she'd taken the opportunity, during Sarah's nap, to go talk to the sheriff. She hadn't had any idea what would happen when she left. That she would crash.

She wanted to talk to Luke again and find out how that had happened, how the van had suddenly shut off like it had. She didn't believe that a ghost had done it.

But she saw Sarah glance out that window again. And she wondered . . .

River used to meet Michael out there, at the grave digger's grave, except for that last night. When he hadn't showed . . . she'd thought she'd seen something, something that she really couldn't explain . . . even now . . .

"After breakfast, maybe we should leave," she suggested.

"Leave? What do you mean?" Sarah asked, her body tense.

"I mean that we should get plane tickets and fly back home," River explained.

"What? Now? Why?" Sarah asked, her voice going a little high as if she was panicky at the thought.

"You know I hate this place," Mabel said. "But I don't think we should leave before the funeral is over, and *you* definitely shouldn't leave before the will is read."

"I don't care about an inheritance," River said. As she'd told her mother when she'd refused to come home all those years ago, she didn't need or want any Gold money.

"What about your mother?" Mabel asked. "Do you care about her?"

River sucked in a breath. "Of course I do, and I want her to come home with us but—"

"The sheriff isn't going to allow that," Mabel said, speaking River's earlier thought aloud. "And even if he did, your mother won't leave here. I've tried to talk some sense into her, but you know how she is . . ."

Was that what Mabel and Fiona had been arguing about so much over the past few days?

"She might be a little too concerned about what her inheritance is going to be," Mabel muttered.

River wondered if her grandmother had doubts about Fiona's innocence as well.

"We can't leave," Sarah said, and there was definitely panic in her voice. "We just got here."

"Days ago," River reminded her. "And that is usually only as long as you have to be somewhere when someone dies, just a few days."

"I don't know that," Sarah said, her tone getting a little snarky now. "I don't know anything about funerals and this place because you've treated me like a little kid who has to be protected from all that stuff."

River's head began to pound a little harder. "I think you can see why I want to protect you from all of this . . ." she murmured as she touched that bandage on her head.

Sarah jumped up from the daybed and rushed over to her. "I'm sorry, Mom. I know you got hurt last night. And I never want that to happen. But I don't think we should let someone scare us into leaving, either."

River narrowed her eyes and studied her daughter's flushed face. She was really worked up about this. "Then why did you choose to do online school instead of going in person?" she asked. She'd asked the question before, but Sarah had never given her a real answer.

"It wasn't because I was scared," Sarah said, but she looked away from River as if she was unable to hold her gaze. "I was just sick of it . . ."

"Of what?" River asked.

Sarah shrugged. "Stupid stuff. Stupid teenage games and pranks and . . ."

"You were being bullied," River said, and that dread churned in her stomach now. "Why didn't you tell me?"

Sarah sighed. "Because you would have tried to stop it in *your* sweet, nonconfrontational way you have of dealing with things."

"What are you talking about?" River asked.

"You wouldn't have wanted to get them in trouble, so you wouldn't have reported them. You would have invited them over and tried to get them to be friends with me or something."

Mabel snort-laughed and nodded. "Sounds about right."

River felt compelled to defend her methods. "But if it worked—"

"It wouldn't have worked for me," Sarah said. "I don't want shitty, shallow friends like that."

No. River had a pretty good idea who Sarah wanted as a friend. A certain boy who was definitely not shallow and was handsome and a little bit older than she was, just like Michael had been to River. And because of Michael, River had wound up having a baby in her teens.

"And being friends or even family doesn't stop people from treating you like crap and taking advantage of you," Mabel said now. "Sometimes nice doesn't work, River. And sometimes you have to fight instead of run."

River sucked in a breath. "I wasn't talking about running away," she insisted. "I was talking about protecting you and my daughter."

"GG Mabel and I are pretty tough, Mom," Sarah said. "You don't have to worry about us."

Mabel nodded in agreement. "She's right. You and your mother are the ones we need to protect."

River knew what the best way to do that was: to find out the truth. But that might not protect her mother at all.

Luke had that recording, but that wasn't all he had. He had a hell of a lot of questions for all the Golds. He also had a need to check on River and make sure that she was all right. She wasn't safe, not in this house, not with these people.

He was there, too, standing outside the dining room where all the family was having breakfast. Or almost all the family. He hadn't heard River's or Sarah's voice yet. Taking a page from Lawrence Gold's book, he was sticking to the shadows outside the open door, hidden behind a bookshelf against one wall of the wide corridor. From the shadows, he was listening. The voice on that recording had been disguised as a raspy whisper, so he had no way to tell who had placed that call. It could have been a man. Or a woman. Or even one of those kids.

But not Sarah. She wouldn't have done anything that might have put her mom in danger. She stuck close to her now as they walked toward the doors to the dining room. Fortunately, they had come from the other direction, so they didn't see him behind the edge of the bookshelf.

But he could see them. Sarah was dressed in leggings and a big sweater. She fit in more in Michigan in the fall than her mother, who wore a summery yellow dress. At least she had a sweater on over it. Her grandmother was dressed in bright colors, too. And she stuck as close to River's side as Sarah did.

Everyone else must have seen them, too, because that conversation inside the dining room suddenly ceased. The only sound was the clatter of silverware, as if someone had dropped theirs when they saw River standing there with the bandages on her forehead and her hands. Were they shocked to see her hurt or to see her alive?

"River, my God, what happened?" Noah asked the question with concern in his deep voice. "Are you all right?"

She began, "Yes . . ."

"Somebody caused her to crash," Sarah said.

"Crash?" Gregory Gold II asked. "You were in one of the company vans?"

Like he hadn't known for certain . . .

"You said she could borrow one," his son, Gregory Gold III, said as if reminding him.

So he'd known.

"Was there something wrong with the vehicle?" Lawrence asked.

"I make sure those vehicles are serviced regularly," Noah said. "There is no way something was wrong with it."

Sarah raised her voice. "My mom didn't cause the accident—"

"Of course it was an accident," Gregory Gold II insisted. "Everyone understands that sometimes these things happen. Don't worry about the damage, River."

She sucked in a breath then.

"Don't worry about her suing your ass off for getting hurt in

THE HOUSE BY THE CEMETERY 175

that malfunctioning vehicle," Mabel said. "Just give her the damn settlement she deserves."

"The will won't be read until after the interment," Gregory II said as if that was what Mrs. Hawthorne meant. "We are rescheduling the funeral for tomorrow, and then after the interment Colson Howard can read the will."

"Once you get what you want, you can go back to California," Mrs. Gold said. From the shakiness of her voice, it must have been the oldest one. Carolyn.

"What I want is the truth," River said. "I want to know what really happened to my . . ." Since she was still in the doorway, Luke could see how her throat moved as if she was struggling to swallow. ". . . father. And I want to make sure that nobody tries to lay the blame for that on my mother."

"Yes, the sheriff was way out of line," Fiona agreed. "He has no idea what he's doing. He has no business trying to run any sort of investigation."

Luke chuckled, drawing Sarah's attention as she turned in the doorway and looked back into the hall. He stepped out from behind the bookshelf and joined them all inside the dining room. "My business is investigating crimes," he said. "And right now, right here, my business is booming nearly as much as yours."

"That's crass of you," Mrs. Carolyn Gold remarked with a disdainful sniff.

"That's the truth," Luke said. "I'm investigating Gregory Gold the first's murder as well as the murder of Justine Campbell."

"You're sure?" River asked, her blue eyes wide with a faint sheen of tears. "She was so young and . . ."

"Yes, she was," he agreed. "That is why she wouldn't have willingly taken the filler, with the high concentration of botulinum A toxin, that caused her death just like it did Gregory Gold the first's."

Sarah's brow wrinkled. "Botulinum A toxin?"

"It's in cosmetic fillers," Fiona said. "And it doesn't kill people unless they inject way too much of it."

"It has killed two people," Luke said. "And last night someone tried to kill your daughter, too."

"I knew it!" Sarah exclaimed.

The color drained from River's face, leaving her as pale as she'd been last night and with that same shaken, horrified expression. "The van just shut off . . ." she muttered like she had last night.

"Someone shut it off," he said. "They placed a call to the vehicle security company, said it was stolen, and demanded that the engine get shut off immediately."

"Who did that?" Sarah asked.

"Someone in this house," Luke said. "They called from the main office line."

"Who?" Sarah asked again, but instead of looking at him, she was looking at all of the Golds sitting around that long table.

"We have a recording of the voice, but it's whispering," he said. "The techs will go over it, see if they can get enough to do a voice match." He followed Sarah's gaze around that table now. But none of them were looking back at him. They were looking at each other, as if wondering if the person sitting next to them had made that call and had tried to kill an innocent woman.

Because he had no doubt that River was innocent, that she had nothing to do with those murders. She probably didn't even have anything to do with Michael running away because Michael hadn't run away with her. His daughter knew nothing about him. And River hadn't seen him since she'd run away.

"You'll need warrants to get any of our voices to use for comparison," Honora Gold remarked. And she slung her arm around the back of her son's chair, as if protecting him.

But why would Garrett go after River? He had as good a

motive for killing his grandfather and girlfriend as Fiona Gold had. But why try to hurt River?

Unless she'd seen something yesterday . . .

Unless she knew something she didn't realize she knew . . .

Luke stepped closer to her and whispered, "I need to talk to you. I have a few more questions."

"I told you what happened last night," she said, but she didn't sound a hundred percent certain that she had.

Had she remembered something else?

"Don't interrogate her like she's some criminal," Sarah chastised him. "She hasn't done anything wrong. Ever."

"I know that, Sarah," he assured the girl. "I just need her to answer a few more questions. Then hopefully I can figure out who tried to hurt her."

River bobbed her head in a quick nod and moved back out into the hallway. "Of course I'll answer your questions, Luke, but you should be focusing on who killed that poor girl." She shuddered and blinked rapidly again as if the thought of her death had brought tears to her eyes.

And the evidence of her empathy and compassion affected him, making him more aware of her than he'd ever been and not just as a beautiful person on the outside but about how beautiful she was on the inside, too. "You are incredible," he murmured.

Her face flushed now. "What do you mean?"

"Someone tried to kill you last night, but you're more upset about what happened to someone you don't even know."

She moved her shoulders in a slight shrug. "I'm fine," she said. "I survived. And I'm not sure that someone was actually trying to kill me or just scare me."

He actually wasn't sure about that, either, especially if that call had come from her mother. Even if Fiona was trying to get away with murder, he doubted that she would have tried to kill her own daughter to do it.

"But someone did kill Justine Campbell, and I don't have to know her to care about her. She was young and pregnant with her whole life ahead of her and her baby's life." She blinked furiously against the tears that filled her eyes. "Maybe I am thinking about myself because I know what it feels like to be her."

"Young and pregnant."

"I was even younger than she was," River said.

"Too young," Luke said. "That was why I said what I did about you and Michael giving up your child." He glanced toward that open door of the dining room where Sarah stood watching them, and he lowered his voice when he continued. "You were children yourselves. But I see that you did a good job with her. The woman who gave birth to me and to Michael was young when she had me, much too young, and she never grew up, never learned how to take responsibility for herself or for her actions."

"Or for her children," River said, and she reached out and touched him. But her hand was bandaged, so he couldn't feel her skin, just the cotton bandage.

But he was reminded of his job and his reason for doing it. To keep people safe. To keep them from getting hurt like River had been. And Justine Campbell . . .

"I need you to tell me exactly what you saw during the wake," he said.

"During the wake . . . what . . . why?"

"Because maybe you saw something and that's why someone messed with the van you took out last night."

She sucked in a breath, and as she tried to remember, she touched the bandage on her forehead. "I was talking to those old ladies . . . you know the ones . . . the funeral groupies . . ."

"Or my father's groupies," he said with a smile. "They love attending all his services."

"They are fans of my mother, too, apparently," she said. "They were talking to her and to me and Sarah and then Justine continued down the receiving line. She and Garrett exchanged words and he ran out. His mother ran out after him and then Justine kept going and kind of stumbled and knocked over that flower arrangement . . ."

So had Garrett or Honora caused that needle mark and her death? By running out, they'd given themselves the opportunity to get rid of the syringe. Or even plant it somewhere or on someone else.

"But I'm not the only one who saw that," she said. "I'm sure everybody saw that."

"What about your mother?"

"I'm sure she saw it, too," River replied. "But she and my grandmother had already walked away from the receiving line and joined me and Sarah. That was when those old ladies approached us."

"So your mother didn't go near Justine?"

She tensed.

"What?" he prodded.

"Fiona didn't leave the receiving line until after she said something to Justine . . ."

So she'd been close enough to Justine Campbell to talk to her . . .

Close enough to stick that needle in her . . .

And then what? Had she gotten rid of it somewhere that River might have seen her dispose of it?

"I know what you're thinking," she said. "But my mother loves me. She wouldn't hurt me."

"Maybe she didn't think you would get hurt, just that you would get scared enough to leave."

"She asked me to come here," she said. "Why would she be trying to get rid of me?"

He shrugged then. "Because you saw or know more than she wants you to . . ."

"She might not be the one who thinks so," she said. "It has

to be someone else. Someone that killed my father and Justine and that caused my crash, and if you're only going to investigate my mother, you leave me no choice . . .'"

Luke tensed now. "No choice in what?"

She crossed her arms over her chest and raised her chin, as if challenging him. "*I* will have to investigate everyone else."

His pulse quickened with concern. "No, you can't do that, River. It's too dangerous," he said.

He did not want her getting hurt again.

And if the killer was already threatened enough by her to try to scare her away, next time they would make sure that she did not survive just as they'd made sure that Gregory Gold I and Justine Campbell had not survived. And the next funeral being held at Gold Memorial Gardens would be hers.

Chapter 19

Sarah and Mabel had already convinced her to stay, but now River was even more confident that it was the right decision. Was it dangerous? Her cuts and bruises proved that it was, that Luke was right.

But leaving without learning the truth would be even more dangerous to everyone she left behind and maybe to her and Sarah and Mabel as well. There was no guarantee that the danger wouldn't follow her back to Santa Monica. Gold Memorial Gardens and Funeral Services had locations everywhere. Even California.

So no. She couldn't go anywhere, and be safe, until she knew for certain who'd killed her father and that girl and who might have tried to kill her. And that person was arrested and prosecuted.

To get them arrested and prosecuted, she was going to have to bring Luke evidence. Was he right? Had she seen something when Justine had died? Something that somebody was worried she would remember, but yet she couldn't remember any more than she'd told him.

She paced the showing room now. The casket was gone. And both bodies.

But the plants and flower arrangements were still there, wilting like the one that had fallen on the ground. The dirt had settled into the carpet now. But they couldn't clean yet, not until the room was released.

And it hadn't been.

River had sliced through the tape that had sealed the doors shut, and opened them so that she could try to jog her memory. Maybe it was the concussion that kept the details from coming back or maybe it was just that so much had happened.

Ever since that call from her mother . . .

Ever since her father died. For so many years she hadn't believed that he was her biological parent. But the way her mom had acted when River had asked if he was, how adamant Fiona had been . . .

She had definitely been telling the truth about River's paternity. And if she was telling the truth about that, then she was probably telling the truth about everything. So who, besides Fiona, had a motive to kill both Gregory Gold I and Justine?

Garrett. Or Honora.

They'd left this room quickly the day before, though. So River left it now, and she sought them out. She found them in the dining room with a few of the others, the Golds by marriage rather than blood, who were lingering over cups of coffee. River's stomach roiled at just the smell of the bitter brew. She preferred herbal teas and green smoothies, but the Gold family lived on coffee, the stronger and the bitterer the better. That kind of described the people, too, or at least how River remembered them.

But she had been gone for many years and her memories of her time, and the people here, were the memories made in the mind of a child and an adolescent who might have been as overly emotional as some of the other women in her family. Like her mother and grandmother.

She found a carafe of hot water and some tea bags. Grandma had probably requested the cook to put some out for her. She dunked the lemon zest tea bag into the cup of hot water and carried it over to the table. Needing something to eat, she picked up a banana and a scone and chose a seat near Garrett.

He looked nearly as bad as she looked. His eyes were as bruised, with dark circles, as she was bruised from the crash. "Hi, Garrett, I haven't had a chance to tell you how sorry I am."

He stiffened. "Sorry about what?"

"About Justine . . ." That poor girl had once meant something to him. And losing her had to have affected him, so much that he had those dark circles. But he'd looked like that even before she'd died. Because he'd already lost her?

"Don't patronize my son," Honora said.

"God, Mom, just stop!" Garrett shouted at her, and he jumped up, knocking her arm off the back of his chair. Then he rushed out of the room.

He wasn't quite a teenager anymore, but he clearly acted as dramatic and childish as one yet. Or as some teenagers.

Sarah had been acting pretty mature lately. And Jackson . . . That poor kid had been through so much that he really wasn't a kid anymore. All his losses had made him grow up faster than he should have had to.

Honora jumped up as if she was going to follow him out. But he stopped at the door and turned back. "Don't follow me. I can't breathe! You're smothering me!"

Honora sucked in a breath before dropping back onto her chair. Then she ran a trembling hand over her black hair, as if checking to make sure it was all in place. She had the Gold vanity for certain. And the fierceness.

She had intimidated River in the past. Anytime that River had made the mistake of trying to talk to her, Honora had made it clear that they weren't really sisters. That they were not anything to each other. But Honora didn't intimidate River anymore. River smiled at her. "I wish I was the mama bear that you are," she said.

Honora glared. "Now you're patronizing me."

River shook her head. "Not at all. I admire you. I wish that I protected my child as much as you do yours."

Honora's glare softened as tears filled her eyes. "I didn't protect him," she said. "I should have done what you did, River. I should have gotten the hell out of here the minute I got pregnant. First I lost my husband because of how hard I work at this damn business, and now I'm afraid I'm losing my son."

River reached out and touched her hand, patting it with her bandages. "I know you did your best, Honora, and I'm sure your son knows that, too."

Honora stared at the bandages on the hand on hers. "I'm sorry you were hurt, River."

And she said it almost as if she'd had something to do with it . . .

Or maybe because she knew who had. Her son.

Then she pulled her hand from beneath River's, jumped up, and rushed out of the room. River didn't know if she was going after her son, or if she was just trying to get away from her.

"I guess I know how to clear a room," she said to the red-haired woman who sat at the table sipping coffee.

But it didn't look as dark as the Golds usually drank it. But then she was only a Gold by marriage. Gregory Gold II's wife, Gregory Gold III's mother. "I appreciate that your husband had your son pick me, my daughter, and my grandmother up from the airport."

Holly Gold just shrugged. "They don't tell me what they do." She said it almost as if she suspected they were up to something. But then she smiled that smug smile that made her every bit of a Gold. "And I don't tell them what *I* do . . ."

What the hell could she be doing that she wouldn't want them to know? Murdering people?

River forced a laugh. "Holly! Good for you! You need your autonomy, especially in this family."

Then the older woman sighed. "Unfortunately, I think my grandchildren have adopted that same attitude. We rarely know what they're up to . . ." She glanced around the nearly empty room as if looking for them.

"They've been sweet to my daughter," River said. That was probably where Sarah was, with them.

Holly smirked again. "Sweet? No. They're not sweet at all. They're Golds through and through."

Was she proud of that or horrified by it? Before River could figure out how to tactfully ask, Holly stood and walked out of the room. Maybe she was going off in search of them or maybe she was about to do something that she had no intention of telling her son and husband she was doing. But what?

"She is proud of her grandchildren," the woman's sister-in-law said. Ellen was married to Lawrence and blended into the background as completely as her husband tended to do. Her hair was dishwater blond with streaks of gray and her face was a kind of waxy beige like she wore too much foundation.

"You don't have grandchildren yet?" River asked.

"Wynn has been totally focused on his career. College, med school, residency, fellowships, he hasn't had time for anything else," Ellen said.

"He was always determined to become a doctor," River said. "You and Lawrence must be so proud of him."

Ellen offered a small smile.

"And what about Taylor?" River asked. "What does she do?"

"Not children. Not relationships. She's locked herself away from the world. I'm surprised she even came back for the funeral." She glanced around as if looking for her. "She's probably locked in her room with a book."

"Sarah is very much like that." Usually locked in her room with a book, until they'd come here. Now she was interacting with people, but these people were hurtful and dangerous and not to be trusted. Any of them.

Not even River's mother.

But there were plenty of other suspects as well. River couldn't trust that Luke would consider any of them, though, unless she found a reason for him to look at them. They all had motives. Money or revenge or power or . . .

River needed evidence.

"You and your daughter seem very close," Ellen said with a trace of envy.

"We were when she was younger," River said. "But once the teenage years hit . . ."

Ellen smiled. "The teenage years are tough. I don't think I ever got Taylor back after hers. I'm not sure who she is anymore."

A killer? Could Taylor want that money badly enough to kill for it? Could any of them?

"But does anyone really know who anyone else is, River?" Ellen asked, as if she actually wanted an answer. But she wasn't looking at her, she was staring instead at the doorway where her husband stood. He hadn't been there a second ago, but then he had a habit of just magically appearing out of nowhere.

Was Ellen's question about her daughter or about her husband?

River answered it honestly. "I don't think so, Ellen. I don't think we can ever know anyone as well as we think we do. Everybody has their secrets."

Ellen smiled as if satisfied with River's reply or maybe because she had a secret, too.

River shivered at how cold all these interactions with her family left her, of how cold her family was. Any one of them could be a killer. Any one of them could have tried to kill her as well.

Maybe staying here wasn't the right thing to do. She didn't know how to investigate a crime. She only knew how to cover up imperfections and highlight assets. She didn't know how to uncover the ugliness she would have to uncover in order to find out the truth.

She needed help.

Luke hadn't come alone earlier that morning. He'd brought in some crime techs. This time he had them going over the phone and the office where that call had originated the night before.

"You're going to find a lot of fingerprints on that phone," Gregory Gold II said. "I used it this morning. I think Lawrence did as well and my son. Even my mother was in here this morning."

"You were all very busy this morning," Luke remarked, letting his skepticism creep into his voice. And Gregory II was very busily providing them all with a reason for having their prints on the phone receiver. But Luke was glad that Gregory II had stayed in the office with him; that way River couldn't be investigating him as she'd vowed she was going to do.

If it wasn't so damn dangerous, her determination would have been commendable. She wanted to find out the truth as badly as Luke did, maybe even more.

But she had to be careful.

He needed to talk to her again, to make sure that she stayed safe. His phone buzzed, and he pulled it from his pocket to check the screen. A text lit up the screen: **Meet me in the cemetery in twenty minutes where I saw you the other night . . .**

River.

Had she already found out something? Something that might help his investigation. And put her in danger . . .

He had to make sure that she didn't walk out there alone, especially when he noticed that Gregory had slipped away when Luke had been looking at his phone.

At that text . . .

Had Gregory seen it, too?

"Sheriff," the tech, Hannah, remarked. "I think there are some video cameras in this room. There should be footage somewhere of the office."

And of the person who'd made that call . . .

"Can you pull it up?" he asked. The voice recording hadn't helped. But surely the video would reveal who'd endangered River's life.

He just had to make sure that it wasn't in danger again. And he had an uneasy feeling that he was in danger, too. Not necessarily from the killer but from River, from how much he was starting to worry about her, to care about her . . .

"Thanks for meeting me . . ."

"I'm surprised *you* wanted to come back out here."

"I figured that after what happened last night, you'd want to stick close to your mom," Jackson said.

Sarah smiled at his understanding. But of course he would understand after he'd lost his mom. He would probably give anything for her to get a second chance like her mom had, like Sarah had to be a better daughter now.

"And it wasn't the cemetery that freaked me out yesterday . . ." He glanced over his shoulder at the three-story brick house and shuddered.

Sarah was staring at it, too, wondering where her mom was inside it. She'd been with the sheriff for a while. Maybe they were still together, which meant that she was safe. Nothing else would happen to her. The pressure on her chest eased a bit. "Me neither . . ." she murmured.

But it was kind of a lie. She'd seen something yesterday, some shadow in the rain.

But that hadn't freaked her out nearly as much as hearing that crash, realizing it was her mom, worrying that it was going to be too late, that she wouldn't be okay.

"I owe you so much," she said. "For letting me know last night where my mom was."

He flinched. "I had no idea that was going to happen . . ."

"I know," she assured him. He was probably the one person she could trust because he had nothing to do with the Golds, though Toby was the one who'd picked him up from his house and brought him here. They knew each other, since Jackson had been going to their same school for the past couple of months, but they weren't friends.

She glanced around, wondering where Toby and Gigi were now. Probably lurking in the shadows somewhere, probably like they had been the day before. But yet when she and Jackson had come back into the lobby, Gigi and Toby had been there and they'd been dry.

So it couldn't have been one of them that Sarah had seen in the shadows . . .

Who the hell, or maybe what the hell, had she seen? The grave digger?

Jackson was walking, maybe just to put some distance between him and that house. Or between him and the Golds . . .

Either way she couldn't blame him, but she was a Gold.

"I'm sorry if I was a dick last night," she said. "I was the one who was freaked out . . ."

He grabbed her hand, and his was so big that it wrapped all the way around hers. "I was freaked out, too, and she's not my mom. I don't blame you."

"And I don't blame you, for anything," she assured him. "You've been real cool."

"Yeah, dragging you out in a thunderstorm, dumping all my shit on you, that's cool . . ."

She squeezed his hand back. "It's cool with me. You'd get how used to drama I am if you knew my grans. They were like subdued last night. Usually they're shrieking about anything and everything."

"You're not like that at all," he said.

She smiled. "No. I'm like my mom." Just a few days ago she would have hotly denied that; she would have said she had nothing in common with the woman who always found the good in everyone and everything. But maybe because Sarah could now see the good in someone, she got it. She got her mom. And she didn't want to lose her. "I think she's in the house with your . . . with Luke."

"With your uncle," Jackson said.

"What is he to you now?" Sarah asked.

He shrugged. "Legal guardian is the official name. Godfather. Because he was my dad's best friend since like boot camp or something, my mom and dad made him my godfather when I was born. I heard my mom telling someone that she was thinking about changing it after my dad died, that it didn't make sense to think Luke would outlive her."

But he had. He had a job, though, that had to be dangerous. At the moment he was trying to track down a killer. And someone who'd tried to kill her mom. Sarah wanted to track that person down, too, and hurt them.

"Now I think he's kind of indestructible," Jackson said. "He's been through a lot and survived."

"You're pretty indestructible, too," Sarah praised him. "I'm not sure I could have gone through what you have." She'd never had a dad, but if she lost her mom . . .

River would be okay, though. But maybe Sarah should have agreed to leave, to get her out of here and back to where they'd been safe. Or at least her mother had been safe.

Sarah hadn't been in physical danger, though. Not even emotional compared to what Jackson had endured. She'd just been embarrassed and uncomfortable. She hadn't fit in there like she somehow did here. With Jackson.

He squeezed her hand again. "Sometimes I don't think I am going to survive. But Luke keeps hanging on to me. He won't let me go. He yammers on about what my parents would want me to do. How much they loved me and wanted me to be happy, and damn it, he's right. He might have known them even better than I did."

"I don't think I really knew my mom at all until we came back here," she admitted. "Now I understand her so much better." And she knew that eventually her mom would want to get back to Santa Monica. She'd built a life for them there.

"Where are we?" Sarah murmured. They'd wandered a long way from the building, so far away that the woods were beginning to overshadow the gardens, leaving the grass dead in some patches and buried in leaves in other places. And here the grave markers were flat and nearly hidden by the grass and leaves.

"This is it," Jackson said, and he swept his shoe across the tombstone, revealing an engraving: *Lyle McGinty, 1899–1990.* "This is him."

"Who is it?" Sarah asked. "And how would you know him? He died long before we were born."

"It's the grave digger, Sarah. He's the guy who dug most of the graves here before he died. And if you believe the legend, he still digs some . . ."

Over thirty years after he died.

A sudden chill rushed over as the wind picked up, scattering leaves back across that stone, obliterating the name. And then Sarah glanced toward the woods again. While the wind had covered up that stone, it had swept away enough leaves to reveal something else.

A body.

Chapter 20

The sky was so overcast that it seemed more like early evening than mid-afternoon, making Luke feel like he'd wasted even more time than he had. And it was a waste. The tech hadn't been able to pull up any video files. Someone had deleted them all. So he was no closer to finding out who'd made that call, who had put River's life in danger. But at the moment, heading out late to meet her, he felt like he had. At least he'd inadvertently done it while someone else had purposely done it and had had the wherewithal to cover up their involvement.

This person was very smart. And while that was never the impression he'd gotten of Fiona Gold, he was beginning to realize that he'd underestimated her. Yet he couldn't imagine her putting her own child in danger. Jackson wasn't biologically his, but Luke would do anything to protect him. To keep him safe.

Like moving him to Gold Creek.

But that hadn't turned out how Luke had thought it would, especially as Jackson suddenly came running toward him with such force that he nearly knocked him down. Luke reached out and grabbed him, holding him tight. The kid was shaking. "What's wrong?" Luke asked. "What's happened? Are you okay?"

"There's another body," Jackson said, his voice cracking. "We found another body!"

Luke started shaking now. "Is it—" His voice cracked with the fear gripping him. "—is it River?"

Jackson's eyes widened with horror, but he shook his head. "No, no, it's a man . . ."

"Wait, who's we?" Luke asked, peering around the kid. "Who's with you?"

"Sarah," he said. "She's back at the grave. And River . . . she told me to come find you!"

The panic gripping Luke eased. River and Sarah were safe. They were fine. They were waiting for him. "Go up to the house," Luke said. "The techs are just leaving. Try to catch them out in the parking lot!" He touched Jackson's back, nudging him. "Go. Hurry!"

He wanted that kid as far away from death as he could get him. But why and how was he even here?

He'd deal with that later. Right now he ran toward the grave that he knew Jackson was talking about even though he hadn't specified. The grave digger's, where he was supposed to have met River already as she had requested in that text message she'd sent him.

He found her and her daughter standing together, their arms around each other like he'd been hugging Jackson seconds ago. But while he'd comforted the kid, he wasn't sure which of them was comforting the other. "Are you two okay?" he asked with concern.

River turned toward him and nodded. "I'm glad Jackson found you."

"I was on my way," he assured her, for some reason not wanting her to think that he'd failed to show up, like Michael had that night she'd run away. "I was just wrapping up inside with the techs. I told Jackson to go get them. Unless . . . does the man need medical help?"

Sarah shook her head then. "No . . ."

"He's definitely dead, and it looks like he might have been here for a while," River said, and she gestured toward where the woods started on the perimeter of the cemetery.

A pile of leaves covered up most of the body but for one arm and part of a face. His eyes were already opaque, the arm stiff but bloated, the gold watch encircling it had already cut into the flesh. He was definitely dead, but Luke walked over to him anyway and brushed aside some more of the leaves. "I don't know him."

He'd never seen the guy before.

"Mom!" Sarah exclaimed. "We know him!"

River shook her head. "No, no, we don't."

"Who is he?" Luke asked.

River shook her head again. "We don't know him."

"Yes, Mom. Look at him," Sarah ordered her. "Really look at him."

River grimaced, and she looked so horrified that Luke wanted to tell her that she didn't have to . . .

That she could walk away. But he was the sheriff and another body had been found under highly suspicious circumstances. And Luke needed to know who he was and what the hell he'd been doing out here in the cemetery.

But he didn't want to touch the body any more than he already had until the scene had been processed. "Just step a little closer, River, and see if you can tell me who he is."

She took a tentative step forward and leaned down to peer at his face. And she shook her head again. "I don't know him."

"Mom," Sarah said, and she sounded impatient. "It's the homeless guy."

Luke glanced at that watch again and the stitching on the

sleeve of what looked to be an expensive suit. "From what he's wearing, this guy is definitely not homeless."

"He was homeless in Santa Monica. He's the guy who was digging through our trash," Sarah insisted.

Luke stared at the girl, who seemed to be really convinced.

"Push the leaves off his neck," she said.

He glanced around, but there was no sign of Jackson and the techs. And the body had already been sitting out here for a while. He probably wasn't disturbing much if he touched him. So he pushed aside a few more damp leaves and pulled back the guy's collar. There was a scratch on his skin that had already scabbed over.

"How did you know that was there?" River asked her daughter.

"Mom, that's the scratch from when GG Mabel jumped on the guy's back and attacked him when she found him going through our trash and thought he was stealing stuff."

River sucked in a breath. "Oh, my God, you're right."

"This guy was at your house in California?" Luke asked.

River nodded. "Yes, I do believe it's him. But I don't understand."

"Yeah, why would some homeless guy follow us here from Santa Monica?" Sarah asked.

Because he wasn't a homeless guy.

Luke needed to find out who the hell he was and what he'd wanted with River that he'd followed her home to Gold Creek. Or had he come for Gregory Gold I's funeral?

Now he was going to be here for his own.

River's head pounded. She'd put off giving a statement or talking to Luke until she'd had a chance to get Sarah inside the house and to make sure that she was really all right even though she kept insisting that she was.

"Mom, it's no big deal," Sarah said once the door to their bedroom closed behind them.

"I hope you don't really feel that way," River said with concern. "A man died."

"I know, and that sucks. It really does," Sarah agreed. "But what was he doing *here* after being in our *garbage* just over a week ago, Mom? That's the really weird thing."

"That is weird," River acknowledged. Luke had pointed out the expensive watch and the suit. "That man probably wasn't really homeless."

"Then why was he picking through our garbage? That's as much of a mystery as how he wound up dead," Sarah said, her dark eyes bright with excitement. "There are so many mysteries here for us to solve."

River groaned, realizing now how she must have sounded to Luke when she'd told him she was going to do her own investigating. Like she was goddamn Nancy Drew or something.

"Is that what you and Jackson were doing out there?" River asked. "Were you looking for something?"

Sarah shuddered. "A body? God, no. I know that's not good for him, not after what he's been through . . ."

He had been so shaken when River had found them standing where Luke was supposed to be waiting for her. If only he'd been the one to get there first . . . before the kids and before she had.

She'd been running late though because of Mabel, who'd been waiting in the lobby for Dr. Jeffries. Worried that she wasn't feeling well, River had quizzed her a bit. But it turned out that Mabel was actually seeing the doctor, who was probably a few years younger than her. Mabel only dated guys younger than she was, though, because women lived longer than men. And because she didn't want to become anyone's nurse.

"I should go find him and make sure that he's all right,"

Sarah said. Her phone buzzed and she pulled it out. "He's waiting for me before he heads home. And Gigi and Toby are looking for me, too. They want to know what happened this time."

This time.

Because there had been other times, other things . . .

"I was wrong to agree to stay here in Gold Creek," River said, her stomach churning with revulsion and regret for all those things her daughter had been through since River had brought her here. They'd come for one funeral, but now there would be two more. Those would be up to Justine's and that man's family to plan, though, and River had no intention of attending either of them even if they were held at this location of Gold Memorial Gardens and Funeral Services.

"I think we should go back to California," she said. Before anyone else died. "It's too dangerous here."

Sarah shook her head. "Mom, that man was there first. He knew where we lived. He was going through our trash for some reason. So what makes you think we're safe there?"

She was right.

"And at least here it's not just us," Sarah said. "We have other people around."

"And that makes you feel safer?" River asked with skepticism. She certainly didn't feel safer around any of them. That was why she'd wanted to meet Luke, to share with him the strange conversations she'd had and her suspicions about Garrett and Honora.

"Yeah, it does," Sarah said.

It or someone?

Sarah was edging toward the bedroom door, obviously eager to get away or get to someone. Somehow River suspected it wasn't her cousins who Sarah was so eager to see.

But her empathetic daughter had every reason to check on Jackson. River knew Luke had brought him here so that he would be safe yet the kid had seen too many dead bodies over the past few days. Maybe he should go back to Santa Monica with them.

"At home we have GG Mabel," River pointed out. "She protects us."

Sarah smiled. "Yeah, and that guy has the scratches to prove it. You think GG Mabel offed him when she saw that he'd followed us here?"

"If she thought she was protecting us, she might have," River said. "But she isn't really high on my suspect list."

Sarah's eyes brightened. "You have a list? Do you want to work this together?"

"No, no," River said. "We should leave the murder investigation to the sheriff." And maybe they should leave entirely. But Sarah was right. There was no guarantee they were safe in Santa Monica, either. After what had happened to Jackson's mother, it was clear nobody was really safe anywhere, though.

"You trust the sheriff now?" Sarah asked.

River hesitated for a moment with words stuck in her throat.

"Mom, remember you promised not to lie to me," Sarah prodded her.

River smiled then sighed. "Then no. I don't entirely trust the sheriff now. He seems a little too eager to find Grandma Fiona guilty."

"Her prints were on the syringe that killed her husband," Sarah pointed out, but she twisted her mouth into a slight grimace at the thought.

"But she had no reason to hurt that girl or this man." At least not one that River could think of . . .

"Do you really know that, though?" Sarah asked. "We don't know what he was doing in California and what he's doing here. And we really don't know Grandma Fiona all that well, either."

"She's my mother."

"You left home when you weren't much older than I am

now," Sarah said. "And I realized today that until we got here, until I saw where you came from, I really didn't know you very well."

That comment struck River like a cold slap. But she couldn't deny that she'd kept so much of her past and her pain from her daughter. "You must know that I would never hurt anyone, though, right?" River asked.

Sarah nodded. "I know that, Mom. I always knew you're a good person and that you try to see the good in everyone else. And maybe that's what you're doing with Grandma Fiona."

"I just want to know the truth," River said.

"That's why we need to stay," Sarah said. She glanced at her phone again. "But right now, can I go?"

"Just be careful, Sarah. No more hanging out in the cemetery, and please don't go anywhere alone."

"Like you were out in the cemetery alone?" Sarah asked with a little smirk. "And last night . . ."

"I know. I know. I'll be careful, too."

Sarah paused with her hand on the doorknob. Then she turned back, crossed the room, and hugged River. "I love you, Mom. And if I ever lost you . . ." Her voice trailed off, thick with tears.

And River held her tightly. "I love you so much, baby. And I can't lose you. So please . . ."

Sarah pulled back. "I know. I'll be careful." Then she pulled away and rushed out the door.

And River worried that maybe it wasn't possible to stay careful enough to stay alive . . . not with the way the bodies kept piling up.

First her father.

Then Justine Campbell . . .

And now some stranger in the woods.

What did they all have in common besides that they were dead?

* * *

There were better places than the woods to hide a body. There were places where the killer could have gotten rid of it as they were getting rid of one now . . .

The cremation casket rolled down the conveyor toward the open door of the oven. There was more than a body in that cheap casket.

There was a syringe.

And the wallet of the man who'd just been found in the cemetery; the wallet had his identification and private investigator license. Russell Malewicz. His gun probably should have been in there with his ID and license. But Russell's killer hadn't known what the heat would do to the weapon. And maybe they would need it.

The sheriff probably didn't have much or any experience solving murders, but that wasn't stopping him from investigating. And River had already been sticking her nose where it didn't belong, just as she didn't belong here.

She never had and neither did her insolent child.

They both had to go. And if they didn't leave on their own . . .

The killer would make them leave the same way Gregory Gold I, Justine Campbell, and that backstabbing, blackmailing PI had left . . . in body bags.

Chapter 21

Luke had another murder to solve. He didn't need the coroner's report back to know that the man in the leaves hadn't died of natural causes. Because if he'd just had a heart attack or stroke, he wouldn't have been able to cover himself with leaves afterward. Somebody else had done that. Somebody who'd been trying to hide him.

Luke stood outside, in the parking lot, watching the coroner's van pull away with that body inside a black bag in the back of it. It was hidden now until it got to the medical examiner's table. Then hopefully, his secrets would be revealed. Like his identity.

Because no wallet had been found on him.

Luke doubted it had been a mugging, though, because of the watch and the location. Who would mug someone in a cemetery? Especially someone who must have been armed since he'd been wearing a holster under his suit jacket. An empty holster.

As the van disappeared through the open wrought iron gates of the cemetery, Luke turned back toward the front doors where Jackson was still standing. "You never told me why you're here." Luke realized that he still didn't know why his godson had been in the cemetery.

Jackson gestured toward the direction of the departing van. "That kind of distracted you."

"What did it do to you?" Luke asked with concern. "Seeing that . . ."

Jackson gave an exaggerated shudder of revulsion. "Not something I ever want to get used to . . ."

"Then maybe you shouldn't come back here," Luke suggested. "Why were you here?"

"Sarah's a friend," Jackson said. And she suddenly appeared behind him in the doorway to the lobby. "I wanted to check on her after what happened last night with her mom."

Luke could understand that; he was worried about her, too, and her mother as well. But he was responsible for Jackson. "I just don't want you getting hurt."

Jackson nodded. "I get that. I know." He turned then and saw Sarah, and his whole expression changed to one of . . . awe and affection.

And Luke wasn't just worried about Jackson getting physically hurt; he was worried about him getting emotionally hurt as well. Because Sarah and River were going to go back to their home eventually.

Part of him wished they would do that sooner rather than later. For their safety.

But if the dead guy had been going through their garbage in Santa Monica, something else was going on here. Something that put them in danger no matter where they were.

Luke's phone buzzed, and he pulled it out, hoping it was one of the techs. They were looking for that gun in the woods and in the cemetery. But the text was from River: **I still need to talk to you . . .**

Luke wanted to know what she had to tell him, and he also

THE HOUSE BY THE CEMETERY   203

needed to take her statement. Not that she'd seemed to know a lot about the man whose body her daughter and Jackson had found. She hadn't even believed he was the homeless guy until Sarah had pointed out the scratch on his neck. He needed to talk to her grandmother, too, but after his experiences talking to her mother, he wasn't looking forward to that. "Sarah, where's your mother?" he asked.

"In our room," the girl replied.

"No, I'm right here," River said, as she stepped around her daughter.

The teenager tensed. "Are you following me? You showed up out at the grave, too."

"I'm not following you," she said. "But I think Toby and Gigi are." The teenagers laughed as they stumbled out through the doors River held open for them.

"We just wanted to see what was going on . . ." Toby murmured.

"Did you really find a body?" Gigi asked.

"Yeah," Sarah said. Then she glanced at Jackson. "I don't want to talk about it, though."

"Why don't you and Jackson get away from here for a bit." River was the one who made the suggestion. "Get ice cream or something. Is Smithville's Dairy still in town?"

Jackson nodded and smiled at her. "Yeah, it's got the best waffle cones I've ever tasted."

"Always did," River said with a smile of her own that made her even more beautiful than she was. "I can give you some money—"

Luke fished out his wallet and handed Jackson some bills. Smithville's Dairy wasn't cheap. "Here you go. But don't be gone long."

"Can we go, too?" Gigi asked almost shyly.

Toby glanced back at the house, and he seemed almost eager

to get away from it, too. "I was Jackson's ride here, you know. I have to go."

So that was how the teenager had made it to the funeral home.

"Me too?" Gigi asked.

Sarah sighed. "Okay, but no gory talk."

Gigi snorted. "You're the one who likes the gory stuff."

Toby nodded. "You should see her comics—"

Sarah elbowed him. "Graphic novels."

And the four teenagers headed across the parking lot together. River stared after them like Luke did. "Will they be okay?" she asked.

"They'll be safer in town than here," Luke said. Especially with that gun still missing.

River had to wait again to talk to Luke because the county crime scene techs interrupted their conversation with a report for him. A report he obviously wasn't happy about because he clenched his jaw and just nodded. And he stared after them as they drove away.

"What is it?" River asked. "What's wrong?"

"Three people are dead," Luke said. "And I need to find out who's responsible before someone else gets hurt."

She nodded so heartily that pain shot through her head, and she flinched.

He stepped closer to her and touched the bandage on her forehead. "And I'm sorry that you were hurt."

"It wasn't *your* fault," she said. But she could tell that he blamed himself. That he was worried he'd failed somehow. "That crash had nothing to do with my ankle, which is fine, by the way."

"I didn't even think of that when you said you wanted to meet out by that grave," he said, and he grimaced. "Why did you want to meet out there, so far from the house?"

She glanced at the house behind her and shivered. "I wanted to be able to talk to you freely."

"Then maybe we should go to Smithville's Dairy, too."

"I don't want to talk in front of the kids," she said. "I'm worried that Sarah is already too involved in all this. That she has some notion of playing amateur sleuth."

His lips curved into a slight grin. "I can't imagine where she got that idea from, of investigating on her own . . ."

Heat rushed to her face. "I just don't want you focusing on my mother and not looking at other suspects."

He sighed. "I do find it hard to believe that she would put you in danger for any reason."

He might have found it a little harder to believe than she and Sarah did. As Sarah had pointed out, it probably wasn't possible to know someone else fully, even someone related to you.

Apparently, Luke hadn't known Michael as well as he'd thought. And neither had she.

She sighed now. Feeling a little guilty over her thoughts about her mother, she wanted that distance between them now or at least between herself and that house. She started walking across the parking lot toward the cemetery.

Luke fell into step beside her. "This isn't a good idea," he said. "We shouldn't go out there."

"Because it's a crime scene?" she asked.

"Because I don't want it to become a crime scene again," Luke said. "I noticed that the man—"

"You don't know his identity?" she asked.

"His wallet was missing. So we didn't find an ID."

"So maybe it was just a mugging or something?"

"They would take the wallet and leave that watch?" Luke asked. But he shook his head before she could. "No. It wasn't a mugging. But his wallet wasn't the only thing taken from him."

Her heart beat unsteadily. "No. His life was, too," she said.

"And his gun," Luke said. "He had an empty holster on under that tailored jacket."

She gasped now. "So there's a gun out there somewhere."

"My techs searched for it," he said. "But they didn't find anything. They're going to come back tomorrow morning with more equipment." He glanced at the sky.

What little light had come through all those dark clouds was slipping away now as evening approached earlier in autumn in Michigan. "We should look for it," she said. "Make sure that it's not just lying out there somewhere where anyone could pick it up."

"I'm worried that it was already found," Luke said. "That his killer took it."

"You know for certain that he was murdered?"

"He didn't cover himself up with leaves, River."

She remembered how they'd been piled on top of him. They hadn't fallen off the trees and all just landed on him like that. "No, somebody definitely tried to conceal the body," she agreed. "Maybe they did that with the gun. We could look around a little more." She pulled out her cell and turned on the flashlight feature. "We can look . . ."

"This is a bad idea," he reiterated, but he kept walking beside her down those paved paths that wound between the monuments, fountains, and statues.

The sky was a little lighter the farther they got away from the house. As if the darkest of the gloom was over that big brick building. She turned back and looked at it, and she noticed that some of the darkness was from the plume of smoke rising from one of the stainless-steel stacks at the end of the building. And she gasped as she always had when she'd seen that, the smoke from the crematorium oven.

From someone being burned.

She shuddered.

"If you're cold, we should turn back," Luke said.

She'd already changed into warmer clothes than she'd been wearing earlier. She'd found a pair of jeans and a sweater of her mother's that had fit her. When she'd raided her mom's closest, she hadn't found her in her room, though. Where was Fiona? Why hadn't she come out when the sheriff's department vehicles had showed up again?

"I'm fine," she said. "I'm just worried."

"You have every reason to be," he said. "I'm worried, too. I don't want anyone else to get hurt or to be in danger. And I can't guarantee that won't happen until I catch whoever is responsible for these murders. I need to do that as soon as possible." And his steps slowed as if he was considering turning back.

She reached out and grasped his arm. She'd taken the bandages off her hands, so she could feel the hardness of his muscles now. The tension in him. "It's not your fault," she said. "You didn't even know until you got the coroner's report back that my father was murdered. So how could you know that Justine would be or that that man would . . ."

"There's a killer in Gold Creek," he said, and he shook his head as if disgusted. "I thought it would be so safe."

"For Jackson," she said, and she felt a pang of concern for those kids. They were just getting ice cream, and really, they were probably safer in town than anywhere near here.

"For everybody," Luke said. "As sheriff I am responsible for the safety of everyone in Gold Creek."

"That's a lot of responsibility," she said, and now she moved her hand from his arm to his tightly clenched jaw. She remembered Michael saying that about him, about his reason for entering the military being because of his desire to keep people safe. Like he hadn't believed he'd kept Michael safe from their addict mother.

But he'd just been a child then, just a few years older than

Michael. He hadn't been able to protect him then or even when they'd gotten older and reconnected.

"I knew it when I agreed to run for the open position," Luke said, obviously unwilling to cut himself any slack.

But River was more than willing. She ran her fingertips along his jaw then.

And he shivered and murmured her name as he stared down at her face. "I really want to . . ."

"Catch a killer?" she finished for him.

"That too, but for some reason I want to kiss you . . ."

Her heart did a little flippy thing in her chest at his words and as she realized she wanted the same thing.

"I'm sorry," he said. "That was out of line and unprofessional and—"

So she rose up on tiptoe and kissed him, just brushing her lips across his mouth. But the sensations that raced through her at just that brief contact were sobering. She didn't remember the last time she'd reacted to a kiss like that. Maybe because she hadn't had a kiss in a long time. She'd been so focused on Sarah and Mabel that she hadn't been interested in dating beyond more than a casual coffee or dinner now and then. But if those men had kissed her, she hadn't felt anything like this.

Not even with Michael . . .

The thought of him had her stumbling back a step, like she was betraying him by kissing his brother. "I'm sorry now," she said. "That was out of line."

"Don't worry," he said. "I won't press charges."

She chuckled. "Thank you."

"We all have a momentary lapse of judgment now and then," he said. "Like I did when I thought being sheriff would be a good idea . . ."

"You couldn't know that any of this would happen," she assured him.

"The kiss or the murders?" he said, his green eyes twinkling in the dim light as he teased her.

"The murders," she said. "I honestly thought Gregory Gold the first would live forever."

"So did he from what I understand," Luke said with a slight grin. "That was why he made Dr. Jeffries promise to do an autopsy if he died."

"Did he have any idea who would have caused his death?" River asked. "Did he give Dr. Jeffries any names?"

"His family," Luke admitted. "He thought one of his family would kill him."

And so did River. She shared with Luke then the conversations she'd had earlier with Garrett and Honora and Holly and Ellen as well.

"You think it's one of them?" he asked. "Why?"

She shrugged. "I don't know. They just all acted so weird."

"They are weird," Luke said. "You're so different from all of them."

"That's why I could believe that I wasn't a Gold."

"But now?"

"My mom swore to me that I am," she said. "And I want to believe her."

"But you can't quite bring yourself to accept that . . ." His mouth dropped open a bit as if something had shocked him like that kiss had shocked her. "What was that man taking out of your trash?"

She shrugged. "Mabel thought he was trying to find checks or credit card statements to steal our identities or something. But he was pulling out half-eaten food and one of the containers from the smoothies I get from my favorite organic place. He was just hungry."

"He wasn't hungry, River," Luke said. "He was trying to find something with your DNA on it."

"Why?"

"Maybe he was trying to find out for sure if you are a Gold heir or not."

She shook her head. "But that happened a week ago, a few days before Gregory died."

Luke nodded. "Yeah . . ."

She shivered and not just because the wind picked up again, hurling leaves and swirling the smoke around so that the scent grew heavier. She nearly gagged at the odor and the horror of what Luke was suggesting, that somehow her DNA had something to do with the death of the man who was probably her father.

"What is that smell?" Luke asked. "Is something on fire?"

"Somebody," she corrected him. "That's the smoke from the crematorium oven." Though there were special filters in the stacks to limit the odors and anything else from escaping into the atmosphere. Mostly it was just heat that came out of the stacks.

"No! They're not supposed to be doing any business until I release the crime scene from Justine Campbell's murder." He turned back then and started toward the house. But he didn't get far before shots rang out, echoing all around them. He ducked down, or maybe he fell.

Or maybe he'd been hit. River couldn't be certain and then she was falling, too.

Chapter 22

Luke knew where that gun was now. In the hand of a killer. He just hoped that person wouldn't become his and River's killer.

He dropped to the ground fast and then he pulled River down with him behind a tall granite headstone. "Are you all right?" he whispered to her. Hopefully, she hadn't been hit with those first bullets. Since he'd been between her and the house, she shouldn't have been since he wasn't or at least he didn't think he was. Unless . . .

"I'm okay," she said. "Are you?"

With the adrenaline and anger coursing through him, he probably wouldn't realize that he had been hit until later. Like what had happened before with the shrapnel from the bomb that had killed his best friend. Luke hadn't even known that he, himself, had been wounded, physically, then. Jack had noticed, and with his dying breath, he'd made Luke promise to take care of himself so that he could take care of Jack's wife and son for him. Luke had been more concerned about his friend than himself, though.

"I got you. Hang on . . ." Luke had said. But he hadn't had him. Jack had died in his arms.

Luke had to make sure he had River now, that he kept her from getting hurt again. Or worse . . .

"We have to get out of here," he said. He reached out and shut off the light on her cell and on his, plunging them into almost total darkness now. But River was wearing a pink sweater, such a pale pink that it nearly glowed in the deep shadows. He had to stay between her and wherever those shots were coming from.

Where the hell were they coming from?

The gunfire continued to ring out sporadically, maybe from the direction of the house where that fire continued to burn inside the crematorium oven. What the hell was burning?

A body or evidence?

He needed to get back to the house and get River back to safety without either of them getting hit. "We're going to run," he said. He knew that a moving target was harder to hit, especially if the shooter wasn't an experienced marksman.

And Luke didn't think he or she was because of what the bullets had already struck, the stream of water in the fountain and the arm of a statue, sending sprays of water droplets and shards of concrete flying around them. The shots weren't coming close because they were ducked down so low behind that tall granite headstone. But to run, they would have to stand.

"With your ankle, how fast can you go?" he asked her in a whisper.

"I'm fine," she said. "Just scared." And there was a crack in her voice that betrayed that fear.

"Me too," he said. He was scared that he wouldn't be able to shield her, that he wouldn't be able to protect her. And he did not want to lose anyone else. "Please run as fast as you can toward the house, toward the lobby." Hopefully, there would be other people there and that would deter the shooter from following them.

Unless the shooter was already there . . .

The shots were being fired from that general direction, so Luke had to make certain they didn't run right into the line of fire. He had no idea how much ammunition the person had. They would have had to reload once already, and there hadn't been a big enough gap in the firing for them to make it all the way back to the house.

"Stay behind me," he said, "and stay as low to the ground as you can, taking cover behind everything you see. Every monument and statue . . ." But the way the bullet had chipped away the concrete of the statue's arm concerned him.

He had to stop the shooter from firing at them. At her . . .

He drew his weapon and started to rise up. In the dark he could see the little spark as the gun fired, and he pointed his Glock in that direction and returned fire.

"Run!" he told River, and he held her hand with his free one and pulled her along behind him while he fired the weapon in his other hand. He had to hit the shooter or at least stop them from shooting before he or, worse yet, River got hit.

But the bullets kept coming, too close to them. They struck the ground, kicking up dirt and chipping at asphalt and marble as the path and tombstones got hit, too. Luke kept his finger pressed hard on the trigger of the Glock, firing the gun over and over, and hoping he hit his target before he got hit.

He couldn't protect River or Jackson or anyone else if he didn't make it himself.

Years ago, when they were teenagers, Michael had taken River to a carnival, one of those traveling ones that set up their rickety rides and game booths in empty fields or town squares. The carnival they'd attended had been in the empty field next to the high school, and Michael had tried hard to win her a stuffed animal or a plastic ring. But all those games had been rigged for him as well as every other participant to fail. Every shot he'd fired at the row of ducks had missed.

River felt like one of those ducks right now, set on a course toward the house, blindly following Luke, who pulled her along behind him. But that meant he was in front, he was that first duck in the row heading directly toward the barrel of that gun.

A scream burned the back of her throat while her heart pounded fast and frantically. She didn't want him to get hit. She didn't want to get hit, either. She just wanted to throw herself on the ground and hope that the shooter went away.

But Luke was right; they had to keep moving, like those ducks. Because if they stayed in one place, they might become sitting ducks. Easier to hit, easier to kill.

That had to be what the shooter was trying to do. Kill one of them or both of them. And River was so damn scared that the killer was going to be successful this time.

If Luke got hit first, River didn't know how to shoot a gun, how to defend them, how to protect them like he was trying so hard to do, like he might be giving up his life to do.

They had only been gone a short while, the four of them. Or maybe it had been longer than Sarah had thought because the lines at the dairy had been long. The place was popular. And it was good, the ice cream tasting rich and creamy while the waffle cones were sweet with a hint of cinnamon.

Sarah had enjoyed the outing and the treat. The girls she'd gone to school with would have mocked her for eating as much as she had while Gigi had competed with her to see who could eat more. They'd both beaten Toby and Jackson, eating even more than the much taller and bigger boys. Being with them, teasing and even being snarky with each other, made Sarah feel normal for once.

With how much and how hard they'd all laughed, they'd all seemed to have a good time, not just her. Even Jackson had seemed happy. And that made her even happier.

Until they started back toward that house by the cemetery. Maybe they all dreaded going back there because they fell silent until the wail of sirens shattered that silence. Police cars, with flashing lights, sped past them. An ambulance followed them.

"It might be going somewhere else," Gigi murmured, but she sounded as doubtful as Sarah was.

She started shaking in the passenger's seat while Toby gripped the steering wheel in tight fists. Jackson turned toward her, their gazes met, and he looked as scared as she felt.

Something had happened. And somehow she knew it involved her mother and Luke . . .

Chapter 23

River heard the screaming in the distance. Then the yelling, "Let her through. Her mom is in there." It was Jackson's voice, sounding surprisingly calm and determined while Sarah cried. "Mom! Mom!"

"She has to see if her mom is okay," Gigi added, her voice cracking with tears of her own.

River pushed past the deputies guarding the doors to the lobby and stepped out under the portico. "Sarah, I'm here. I'm all right!"

Thanks to Luke. She wouldn't have survived without him, without him using his body to shield hers.

Sarah rushed toward her and threw her arms around her. "Oh, my God! The police cars and ambulance passed us and I was so scared." She pulled back and looked at her. "You really aren't hurt?"

Her sweater was torn and dirty, her hair mussed. She might have had a bruise on her cheek from falling onto the asphalt path or from a chunk of flying concrete or marble. But she was fine. "I'm okay. Really."

Jackson came up behind Sarah then and his dark eyes held fear despite his calmness. And she knew who he was worried about and with a damn good reason. Luke had been willing to sacrifice his life for hers.

But he hadn't had to. Either he'd scared off their assailant with his gun or the other shooter had just run out of ammunition. He or she had fired so damn many bullets at them.

"Luke's fine," she assured Jackson. "He saved my life."

"Where is he?" Jackson asked as he peered around her and into the lobby.

She shrugged. "I don't know . . ."

Once he'd gotten her safely inside the house just as his deputies arrived for backup, he'd taken off. She suspected he'd gone back outside to find the shooter. So maybe she shouldn't have assured Jackson that Luke was all right because what if he found that shooter? And what if that shooter hadn't actually run out of bullets?

But she hadn't heard any more shots fired. He had to be all right.

"What happened?" Sarah asked. "What did Luke save you from?"

She hesitated a moment, reluctant to share with her daughter how serious an attempt this had been, how close she and Luke had come to losing their lives.

"Mom, remember, honest always," Sarah prodded her.

"Someone was shooting at us," she admitted. Luke's fear had been confirmed; the killer had found that missing gun before he had.

Sarah hugged her again, holding on to her tightly, and behind her Jackson looked horrified, his eyes wide.

"We're all right," River assured them both again. "Luke is, too. He protected me."

Jackson nodded. "Good, he already blames himself too much for other people dying. Like he had any way of knowing that bomb was going to go off . . . and my mom . . . he wasn't even in the country when she died . . ."

But still, Luke had taken responsibility for those tragedies, like he somehow believed he could have stopped them from happening. While his brother had run away from his responsibilities, from her and from their child, Luke took too much on himself.

Earlier she'd been a little embarrassed that she had kissed him. And now she was damn glad that she had. And she wanted to do it again. She wanted him to really be okay probably just as much as Jackson did. She reached out from Sarah and put her arm around the boy, too, her heart aching for all of his losses.

He couldn't lose Luke, too. And even though she didn't really have him and never had, she didn't want to lose Luke, either.

Luke had lost . . . the shooter. And he'd probably lost something else, too. Whatever, or whoever, had been in that damn oven. He suspected there had been some evidence of something in there . . . maybe the ID of the man in the woods and something else . . .

The murder weapon? Because Luke hadn't noticed any gunshot wounds on the body, so he'd been killed another way. But Luke had nearly been killed with the murder victim's gun. He and River.

But she was all right. He was sure of that, that she hadn't been hit. Or he wouldn't have rushed down here. The door was locked. He'd had to send a deputy to find somebody with the key. And finally Lawrence Gold, in his pajamas and robe, appeared with the female deputy. He opened the door and led the way into the room with the ovens that looked more like two big furnaces with doors on them. Heat emanated from one of them.

"Shut it off!" Luke shouted.

"It's off," Lawrence said. "But they're brick-lined and take a while to cool down."

"I don't want it to cool off," Luke said. "I want it open."

"The heat—"

"Open it!" Luke shouted. He needed to see what was inside and if anything could be salvaged.

"I don't know what's in there—"

"There's not supposed to be anything in there," Luke said. "You weren't allowed to resume any operations until the crime scene was cleared. There could have been evidence . . ." And if there had been, he had a sick feeling that it was gone now.

Lawrence pulled on some long gloves that were thick like oven mitts. Then he pressed a switch that raised that door. As it lifted, it revealed the contents atop a tray . . . that appeared to be a skeleton outline, the bones brittle and ashy but not yet dust.

Oh, God, had there been another murder? Another victim?

"Whose body is that?" Luke asked, his voice gruff with concern.

Lawrence shrugged. "I don't know. We interred the body that the kids had out that night, and we don't have any other remains here except for . . ."

"Your father," Luke said. "Where's his body?"

"He didn't want to be cremated," Lawrence said. "That can't be . . . it can't be . . ."

He touched another button and that tray rolled out of the oven, smoke wafting yet from the remains. There were the bones but there was also a melded mass of metal on one side of it. A watch . . .

The skull was hollowed out and had almost collapsed entirely upon itself and within the ash beneath it glittered some gold teeth.

"The watch, the teeth . . ." Lawrence murmured with horror.

"Where's his body supposed to be?" Luke asked.

"In the cold storage . . ." Lawrence crossed the room and exited into the hall again.

Luke glanced once more at the smoking tray of what had once been a human. He couldn't tell what else might have been on that tray. What else had been destroyed . . .

But he suspected there'd been some evidence, something he'd needed to lead him to the killer who'd escaped out in the cemetery. Had he come inside the house? Was he here with them, with River?

Sweat beaded on his brow and dripped down his face, and he whirled and headed out into the hall where Lawrence had just unlocked another door. He pushed that open and Luke followed him inside, gasping at the shock of cool air after the heat. Lawrence crossed to a casket that had been rolled to one side of the room. He was still wearing those padded gloves when he reached out and fumbled with the lid, throwing it open.

It was empty.

Gregory Gold I was gone. It hadn't been enough to kill him; his killer had wanted no trace of him left behind.

Fiona was on the outside looking in, like she had been her entire life. Back home in California, she'd never fit in; she hadn't been quite beautiful enough or talented enough. So she'd learned how to make herself more beautiful, more talented . . . but still it had never been quite enough to make her the star that some of her classmates had become.

The one thing she had always been, though, was smart enough. Smart enough to figure out how to make others think she wasn't smart enough. Let them underestimate her.

The Gold family certainly had. She suspected even her own family had. They were who she was watching now . . . from the outside. Her daughter, her granddaughter, her mother . . .

They were clustered together in a corner of the lobby area, their arms around each other. There had been a boy there earlier with them. Tall, dark, and handsome, and Sarah had certainly been fascinated with him.

Fiona had thought maybe Sarah would take after her. But Sarah was her mother through and through. While the teenager looked nothing like River, she was her clone in personality. Especially when River was younger.

Fiona wasn't like any of them, not even her own mother. Her mother was too blunt, too forthcoming. Sarah took after Mabel in those ways; while River was always honest, she was sweet about it. She was just a sweet girl.

She deserved so much better, so much more from Fiona than Fiona had ever given her. Until now . . .

Fiona was smarter than they'd thought. Smarter even than the sheriff.

He'd summoned them all to the lobby. Even Colson Howard.

She had been *with* the lawyer when Sheriff Sebastian called him just moments ago. So Colson hadn't had far to come to get to the lobby.

Just down the back stairs from her bedroom. Had anyone noticed? From the way Honora had looked at him, Fiona suspected she had. Her stepdaughter had had him first, but she'd lost him just like she had every other man she'd married or dated. She was nearly as consumed with the business as her father had been, but whereas that work ethic had drawn women to Gregory, it repelled men from Honora. Because that girl had to prove to everyone, mostly her father, how smart she was, whereas Fiona was content being the only one who knew how smart she was.

She fought the smile from curving up her lips. She couldn't give in to it. Not yet.

Then the sheriff appeared, and the temptation to smile disappeared. But this was okay. She had a good idea where this was leading . . . exactly where she wanted it to . . .

"Sheriff, what is going on?" Gregory II demanded to know.

He'd appointed himself the head of the family since his father's death. Or maybe his mother had appointed him that. Either way . . .

It wasn't what Fiona wanted. As the surviving spouse, she was the head of the family. And the Golds were just going to have to damn well deal with a matriarch.

"You want me to run down the list?" Luke Sebastian asked with an insolence that had Gregory II's lips curling. Gregory was thin-lipped like his mother, snooty, above it all with the firm belief that everyone else was beneath them. "Let's see," the sheriff continued. "A body was discovered on the property earlier—"

"Was it?" Carolyn interrupted. "I saw the police in the woods."

"At the edge of the cemetery," Luke said. "Right near the grave digger's grave."

"Did some kid OD?" Gregory III asked. "They like to party out there." And he glanced at his own children, as if to confirm that they were present and accounted for. He had no idea what his children did. Neither did their mother or they probably wouldn't have been hanging out with the sheriff's foster kid and with Fiona's granddaughter.

"No. This was no kid," Luke said, his voice short and gruff with impatience and anger. "And you can't tell me that none of you heard the shooting earlier?"

Carolyn arched an eyebrow. "That wasn't you?"

Fiona nearly laughed. Once in a while the old bitch was actually funny.

"I was getting shot at. So was River."

"And you didn't fire back?" Carolyn asked as if taunting him.

Fiona wondered just what that old bitch was capable of doing . . .

She hadn't aged as well as her former husband had. Mostly

because she'd aged and Gregory had refused. She also had Parkinson's disease, but that didn't mean she still wasn't able to manipulate others to do what she wanted. Like either of her idiot sons . . .

"I did fire back," Luke said, his jaw tightly clenched as if he was gritting his teeth. "And the person ran off. Probably into this house . . ." He swung his gaze around the room, pausing on each of them for a moment.

Did he look at her a little longer than the others? A little harder?

Apparently, she was still his prime suspect even though he couldn't possibly believe that she would put her own daughter in danger. She glanced over at River, who was staring at her, too. Could River believe that?

"So is that why you called us all to the lobby?" Gregory II asked. "You're going to search us for a weapon?"

"Oh, I'm pretty sure it's been hidden or destroyed by now," Luke said. "Just like someone destroyed other evidence when they fired up the crematorium oven."

"I thought I heard that . . ." Carolyn murmured. As if she would have heard anything with as deaf as she was getting. Well, she did hear things that people didn't want her to . . .

Noah looked around at his half siblings and cousins. "You told us not to resume any part of the business until you cleared the crime scene," he said to Luke.

"Yes, I did. But someone fired up that oven anyway and they fired up Gregory the first's remains along with it."

"No!" Carolyn gasped. "He didn't want to be cremated." She glanced at Lawrence as if he'd done it. "You know that . . ."

Fiona felt a little sick herself. Gregory had wanted an open casket funeral and a massive monument. He'd wanted everyone to see him and admire how handsome and young he looked and to sob over him, like that silly girl had done. Well, at least he'd had that . . .

Gregory II was shaking his head now. "No . . . nobody would have done that . . ."

"Somebody did," Luke confirmed.

Gregory II shook his head again.

"It was him," Lawrence said.

"Why did you do that?" Gregory asked his brother, and rushed toward him like he intended to punch him.

Fiona's pulse quickened in anticipation of seeing her step-sons brawl. Her money was on Lawrence. You always had to watch the quiet ones . . .

"I didn't do that," Lawrence protested. "I know that Father didn't want to be anywhere near those ovens alive or dead. I honored his wishes."

"Why would someone do that?" Linda, the second wife, asked. "Knowing that wasn't what he wanted . . ."

And they all turned to look at Fiona now, like she would have had a reason to destroy his remains.

"It must have something to do with the money," the sheriff spoke up. "His murder, Justine Campbell's . . . and the man whose body was found today."

"What could some stranger have to do with anything?" Carolyn asked disdainfully. She'd never taken to the people she'd considered outsiders: like Fiona.

"I intend to find out," Luke said. "That's why I want his will read now. Tonight."

Colson shook his head, and his thick salt-and-pepper hair was slightly mussed from her pillow, from her hands . . .

Did he smell like her yet?

"I . . ." He cleared his throat. "I can't read the will until after his interment."

"There's nothing to inter now," Luke said. "But ash and bits of bone . . ."

And teeth. Nobody understood how much was actually left of a person after cremation. They didn't disintegrate into the neat little pile of ashes that someone expected, like what you would get from burning a bunch of newspapers. That wasn't what real cremated human remains looked like.

"We can still bury him," Lawrence maintained.

"Well, the cemetery is a crime scene now, and since someone already violated my order to not do any more business here, we're going to do things a little out of order with the damn will," Luke said, and there was definitely impatience in his voice now.

Fiona smiled at him. Now he knew how she'd felt dealing with these entitled, stubborn Golds all these years.

"What do you hope to find out from forcing this reading?" Colson asked him.

Luke looked at her then but his gaze didn't linger too long before it moved onto the others. The only ones he didn't look at were River and her daughter. Then he finally replied, "I intend to find a killer."

Chapter 24

At the late hour and with the lights dim and everyone gathered in a circle around the formal dining room table, River felt more like they'd been gathered for a séance rather than the reading of a will. As if on cue, thunder rumbled and lightning crackled outside, flashing through the thick draperies pulled across the windows.

"Why am I expecting a medium with a crystal ball to show up?" River muttered to the man sitting next to her.

Noah chuckled. "What? To summon our father's spirit? I don't think we need a medium to do that. I'm sure he's here. He's going to haunt the hell out of whoever put him in that oven."

"Of whoever killed him," River said, and she felt a sudden sense of loss despite never having been close to the man. But now she would never have the chance to get to know him.

He was gone.

And someone had tried to reduce him even more . . . to nothing. She glanced at her mother then. Fiona was not sitting near her. She was seated to the right of the lawyer who sat in

Gregory Gold I's place at the head of the table. Carolyn sat at the other end, opposite Colson Howard, all the way down that super long mahogany table that could easily seat forty or fifty people for a dinner party.

Or a celebration of life.

Or apparently for the reading of a will.

Since the children were minors, they hadn't been allowed into the reading. Nor had Mabel despite her insistence. But the sheriff was here. Despite all those open chairs, he didn't sit.

River could feel the tension radiating off him. He was furious. From getting shot at? Over someone destroying evidence?

She suspected he was the angriest at himself for not catching this killer yet, for not keeping everyone as safe as he wanted them to be. As he needed them to be . . .

Had she thanked him for saving her life? For putting himself in danger to protect her? She hoped she had, but everything had been so crazy. They'd done that mad dash through the cemetery to the house and then once they'd gotten inside, he'd just about disappeared.

Now she knew where he'd been. Downstairs. Where the crematorium was.

Where her father's body should have been in the cold storage area.

But he was gone now.

Unless . . .

Goose bumps rose on her skin and she leaned closer to her half brother and whispered, "Boooo . . ."

"I've missed you," Noah said. "You were the only light in this house for so many years."

"I never knew you felt that way," she said. Whenever he'd actually been inside the house, Noah had always been so quiet. Like Sarah had been back home. But here she was more social, and despite all the horrible things that had happened, she seemed happier, too.

"It would be nice for you to stay," Noah said.

"Nice for whom?" she asked with a smile.

And Noah cocked his head toward Luke, who was standing near the lawyer talking to him in a low and furious-sounding whisper. Fiona was close enough to hear, but instead of seeming concerned, she seemed . . .

Smug. Like how the rest of the Golds usually seemed. And River felt that sick churning in her stomach again. And her head began to pound with the tension gripping her.

"Can we get this over with?" Carolyn Gold asked.

"Past your bedtime?" Fiona asked with heavy sarcasm.

"You're in bed more than I am," Carolyn said, and she glanced at the man sitting across that long table from her.

Colson Howard.

Was there something going on between him and River's mother?

"We are going to do this now," Luke said.

"You know this all has to go through probate and trusts before it's official," Colson said.

"But you intended to read it aloud after the interment," Luke reminded him.

"Yes, because that was per Gregory's last wishes," Colson said.

"For all intents and purposes, he's been interred now," Luke said. "So do it."

Colson sighed and pulled out his phone. It was one of the big ones that doubled as a tablet, and it must have contained some of his documents because after a few swipes he began to read:

"I, Gregory Gerard Gold the first, being of sound mind and exceptional body, do hereby declare this my last will and testament. I am not sure which ones of you will survive me and which ones will die before me. Or which of you will even survive until this will goes through probate without me there to protect you and to keep you in line. So I will bequeath only to my survivors at the conclusion of probate the following shares of my estate, which includes my business and all my properties and business and personal accounts in the following percentages. My current spouse will receive twenty-five percent. My former spouses will receive a percent equal to the percent that each of my children and grandchildren will receive of the remaining seventy-five percent. However, in order to inherit, each of these children and grandchildren will have to submit proof that they are in fact my biological descendants."

Carolyn laughed and slapped the table with one of her tremulous hands. "There it is. There you have it, Sheriff. Your motive. And your killer." And she pointed that trembling finger at Fiona. "That is why Gregory had to die before their divorce went through."

"What divorce?" Fiona asked. "I am legally Gregory's current wife."

"He was going to divorce you and marry Justine," Honora said. She put her arm around her son, who sat slumped in the chair next to her. "She broke Garrett's heart when she fell for his grandfather and got pregnant with his child. So whoever killed her wanted to make sure that she and her child didn't inherit, either."

Fiona sighed. "Yes, heartbroken people do crazy things, Honora." And Fiona emitted another sigh, a pitying one, as if she felt sorry for Garrett.

Was he the killer of both his grandfather and former girlfriend? River stared at him, but she just couldn't believe he would have the wherewithal to pull off murders like that. Someone more calculating had planned those murders.

Fiona leaned back in her chair and smiled. "I am more than happy to have my daughter and granddaughter undergo a DNA test."

"That's why Father's body was destroyed," Gregory II remarked. "Now we can't do it."

Carolyn shrugged. "It doesn't matter. With all of us . . ." She gestured toward her sons. "We have the controlling percentage."

"So you already know that I'm a Gold," River remarked. "That's why that man was sent to dig through my trash. He proved it to whoever hired him, didn't he? Is that why he was killed?"

"You're not making any sense," Noah whispered to her as if he was concerned for her sanity.

"Someone went through your trash? The man found outside?" Fiona asked her.

She nodded.

Fiona laughed. "So now whoever the killer is knows that my claim is real. Through myself, my daughter, and granddaughter, I have thirty-five percent."

That was assuming that River would side with her. But she didn't dare to point that out.

"And like I said, we have more," Carolyn repeated. "And you only inherit if you are not complicit in his death. Right, Colson?"

"Does it say that?" Luke asked the lawyer.

Colson cleared his throat. "It doesn't have to. Michigan has the slayer statute ensuring that a killer or felon cannot profit from his or her wrong. But yes, Gregory also had me include that stipulation as well just in case the law was too ambiguous."

"And because of that law, you might not have controlling interest, Carolyn," Fiona pointed out.

"You're accusing one of us of being the killer?" Carolyn asked, as if murder was beneath her. And maybe it was.

"And you're also assuming that your children and grandchildren are all legitimate heirs," Fiona pointed out.

"And that they would all side with you," Linda said, and she shared a look with Lawrence that had Carolyn glaring at her son.

"I have no issue taking a DNA test, either," Honora said,

and she exchanged a look with her mother as well. "And if anyone refuses, they should be excluded from inheriting."

"That is the way the will reads," Colson admitted.

"More of Gregory's fine print?" Fiona asked, and she reached out to pat the lawyer's hand, hers lingering just a bit on it.

River had that chill rush over her again. It had nothing to do with any ghost, though. It had to do with divorce papers and secret alliances, and what the hell her mother was really capable of . . .

Sarah was right; River really didn't know the woman who'd given birth to her. And she certainly didn't trust her right now. Probably the only person she could actually trust in this room was Luke. But he wasn't looking at her. He was watching all of them turn on each other.

"Is there fine print to address how we do this when there is no DNA left of Grandfather to compare it to?" Gregory III asked.

"The body wasn't completely destroyed," Luke said.

But the others looked skeptical, as if they suspected he was lying. Or maybe they were hoping . . .

"And, because of the suspicious nature of his death and your rush to have the funeral, I had the medical examiner keep several tissue samples," Luke said, and now he was the one looking smug. "I'll be back in the morning to collect DNA samples from all of you."

When he started for the door, River jumped up to follow him out, but Honora beat her to him and followed him out into the hall. River couldn't hear what she was saying, but she rushed off when she saw River standing just outside the open pocket doors.

River walked with him as he headed toward the lobby doors that led to the outside. "Thank you for earlier," she said. "For protecting me."

He turned back and touched her cheek, and she flinched slightly at the sting as his finger ran over the bruise on it. "I didn't do a very good job," he said. "And I need you to be careful. I'm keeping deputies outside, but in here make sure that you're never alone."

She smiled slightly. "Wouldn't I be safer alone than with someone I can't trust?" she asked.

"Don't trust anyone," he said.

She knew that he was referring to her mother. Fiona was obviously still his prime suspect. The contents of the will only gave her a bigger motive for murder.

But River just couldn't accept that her mother would hurt her. Maybe that was because she would give up her life for Sarah. "I'm not worried about me," she said. "I'm worried about my daughter."

"I'm worried about both of you," he said, his voice gruff with that concern. His fingers trailed down her cheek to her jaw. "Just please be careful." And he started leaning forward as he raised her chin, as if he intended to kiss her.

"Is that how you're going to get her DNA, Sheriff?" Noah asked.

After the twinge of disappointment she felt, River chuckled. And when she turned back, she saw why Noah had called out to them because he wouldn't have been the only one witnessing that kiss. Most of the others had filed out into the lobby as well. At least that was why she hoped he'd stopped them.

"I was telling River to be careful," Luke said. "You all need to heed that advice. I have deputies outside, so if anything happens, help is nearby. And I will be back in the morning."

River started to turn away then and head toward the stairs like the others, but Luke caught her hand and held her back for a moment. "Go to your room and lock you, your grandma, and your daughter in for the night. Don't come out again until I get here in the morning."

She shivered at the intensity of his tone, of his concern. "Luke . . ."

"You know how dangerous this person is," he reminded her. "You could have been killed tonight. Please be careful." Then, despite whoever else might have been watching them, he kissed her.

And River realized that he was a little dangerous to her, at least to her heart.

Sarah knew she was supposed to stay locked inside the bedroom for her safety and really for Mom and GG Mabel's, too. But the text tempted her: **Want to see a cremated body?**

Of course it was from Gigi. Sarah wasn't even sure if Toby intended to meet them down there. Or maybe he was already there and intended to pop out of the oven to scare her like he had jumped up from the casket that first night. That hadn't been that long ago, but it felt like it anyway.

So much had happened since then.

So many bad things.

And so many good things.

Sarah didn't necessarily want to see a cremated body. But she was curious, too. What would it look like? What would be left to even tell that it had once been a person?

Not just any person but her grandfather.

What the hell was going on? Mom swore that the sheriff was getting to the bottom of it, that Luke would figure it out soon. And that in the meantime he wanted them to be safe, to lock themselves inside, and that was what she'd done when she'd come to bed a few hours ago.

Despite GG Mabel's snoring, Sarah had actually been asleep when Mom had returned from the reading of the will. But once she'd shared with her what was going on, Sarah hadn't been able to sleep. She'd kept running numbers and scenarios through her head like little thought bubbles chasing each other across the ceiling.

And she'd been more concerned about who the killer was than what had happened to her grandfather. But the only reason someone would have wanted to burn him up was because they didn't want anyone to realize they weren't an heir.

Mom wouldn't have done that. She probably would have been relieved to know that she wasn't a Gold. But Grandma Fiona . . .

She wouldn't have tried to shoot her own daughter, though, or caused that crash. At least Sarah hoped not . . . because if she had, Mom would be devastated and Sarah would have to kill the bitch.

She needed to figure out who had tried to hurt her mom. And maybe they'd left a clue down in the crematorium room, something that the sheriff's crew had missed. Sarah had been the one who'd found the body earlier, so maybe she would find something else . . .

Slipping beneath the covers, she eased out of bed. After standing outside earlier, waiting for the deputies to let them inside, she'd been cold. So she wore sweats and a sweatshirt already and didn't need to dress. She shoved her feet into her slippers and headed for the door.

Her mom shifted in bed and murmured something, and Sarah tensed with her hand on the doorknob. When Mom's breathing evened out again, she unlocked and opened the door. She slipped out quickly, so that the light in the hall didn't wake Mom or GG Mabel. Once she closed the door, she held her breath for a moment and waited. But nobody stirred inside the room. Nobody stirred in the hall, either; Gigi wasn't waiting for her like she had in the past. Maybe she was going to meet Sarah downstairs. She hurried off in that direction, walking as softly as she could so that she didn't wake up anyone else, either.

Once she descended the first flight, she headed across the lobby and down the hall toward the stairs to the basement.

Crime scene tape was stretched across that door, but someone else had already broken the seal on the jamb.

Yeah, Toby and Gigi were both probably waiting for her. She pushed open the door and ducked under the dangling piece of tape. These steps weren't like the fancy double stairwell in the front of the house. These were concrete and the walls were stone with just a dim sconce for light. Sarah felt like she was descending into a dungeon.

Or hell . . .

She'd once thought that was high school in Santa Monica; now she knew that was nothing. Not compared to what Jackson had been through. She wished he was here now, holding her hand like he had in the cemetery. But that wouldn't be fair to him.

She liked stuff like this, liked being scared.

He hated it. Probably because he'd known real fear. Mom did, too, after the things she'd been through lately. And Sarah felt a pang of guilt for begging her to stay. River clearly had had a damn good reason for hating this place and never wanting to come back.

But Sarah . . .

She felt like this place was part of her somehow, like it was in her blood. So Grandma Fiona probably had been telling the truth about River being Gregory Gold I's daughter, meaning that Sarah was his granddaughter. She looked like them, but she also felt like them or at least some of them. Like Gigi and Toby. They could be asses, but she could be, too. She liked them. And she liked who she was with them. She liked who she was with Jackson even more. Here in Gold Creek she felt like she could be herself and she fit in just fine. And if she actually inherited part of this place, would she have to leave?

Or would she be able to convince Mom to stay?

The basement must have high ceilings because the stairwell was deep, and she couldn't see that far ahead in the dim lighting to see how close she was to the bottom. But the air got thicker and damper, and she had to be close. And then she saw the floor . . . or what she could of it beneath the woman lying at the bottom of the stairwell, blood pooled beneath her head as her eyes stared up at Sarah.

Honora . . .

Aunt Honora? Was she dead?

A scream burned the back of Sarah's throat as it clawed to get out. But Sarah held it down, just as she held down the panic.

Oh, God, no . . . not another body.

Honora held a cell phone in one hand as if she'd been calling for help. But on the screen of it was the text that Gigi had sent to Sarah. That was Gigi's phone.

"Gigi?" Sarah called out. This was no prank.

This was murder. A shadow fell across the body as someone moved toward the stairwell from the hall.

"Gigi?"

The person didn't step into the light, so Sarah couldn't tell who it was, just that they were carrying a gun . . . with the barrel pointed at her.

Luke shouldn't have left. He'd known he shouldn't have even before he'd started driving away. He'd known when Honora had rushed out of the room after him and whispered a name to him. "Russell Malewicz."

"What?"

"Russell Malewicz. Was that who you found?"

Luke shook his head. "I didn't find him. Sarah did." And Jackson. And he needed to check on the kid. He'd seemed fine when he'd left for ice cream with the other kids, but then they'd come back to find the police cars there and the ambulance. Someone had called that in as well as the deputies in case they'd been hit.

He could have been. Had that scared Jackson? Would he

have an anxiety attack? Ever since the shooting at the mall, where he'd lost his mother, the kid had had panic attacks. PTSD like he'd been in the battles Luke and his father had been in, but his had been even worse . . .

He'd had no way to defend himself or his mother.

But Jackson had been fine when Luke checked on him, stopping there after leaving that house and before heading into the sheriff's office. He'd had no sleep, but he knew it was pointless to even try. He wasn't going to rest until this killer was caught. He did not want anyone else getting murdered.

Like Gregory Gold I, Justine Campbell, and Russell Malewicz. Luke had just confirmed that the body in the woods was his. After Honora gave him the name, he pulled up Russell Malewicz's driver's license and his PI license and his gun permit on his computer at the sheriff's office. How did Honora know him? Had she hired him?

He had to ask her those questions and this time get the answers she'd refused to give him when he'd tried to ask her at the house. She'd just rushed off after whispering that name to him. So he started driving back, intending to wake her up and bring her in so that she would answer his questions.

Then he got the text from River: **Help. Someone is holding a gun on Sarah in the basement, and I think Honora is dead. No sirens.**

Luke read the words and instantly felt the panic that River had to be feeling.

Even though River had texted him, Luke knew that she wouldn't calmly wait for him or for one of his deputies to arrive before she stepped in and tried to save her daughter. She would put herself between Sarah and that killer, she would take a bullet for her daughter. But then the killer would claim two more victims: River and Sarah.

While Luke could have called in one of the deputies from the parking lot, he was worried that none of them had experience handling this type of situation. They might rush in and get both Sarah and River and maybe even themselves killed.

He had to handle this himself. And thank God he was close, just seconds away. Luke didn't turn on the siren or the flashing lights as he turned into those open gates to Gold Memorial Gardens. He was here, but he still had to figure out a way to save them that wouldn't get them all killed.

Chapter 25

River had no idea how long she'd been asleep before she'd awakened to find Sarah gone. So she had no idea when Sarah had left the room or if she'd left of her own free will or if someone had taken her.

River knew she'd locked the door, though, just as Luke had advised. She'd locked them in where they would have been safe had they stayed inside, but Sarah had slipped out. If someone had been outside the door and managed to unlock it, River hadn't heard because she'd been sleeping so deeply. So deeply that she hadn't even been aware of Sarah leaving.

Had she gone off to investigate the murders like she'd mentioned earlier that she'd wanted to? Or was she just meeting her teenage cousins?

Knowing where they'd gone last, River had headed straight for the showing room. It was still a crime scene from Justine's murder, though. But maybe that was the draw since Sarah had made that same bold claim River had to Luke, about investigating on her own.

But Sarah hadn't been inside the showing room. She could

have gone back out to the cemetery. Maybe she was even meeting Jackson there. Though after they'd found that body, River doubted that Jackson wanted to ever go back out there. But the dead bodies hadn't bothered Sarah much. Maybe she was really a Gold.

Then River had remembered the other crime scene, not that Gregory Gold I had been murdered in the crematorium oven, but his remains had been disposed of, evidence destroyed. And DNA . . .

That was what this was all about . . .

DNA because, with the Golds, that equaled money.

And power . . .

Someone wanted control of the company so badly that they were willing to kill for it. Over and over again . . .

River had to find Sarah. Seeing that ripped tape across the door to the basement stairwell, she knew where her daughter was. The stairwell was long and dark, and she had to get within just a handful of stairs above her before she saw Sarah. Her daughter was standing over Honora's body at the bottom of the steps, her hands held up because someone, with most of their body concealed with shadows but for their arm, pointed a gun at her.

Fear gripped her so intensely that she lost her breath for a moment, even seemed to lose her heartbeat. Then it resumed at a frantic pace. She was worried that if she rushed forward whoever was holding that gun would fire it. And with as close as the barrel was to Sarah, there was no way they would miss this time. So River steadied her shaking fingers as best she could and quickly sent that text to Luke, praying that he was close or that he would send in those deputies he'd posted outside the building.

She wanted him to be the one who handled the situation, though. He'd saved her before; she wanted him to save her daughter, his niece, this time.

She didn't care about herself.

Sarah was talking. "Hey, we need to get some medical help for Aunt Honora. Let me call for an ambulance."

Pride warmed River. Her daughter was so caring and so smart. Calling for help for Honora would also get help for her. She didn't know that her mother was here, that she'd already sent that text.

So where was Luke? Or one of the deputies?

"You don't want to help her!" The gun barrel pulled back and then shoved closer to Sarah. "You did this!" And there was that thrusting motion with the gun. "You shoved her down the stairs!" And this time Garrett moved out of the shadows with the gun as he moved even closer to Sarah with that barrel. If he fired it now, there was no way that he would miss.

Her heart pounding hard, River slipped down a few more stairs, close enough that she could throw herself onto them. But Sarah was speaking to him yet in that calm voice.

"No, I didn't hurt her," she said. "I just got here, and I found her already lying down here."

"She was meeting you here. This is all your fault . . ." Tears cracked in his voice now and ran unchecked down his face.

"I thought I was meeting Gigi," Sarah said. "She was texting me from Gigi's phone."

"She didn't think you would come if she texted you from her phone."

"Or was there some other reason she didn't want to use her phone?" Sarah asked him. "She didn't want the police to see that she was the one who lured me down here. Because that was what she did, pretending to be someone else like she did to get me out of my room and down here by myself."

"Is that why you pushed her?" Garrett asked.

Had Sarah been defending herself from the trap her aunt must have set for her? Pain gripped River that her daughter had had to fight for her life like that. And take a life in the process . . .

"I swear to you I didn't push her," Sarah vowed. "I just got here. You must have heard me coming. You know that. I'm sorry, Garrett, but she must have fallen."

"No. No," he insisted. "I was coming from the other entrance, from outside, like we'd planned. And I heard her scream. Then I heard footsteps running back up the stairs right after she . . . hit the bottom . . ."

From the look on Honora's face and the amount of blood beneath her head, she must have died pretty quickly. Hopefully painlessly . . .

"If I ran away, why would I have come back?" Sarah asked. "I swear that wasn't me. I didn't hurt her. I don't even know why she wanted to see me. But Garrett, we need to get her help."

"She's dead!" he screamed. "Can't you see? Look at her!" He looked down then, and the barrel of the gun pointed down.

"Garrett," River called out.

Both he and Sarah jumped. Then Sarah turned toward her, her eyes wide. "Get out of here, Mom! Go! Now!"

Panic and pride warred within River. She had to do something, had to try to save her baby, but that her baby was trying so hard to save her, too, had tears rushing to her eyes. She blinked them back to clear her vision and saw now that the gun was pointed directly at her. That was good. She wanted it pointing at her, not her daughter. So she started down a few more steps.

"No, Mom," Sarah cried. "Go, go get help for Aunt Honora. We can help her. Tell Garrett. Tell Garrett you're getting help."

River glanced down at the crumpled body of her half sister. They had never been close; she couldn't remember Honora doing much more than glaring at her. But still, they had been raised as sisters, and River's heart ached with the loss and with pity. Standing closer to her confirmed her earlier thought that

Honora must have died quickly. From her blank stare to all that blood pooled beneath her head, Honora was beyond help.

River felt at the moment that she and Sarah were, too. Sarah had bought some time by talking to her cousin, but nobody had arrived yet. And those deputies were supposed to be close in case they needed them. And they needed them. But they needed Luke even more.

"Garrett, you know Sarah had nothing to do with this," River said. "You heard the running footsteps. Whoever pushed your mother ran away. They just left her here while Sarah and I want to help."

He shook his head as those tears kept streaming down his face along with snot that ran from his nose into his mouth like he was a little boy throwing a tantrum he couldn't control. "No, no, Mom wanted to talk to Sarah."

"Why?" Sarah asked. "What did she want to talk to me about?"

"She wanted to find out if the dead man you found in the cemetery was Russell . . ."

"Who's Russell?" Sarah asked. "And how would I know if he was the dead man?"

"Was the guy you found in the cemetery, was he the man you caught in your trash back in California?" Garrett asked. "He's a private investigator that Mom hired to get something from you and your mother, something that could be used to check your DNA."

So Honora had already known the contents of Gregory Gold I's will before his death.

"Because of that DNA, you know that Sarah and I are no threat," River said. "We have no claim on Gregory's estate."

Garrett snorted, and a snot bubble protruded from one nostril. "You do. You're a Gold. Your daughter is, too. You both have a claim on it. That's why Mom hatched that whole damn plot, using Justine to get to Grandfather, to break up his marriage and make sure she got pregnant . . ."

"Your mother was behind all this?" Sarah asked. And River couldn't tell if she was horrified or awed, probably because she didn't want Garrett with the gun to know. "She set up *your girlfriend* with *your grandfather*?" From the way she nearly gagged as she said it, she was clearly horrified.

Garrett let a little sob slip through his quivering lips. "Justine loved me so much. She would do anything for me, anything for us to get what we wanted . . ."

"But did you want it?" Sarah asked. "Or did your mother?" She glanced down at that body as if Honora could give them any answers.

"Mother was going to take over first," he said, "and then, when I was done with college, I was going to work with her."

"For her," River corrected him. "That was what Honora really wanted. Everybody working for her." All of her brothers and nephews because she'd never felt like she got enough respect from them, but what she'd really wanted was her father's respect and his love. "Is that why she lured Sarah here? She wanted to kill her? No, she wanted *you* to kill her. Is that why you have that gun, Garrett?"

Pointing his job out to him probably wasn't a good idea in case that did remind him to see it through. But maybe he would realize how badly his own mother had been using him and setting him up to take the fall. Or maybe he had already realized it and that was why his mother was at the foot of those stairs. Once he'd figured out that Honora was manipulating and using him, he'd pushed her and he was just lying about hearing footsteps running back up the stairs. Or maybe someone had seen what he'd done and ran back up for help.

But where the hell was it?

If Garrett had killed his own mother, he would have no

compunction about pulling that trigger and killing a cousin he had just met a few days ago.

"My mother wanted me to use this gun to protect myself," he said. "That's why she gave it to me. She said if that was Russell whose body Sarah found out in the woods, then someone had murdered him, and she was scared that one of us would be next." Another big sob slipped out. "And she was right."

"Why would anyone kill her?" Sarah asked. "Or you? What's going on, Garrett?"

He shook his head. "I don't know. She said Russell took it too far, that he knew more than she did, and that he was using it to his advantage somehow. And that if someone killed him, they might think she knew and that they would kill her, too."

"He is dead," Sarah confirmed. "The man that was buried under the leaves was the same man who went through our trash back in Santa Monica."

"She was right . . ." he murmured. "She was right . . ." He gazed wildly around then, as if there was someone lurking yet in the shadows, ready to pounce on him.

And River hoped like hell that there was. But she couldn't be certain and the more they talked to Garrett, the more unhinged he became. She spoke softly and gently when she said, "You have to know, with your mom dead, it's all over now."

He let out a scream then that was so unexpected and primal that River didn't know what would happen. So she jumped down those last few steps, stumbled over Honora's body, and knocked Sarah back against the wall, behind her.

And as a shot rang out, she closed her eyes and braced herself for the impact of the bullet.

Luke squeezed the trigger, firing the shot that dropped Garrett to his knees. With the way Luke's bullet had struck the young man's shoulder, Garrett should have dropped the gun, too. But Garrett still grasped the weapon, even as blood ran down his arm, and he had the barrel pointed right at River now since she had jumped between him and her daughter just as Luke had been afraid that she would.

Luke had hurried as fast as he could through that outside entrance to the basement, but getting through the locked door and down the long, winding hallway had taken too long. During one of the times he'd gone over the house during the past few days, he'd learned about that basement door to the outside. While he'd come in through that way, he'd had a deputy stationed at the other door to the stairwell, ready to storm inside at his say-so.

As he'd started down the hall, he'd heard them talking. Sarah and River must have been doing that to keep Garrett distracted or maybe they had been buying time for Luke to get there, to help them.

They'd been counting on him. But then River must have given up on him, like she'd had to give up on Michael all those years ago when he hadn't met her. And she'd decided to protect her child all by herself. She'd hurled herself between Sarah and that deranged kid. Because of the way Garrett swung the gun toward her, Luke knew he was going to fire.

So he'd fired first.

Garrett screamed again like he had just moments ago. But this time his pain was physical, not emotional. But despite the pain he lurched to his feet again and toward River, who stood between him and her daughter, who was pressed against the stone wall behind her.

"Drop the gun!" Luke yelled. He didn't want to shoot him again, but he would. And this time he would follow his training and go for the kill shot. He wouldn't just try to disarm him.

River must have sensed that and maybe she didn't want her nephew to die because she grabbed for Garrett's weapon, like she could wrest it from him. But even injured, the young man was stronger than she was, because he was bigger and maybe he was even on something. He had seemed pretty erratic every time Luke had seen him. But he'd attributed that to grief. Now he figured it was guilt and probably drugs.

"Drop the gun!" he yelled again. But he was talking to both of them now as they grappled together over it. Too close for him to be certain that he would hit Garrett and not her, especially with the way they kept moving.

"Mom!" Sarah was shrieking.

River couldn't get the gun away from Garrett. She couldn't even get his finger off the trigger because another gunshot rang out. And this time Luke hadn't fired it; it had come from Garrett's gun. Fear gripped him as River and her nephew both dropped to the ground atop the body of Honora.

And Sarah screamed.

Chapter 26

Her child was screaming, and River couldn't remember the last time she had before they'd come to Gold Creek. Growing up, Sarah had never been a screamer like other little girls were. She hadn't even screamed when she'd found the body. But she had been yelling earlier when the deputies had kept her and the other teenagers outside after the shooting. She'd cried then, too, and River couldn't remember the last time that Sarah had cried before they'd come to Gold Creek.

Her daughter was so strong. Even when River could tell that something had been bothering her, Sarah had insisted that it wasn't, that she was fine.

Since she was screaming, she had to be in pain. She had to be hurt.

River roused herself. She had to wake up, had to check on her baby. "Sarah . . ." she murmured. And she blinked her eyes, clearing the darkness from her vision.

"Don't move," another voice said. A deep voice . . .

And everything came rushing back to her. Garrett holding that gun on her daughter . . .

Honora dead . . .

River turned her head and stared straight into the face of her dead half sister. "Where's Garrett?"

And the gun . . .

A low groan emanated from somewhere around River, and she turned her head again to the other direction and saw Garrett lying beside her. While she was on her back, Garrett was on his stomach with Luke pulling his arms behind him, cuffing his wrists. But the kid was bleeding.

Had she hit him when they'd fought over the gun? Or was that from when Luke had fired the first shot? The one that had struck Garrett's shoulder. But he hadn't dropped the gun. He'd kept pointing it toward her and Sarah, and she hadn't wanted Luke to have to kill him. She'd thought he would give up the gun if she grabbed it from him. He was hurt, bleeding . . .

How the hell had he been so damn strong?

"Don't move," Luke said. But he was looking at River instead of Garrett. "You hit your head again. You fell when you were fighting with Garrett over the gun and hit it on one of the concrete steps."

So that was why everything had gone dark. "Am I . . . did I . . . get shot?" she asked.

"Mom!" Sarah was on her knees next to her, touching her head while she leaned over her. "Where does it hurt?"

River couldn't feel anything but that dull ache that had already been in her head since the crash.

"You haven't been shot," Luke said. "But with that head wound, you need to stay still until the paramedics get down here."

She could hear footsteps now, pounding down the stairs. "I'm fine," she said. "As long as you are . . ." She reached up and cupped Sarah's cheek, which was wet with tears. "Are you okay?"

Sarah nodded. "But you shouldn't have done that. You could have gotten killed."

"I had to protect my baby," River murmured.

Usually Sarah would have gotten snippy about River calling her that, but this time she smiled even though the tears flowed faster. "I love you so much, Mom."

"I love you, too, baby," River said.

"I know," Sarah said. "But please, Mom, promise me that you won't do anything like that again."

River smiled. "I won't. It's all over now." It had to be. But even as she said it, she wondered . . .

Some of the things Garrett had said, some of the things just didn't add up completely. But with the grief he'd been going through over Justine and now his mother, he couldn't be thinking clearly.

And with the pounding in her head increasing, neither was River. She would go over everything later. Right now she was just happy that she and her daughter had survived.

Was it all over? Luke had heard River assure her daughter that it was. But he wasn't convinced.

At least she and Sarah were all right. They'd been at the hospital earlier, checked out and then released again. He was still here, waiting for Garrett to wake up from anesthesia. He'd had to have surgery to have that bullet removed from his shoulder. Luke wasn't going to leave until he talked to the kid. He had a lot of questions he needed answered.

Like where was the private investigator's weapon?

The gun that Luke had taken off Garrett hadn't matched the weapon listed on Russell Malewicz's permit. And while it had been fired, in the stairwell when River and Garrett fought over it, Luke didn't think it was the one that had been fired at them in the cemetery. The caliber was too small. It wouldn't have damaged the concrete statues and marble headstones the way the caliber of gun on the private investigator's concealed weapons permit would have, and probably had.

So there was still a gun missing.

And too many other pieces of the puzzle as well.

If Honora had really wanted confirmation that the body in the cemetery was Russell's, then she hadn't been the one who'd killed him. But someone had. While Garrett had been in surgery, the coroner had confirmed to Luke that the PI died from the same high dose of botulinum A toxin that had killed Gregory Gold I and Justine Campbell.

A moan emanated from the bed that Luke sat beside, and then metal rattled as Garrett moved his uninjured arm, trying to free his wrist from the handcuff that shackled him to that bed. "What happened? Where am I?" Garrett murmured.

"You're in the hospital," Luke said.

Garrett glanced around. "Where's my mom?"

In the morgue. But he didn't have to answer because Garrett started crying as he remembered.

"Oh, no, oh, no, nooooo . . ." he moaned as he twisted his body beneath the covers like a child curling into the fetal position.

Luke felt a twinge of pity for him until he remembered how the kid had held that gun on Sarah and River. How he could have killed them. Had that been his intention? Or at least the order he'd been given but hadn't been able to carry out.

And Luke didn't know if that was because of him, because he'd fired that bullet into Garrett's shoulder or if it was because the kid just didn't have the killer instinct himself. In that moment Luke hadn't. He'd killed before, but to do it right then, in front of River and Sarah, he hadn't thought he would need to. He'd thought that hitting the shoulder of the arm that had held the gun would get Garrett to drop his weapon. But the kid hadn't let go of it.

And then River had grabbed for it.

If something had happened to her or to Sarah, it would have been Luke's fault. Because he hadn't wanted to take another life when so many had already been lost.

Luke read him his rights. "You're under arrest, Garrett, for the attempted murder and assault of Sarah Gold and River Gold. And I will also be charging you in the deaths of your grandfather and your girlfriend, Justine Campbell, and Russell Malewicz. I just don't know yet if you were an accomplice, or the one who actually committed the murders."

"No . . ." Garrett shook his head again. "I didn't kill anyone."

"Did your mother then?" Luke asked. "You told Sarah and River that it was her plan."

"Not to kill anyone," Garrett said. "She didn't want anyone to die. She just knew that Grandfather was getting older, and he wasn't going to live as long as he thought he was. And she wanted to be ready."

"She wanted to take over the business."

Garrett nodded. "But she didn't want to kill anyone. And now she's dead . . ." He dissolved into tears again.

Luke waited until the sobbing subsided. Then he asked, "So tell me what the plan was."

Garrett uttered a shaky sigh and lay back against the pillows. He was clearly exhausted and broken and, hopefully, ready to confess to everything to unburden himself. "She had to break up Grandfather and Grandma Fiona to get that twenty-five percent away from her."

So Honora had definitely known about the contents of the will. Maybe her father had told her, but that didn't seem like something Gregory Gold I would talk about when he had had no intention of dying anytime soon or maybe ever.

"Did she get the lawyer to tell her what was in the will?" Luke asked.

Garrett shrugged then flinched. "I don't know, but she knew what was in it. And that she needed somebody else to get that

twenty-five percent. That was why she talked Justine into helping us."

"She used your girlfriend?" Luke had overheard how disgusted Sarah had been over that, and he nearly smiled. His
niece wasn't as sweet as her mother, but he liked that about her.
"And then she killed her when Justine wasn't able to get that
twenty-five percent?"

"Mom loved Justine," Garrett insisted. "She loved Grandfather, too. She didn't want them to die. That ruined the plan.
Grandfather had to live long enough to divorce Fiona and
marry Justine and for them to have that baby. Whoever killed
them didn't want that to happen."

The kid actually made sense. The only way that Honora
would have had controlling interest was if her family had that
twenty-five percent that the current spouse inherited.

Fiona Gold would receive that twenty-five percent now because her husband had died before he was able to divorce her.
And then his mistress had died as well so that there wasn't yet
another biological heir.

Once again that woman, River's mother, Sarah's grandmother, was his prime suspect in the murder of her husband
and his lover. But why would she have killed that private investigator and put her own daughter in danger?

Was there more than one killer?

Or was Fiona Gold just so determined to get what she
wanted that she didn't care who she had to hurt in the process,
even her own daughter and granddaughter?

Fiona walked down from the second story just as they were
carrying up Honora's body from the basement. She'd just made
certain that River and Sarah were settled into their beds and
resting since their return from the hospital. Now that they were
okay, Fiona could focus again on making sure she, and they,
got everything they deserved.

She sighed as the county morticians carried her stepdaughter's body out, zipped in a black bag, through the double doors of the lobby. Honora had no chance anymore of getting everything she'd wanted, that she'd thought she needed.

Fiona had figured out Honora's plan a while ago. Once Colson had admitted to sharing the contents of the will with his former lover, Fiona had known that Gregory's oldest daughter had hatched a plan to take over Gold Memorial Gardens and Funeral Services.

She'd even admired her ambition despite how her plan affected Fiona. Or how it would have affected Fiona had it worked. But Honora was dead now, her body being loaded into the back of the coroner's van that was parked at the end of the covered portico.

They'd made a lot of trips out here, taking bodies away when usually this was where they brought them, to the embalmer and to Fiona. Fiona wasn't sure why the sheriff was wasting his time with an autopsy on Honora. Clearly, her head had struck the concrete so hard that the back of it had smashed like the pumpkins that teenagers threw at mailboxes and sometimes against the headstones in the cemetery around Halloween.

Fixing the damage to Honora's corpse was going to be a challenge. One that Fiona had met before. She knew how to camouflage a smashed skull, how to reshape the missing section with mesh and plaster and then weave in fake hair with the real hair to cover the plaster and make the head look like its normal shape again. Then she would work on her face, covering the bruises with concealer before evening out the rest of Honora's blotchy skin tone, and she would make Honora more beautiful than she had ever been alive.

Too bad Honora hadn't had more beauty to go with all that ambition. Or more brains. Obviously, she hadn't been smart enough or she wouldn't be getting hauled off in that van. She would have been able to pull off her plan. But while Honora had gotten some information out of Colson before he'd dumped her, she hadn't learned everything. She didn't know all the secrets that Fiona knew.

And that Fiona intended to use to her advantage. And to River's and Sarah's, too. Now that they were home, she had to keep them here, and she had to keep them safe.

Chapter 27

River was gathered around another long table, but this was in the room where survivors came to make the funeral arrangements for their departed loved ones. River certainly felt like a survivor after everything she'd been through the past few days. The crash, being shot at, fighting with Garrett for her daughter's life. Honora losing hers just the night before. Nobody was reaching for any of the tissues, though. Nobody was crying over making arrangements for Honora.

Not even her mother . . .

Linda was almost unusually silent. Maybe she'd taken something that had calmed her down.

Noah sat near River, and she reached out and touched his arm. "I'm sorry about your sister," she said.

Noah nodded. "Your sister, too," he said. "And you were probably as close to her as I was. And now I feel like I never knew her at all. I swear I had no idea about any of this, River."

She patted his arm again. "I know."

Maybe Garrett would have been crying, like he had last night, if he'd been there. He was still in the hospital, though.

Since his injury was relatively minor, he would be released soon but into the sheriff's custody. Hopefully, he would be allowed out on bail for his mother's funeral because River believed that Garrett hadn't had anything to do with the murders. If he had, he would have shot her or Sarah, but he hadn't.

She wasn't certain his mother had been behind the other murders, either. But she also wasn't certain that her own mother hadn't been.

Fiona had the greatest motive for killing Gregory before he could divorce her and marry Justine. But even with keeping that twenty-five percent and combining that with River's and Sarah's shares, she didn't have enough to take control away from Carolyn and her sons and children if they all banded together. And the old woman was smirking now like she knew it.

A knock drew everyone's attention to the doorway where Sheriff Luke Sebastian stood. The circles beneath his eyes were so dark he looked like he'd been punched in the face, or like he hadn't slept for days. He probably hadn't shaved for days, either, because there was quite a bit of stubble on his jaw, some of it gray.

River felt as if the events of the past week had aged her, and Luke looked like they had aged him, too. But he was still handsome, maybe even more so with the experience he carried now. That was the thing River's father hadn't understood, that there was actual beauty in aging. But maybe he hadn't been afraid of getting older as much as he'd been afraid of dying.

"Sheriff, what are you doing here?" Gregory II asked. "Isn't it all over with Honora's death?"

Luke held up a handful of packets of swabs and plastic containers with labels on them. "It's time for that DNA testing."

Even though she was sitting and Luke was standing, Carolyn somehow stared down her nose at the sheriff as she condescendingly told him, "That's not necessary since you have your murderer in the morgue, as my son said. And you're interrupting as we're planning her funeral now."

Fiona smiled. "It doesn't matter who the killer was. You still have to abide by the stipulations of the will in order to inherit."

"She's right," Luke said. "Colson Howard made that clear the other night when he read the terms of the will."

"This is not the time or place for you to be pushing this agenda," Gregory II insisted. "And as the Gold in charge now, I am ordering you to leave, Sheriff."

"But you're not the Gold in charge," Fiona said, and she was the one smirking now.

"Lawrence's and his family's shares give us controlling interest," Carolyn said snootily with a glance down the table at her younger son.

Lawrence's children, Wynn and Taylor, weren't even here. They had even less of an interest in Gold Memorial Gardens and Funeral Services than River had.

"That's not what I meant," Fiona said with a pointed stare at the stepson who was at least a decade older than she was. "You're not the *Gold* in charge, Gregory, and you know it." She turned toward Carolyn, and she was definitely smirking now. "And you know, Carolyn, and you thought your former husband had no idea . . ." She chuckled and shook her head and gave the old woman an almost pitying glance.

"Mom, what are you talking about?" River asked uneasily as Carolyn's and Gregory II's faces flushed.

Were they embarrassed or angry?

While Carolyn's shoulders sagged a bit, Gregory II stiffened and reached inside the briefcase he'd left partially open on the table. And he pulled out a gun, one with a much longer barrel than the one Garrett had the night before.

River shuddered at the sight of yet another weapon. "What . . . what's going on?"

"Get down!" Luke shouted as he dropped the packet of swabs and pulled his weapon.

Gregory swung that long barrel toward him and fired. The doorjamb splintered near where Luke's head had been.

River screamed, and other screams echoed hers.

"Don't do this!" Holly, Gregory's wife, said. "Please don't do this. You don't have to. You're not a real Gold, but I made certain that our son is biologically a Gold. Gregory the third is a Gold, and so are his kids. We're all right. Even without yours, we will still have enough shares."

"Oh, my God!" Gregory said, and all the color drained from his face. "I told you all of that in confidence."

"I know, and I made sure that it wouldn't hurt us," Holly said, and now she had the Gold smugness.

"You slept with my father? And you think that wouldn't hurt us? You bitch!" Then he turned that gun toward her. And another shot rang out.

Fists pummeled Luke, trying to knock him down. Trying to hurt him. But he was unscathed. The bullet that Gregory II had fired had just missed him as he'd ducked down in that doorway.

Luke hadn't missed when he'd fired back. And after what had happened with Garrett the night before, he hadn't taken any chances. If Gregory had hit someone with the gun he'd taken off the private investigator, that bullet would have definitely killed the person he shot. So Luke had had no choice. He'd taken the kill shot. And then he'd taken the weapon from Gregory II's limp hand. The older man lay dead on the floor with so much blood and brain matter on the wall behind him that bile rose up the back of Luke's throat.

Carolyn had launched herself at Luke right after it happened, pounding her shaking fists on his chest and shoulders.

But he barely felt her blows. Nevertheless someone pulled her off him.

"Carolyn, calm down," Fiona said, as she held the older woman's thin shoulders. "Don't make me slap some sense into you. I might enjoy it too much."

"You bitch!" Carolyn shrieked. And now she curled those trembling hands around Fiona's throat.

Luke holstered his weapon and handed Gregory's to the deputy who suddenly rushed into the room. Then he pulled Carolyn off Fiona. Instead of coughing or sputtering, Fiona laughed at her attacker.

"You sad old woman," Fiona said. "That's what Gregory always called you. Sad and old . . ."

Carolyn tried to wrest away from Luke's hold. No doubt she wanted to slap Fiona, and Luke didn't entirely blame her.

"Mom, don't make it worse," River said. "This . . . this is all so . . . sad . . ."

But Fiona Gold didn't look sad at all. In fact, she looked triumphant, like this was what she'd wanted. Maybe even what she'd planned.

"I still have a lot of questions," Luke warned her.

Fiona nodded. "I'm sure Carolyn was well aware of what her son was doing. She probably ordered him to kill my husband and that poor girl and even his own sister." She sighed and shook her head. "You're right, River, this is all so very sad."

Her daughter looked at her then, blinked, and looked at her again. And Luke knew he wasn't the only one who had questions.

Now she had another skull to repair thanks to the sheriff, and this one would be even more of a challenge. Usually in deaths like this, other people wouldn't even attempt the reconstruction necessary for an open casket showing. But Fiona had no doubt she could handle the challenge. Thanks to the sheriff,

Fiona also caught that look her daughter just shot at her. The look of doubt.

Like she wondered what Fiona was up to, or what she'd done.

And that look struck her like the bullet had struck Gregory. She didn't want River to keep looking at her like that, to keep wondering.

So she cleared her throat and spoke aloud to the entire room. "Gregory always knew that Carolyn's older child wasn't his, that she was already pregnant when they met. When she was the one who first started the rumor that River wasn't his child, he laughed at the irony of her accusing me of doing what she'd done."

Carolyn shook her head. "That's not true. He didn't know. He wouldn't have married me if he had . . ."

Fiona sighed. "He didn't figure it out until after you were already married. And then Gregory, being Gregory, was too proud to admit that you fooled him. So he just accepted the boy as his kid, but he decided not to write up his will the way that his father had. The way that Carolyn and Gregory II probably thought he had, leaving everything to the oldest son. No, *my* Gregory made damn certain that no one would inherit, other than current and former spouses, unless they proved they had Gold DNA." She bent down and picked up the swab packets that the sheriff had dropped onto the floor. She wanted no doubts ever again about River's paternity. "So you will all have to submit a sample of your DNA in order to inherit."

"You're not the executor of his estate," Linda said with a glare.

No. But Fiona was screwing him. She wasn't about to admit to her affair with Colson Howard now, though. Not after the way River had already looked at her.

"I will be in charge, though," Fiona said. "I think we all realize that. And we all know that Gregory would not want to leave this family floundering like this. He would want the rightful person to step up and take over."

Linda snorted. "And of course you think that's you . . ."

Fiona shook her head. "No. I know my lane. Lawrence is the one who should be running the company." With her pulling his strings . . . "He's the one who works the hardest and makes sure that the Gold standard is met for every funeral we hold."

Lawrence sucked in a breath and choked on his surprise.

He was really very sweet. And he cared nearly as much about the business as Fiona did. "You've been your father's right hand all these years, Lawrence. You were the one taking care of business while Gregory II and Honora were trying to fight for control of the company. He noticed, Lawrence. He knew your value."

Tears filled Lawrence's eyes and he nodded. "I would be honored," he said.

"And you will be appreciated," Fiona said. "I intend to stick to what I do best, but . . ." She turned toward River now. "I'm going to need a little help . . ."

River shook her head. "No, Mom . . ."

"We'll talk about it later," Fiona said.

But she had no intention of letting her daughter run away again. Not when Fiona had finally gotten her everything she deserved.

Chapter 28

Sarah was glad that Jackson had decided to sit this funeral out. It was a triple one. The urn of Sarah's grandfather's ashes sat on something like a raised throne in the middle of two caskets, one holding the body of his son and the other, the body of his daughter. Gregory II had killed his father, and he had probably killed his sister unless he'd just accidentally knocked her down the stairs.

That image of her lying at the bottom of the concrete steps, all that blood and gunk leaking out the back of her broken head, made Sarah shudder in revulsion.

But as Sarah neared the casket and saw how beautiful Honora looked, how peaceful instead of frightened, she wondered if she had dreamed that entire thing. If it had just been a nightmare . . .

In the other casket lay Gregory Gold II or whatever his real last name might have been. And he looked like he always did even though the room where he'd died was still sealed off. Of course, she and Toby and Gigi had broken that seal to check it out, wanting all the gory details.

The way they stood in front of that casket now, crying, it probably would have been better if they'd skipped the details. "I'm sorry about your grandfather."

"He really wasn't," Toby said. "So I don't know why I'm . . ." He hiccupped.

And Gigi laughed, then sobbed harder as she nodded. "I know. He's not but he was . . . you know . . ."

Sarah's mom had explained it all to them. That while Gregory II wasn't biologically a Gold, Gregory III was. His mom, Gregory II's wife, had slept with her father-in-law to make sure that her kid was a Gold. So Gigi and Toby were Golds, but they weren't biologically related to the man in the casket. The man they'd thought was their great-grandfather had actually been their grandfather, just like he'd been Sarah's.

Sarah wrapped an arm around each of her cousins and said, "Your family is fucked up."

Toby laughed now. "God, I love what a bitch you are."

"Me too," Gigi said as she hugged her hard. "And it's your family, too. You are definitely one of the *Ghoul* family."

Sarah's mom had shared how much she'd hated when kids had called her that back in school. But Gigi made it sound like a compliment, and to Sarah it was.

Tears filled her cousin's dark eyes. "You're not really going to go back to Santa Monica, are you?" Gigi asked. "I don't want you to leave. And I know Jackson doesn't, either."

The thought of going back made Sarah feel sicker than when she'd found Honora's body or when she and Gigi and Toby had gotten the gory details in the arrangement room.

She didn't want to leave, either. But after everything Mom had been through here, Sarah couldn't ask her to stay. She couldn't be that selfish when her mom had been so selfless that she would have willingly given up her life for Sarah's.

*   *   *

River had been so worried about her daughter, but as she watched her with her cousins, warmth of love and pride flooded her. Sarah was being strong and supportive for them. And for her.

She was such a good girl. A good human.

"You did so well," her mother said to River, as she slid her arm around her shoulders. "I'm so proud of you."

River smiled. But then she turned and saw that her mother was staring at the bodies, not at her granddaughter. "I can't believe I let you talk me into helping you." Her stomach flipped a little now, but it had been worse when she'd first stepped inside that cold room with the metal tables and all the tools. And the bodies . . .

Those destroyed bodies.

"You know now that it's more work than it seems," Fiona said with pride, "that it really takes two sometimes."

"And Warner would have happily helped you," River said. The embalmer was clearly besotted with Fiona, like the lawyer was and even Lawrence now. Her mother's vote of confidence in him had made him visible, had given him the confidence he'd been lacking.

And damn it, she'd done the same thing with River, charming and praising her throughout the gory process. To her mother it was a calling and an honor, to make the dead beautiful again, to give their mourners that perfect memory of them, that closure. And during that process, which had been so much work, River had come to understand and respect Fiona. She truly loved what she did, and River understood now how important it was, how much it could help people and ease their suffering during the most horrible moments of their lives.

"You did more than help," Fiona said. "You're a natural just like I was when I first started."

The three older women rushed forward then, and River wouldn't have been surprised to learn that her mother had somehow cued them. "Honora never looked so beautiful," one of them praised.

"Nor has Gregory II ever looked as handsome."

"I heard how badly the bodies were damaged," the third remarked with almost malicious delight. "You really worked miracles."

"Look, it's such a comfort to his poor mother."

Carolyn had parked herself near her elder son's casket. Like Garrett she had a monitor on her ankle that had been the terms of their release on bail. Garrett had been charged with threatening River and Sarah with a deadly weapon while Carolyn had been charged as an accessory to the murder of her former husband and his lover and that private investigator. While Honora had hired him, he must have been blackmailing Gregory II when he'd learned that he wasn't really a Gold.

"I'm not sure anyone can comfort her," Fiona remarked, and that little smirk was back on her mouth.

Maybe she was entitled to a little enjoyment of Carolyn's situation after the way the woman had treated her all these years. River had always thought that Fiona should have left like River had, but clearly she loved what she did here, her work, and now she was loving being the matriarch of the Gold clan.

While River still wanted to leave . . .

But could she take her daughter away from her cousins? Away from the place she obviously felt as if she finally fit? Like Fiona, Sarah was also in her element here.

"I hope you're going to stay, dear," one of the ladies said. "You really are a comfort to your mother."

"She is," Fiona agreed with a smile.

"Family should always come first," the most morbid of the trio surprisingly commented. Then she emitted a slightly wistful sigh. "My father always put his work first, so I never knew him that well."

"I'm sorry," River said sympathetically.

"I'm sure you can relate more than anyone else probably can," the woman replied. "Your father was the undertaker and mine was the grave digger . . ."

"You were, you are, your father was . . ." River stammered, unable to form a coherent thought as she remembered what she'd seen that night she'd run away, the night Michael had been supposed to meet her but never had.

"My father was Lyle McGinty, who worked here for so many years." The woman laughed and patted her blue hair. "I know. People always seem so shocked when I tell them he was my father. But he really didn't die that long ago. And some don't think he's even really gone . . ."

"What about you?" River asked. "Do you think his ghost walks around the cemetery at night?"

The woman nodded. "I don't think. I know. I've seen him." She patted River's hand. "And I think you have, too."

River didn't want to believe that ghosts were real, and she definitely didn't want to believe that she'd actually seen one.

Luke wasn't sure why he'd wanted to come to the funeral. It wasn't as if he'd been close to either of the deceased Golds. Or really to any of them . . . dead or alive. He and Noah had been friends in high school, but they hadn't kept in touch much when Luke left for boot camp. And since his return, they'd only gone fishing a few times.

Then he saw River, and he knew that she was why he'd come here. To make sure that she was all right.

She and Sarah.

Sarah was with her teenage cousins. And it was clear that she was being sweet and supportive of them as they alternated between laughing and crying. Luke would have thought once that she'd inherited that from her father. But knowing how Michael had abandoned River and their baby, he knew now that she'd inherited that sweet and supportive nature from her mother.

And maybe that snark . . .

She turned toward him and gave him a look between a smile and a scowl, then she rolled her eyes at him. That snark probably came from him. She was a character, and he wanted to get to know her better.

But would he have the chance? Or were she and her mother and great-grandmother heading back to Santa Monica as soon as the funerals were over?

Her great-grandmother was with Dr. Jeffries, clearly flirting with him as she leaned against him and smiled up at him. And Dr. Jeffries smiled back at her as if he couldn't believe his good fortune. Luke wished him luck. Mabel Hawthorne was more like her daughter than her granddaughter or great-granddaughter.

And Luke didn't trust Fiona.

While he'd arrested Carolyn, he wasn't certain how much she'd been involved with her son's plan. Or even if her son had killed everyone who had died . . .

If only he hadn't had to kill him . . .

If only he'd had the chance to question him first . . .

But Gregory Gold II was dead even though he didn't look like it. He just looked as if he was sleeping. Whatever else she was, Fiona was damn good at her job. Because Luke knew all too well what Gregory's body had looked like, what his head . . .

That image had haunted him the past couple of nights. He'd thought when he moved home to Gold Creek that he wouldn't have to kill again. The former sheriff had assured him that he'd never even drawn his weapon in the all the years he'd served Gold County.

Unfortunately, Luke would not be able to tell his successor the same. But he still wasn't ready to give up the job or on Gold Creek. Would he have to give up on River, though?

She turned away from the three old ladies she'd been talking to and nearly collided with him. He caught her shoulders in his hands and steadied her. She stared up at him, her blue eyes vivid in her pale face. "Are you okay?" he asked.

She drew in a shaky breath and nodded.

"We were just talking about the grave digger's ghost," one of the women remarked as she walked past them.

"You believe in that old legend?" Luke asked River.

She shrugged, dislodging his hands. "I didn't . . . but that . . . she's Lyle McGinty's daughter . . ."

He let out a soft whistle. "Oh, I didn't know that . . ."

"She just unsettled me a bit." She smiled then. "I shouldn't have let her get to me."

River got to him. Something about her had gotten under his skin. Before he'd even met her, she'd unsettled him. He'd thought then that she was bad for his brother. But now . . .

He realized there was nothing bad about River Gold. "When are you and Sarah leaving?" he asked, the question coming out gruffly because his throat was suddenly raw.

"Is this you ordering me out of town like some old-timey western lawman?" she asked with a teasing smile.

"If I was going to order you to do anything, I would—"

Someone suddenly screamed. And Luke's stomach muscles tightened with dread. He turned to find Holly Gold kneeling beside her mother-in-law, who'd suddenly dropped to the floor. The older woman was completely still, her body stiff and her eyes closed. "She's dead!" Holly shrieked. "She's dead!"

Luke nearly groaned. Not again.

He rushed forward, dropping down next to Carolyn just as Dr. Jeffries did. The older man checked her pulse and shook his head. "She is gone, Sheriff. And I know that she has a do not resuscitate order in place. She gave me a copy some time ago, after her Parkinson's diagnosis."

Luke stared down at the wrist the doctor had just checked for a pulse. That hand was tightly clenched around something that poked out and looked unsettlingly familiar. A syringe . . .

He opened her hand and confirmed his suspicion. But he couldn't tell if the syringe was empty because a sheet of paper was wrapped around it. He unrolled the stationery with the Gold watermark on the paper, and he tried to read the shaky handwriting.

It was worse than Jackson's.

I cannot live without my son. I cannot live with my guilt. This was all my fault. I killed Gregory and that stupid girl and that blackmailing private investigator. I thought we could use Lawrence's DNA and pass it off as Gregory's somehow, but now my favorite child is gone. And all my hopes and dreams are gone, too.

Luke felt a pang of sympathy for Lawrence. His mother didn't want to live without her golden child. And she'd even gone to her grave trying to absolve him of his guilt.

Luke really didn't believe she was capable of doing everything she'd claimed. She wasn't as young and strong as Fiona Gold. He glanced at her now. But there was no look of triumph on her face this time.

She'd already won.

And maybe that was really why Carolyn had killed herself. Because she knew it was over . . .

And now Luke believed it was, too.

Chapter 29

What had Luke been about to order her to do before Carolyn Gold had dropped dead? River wanted to know. And she'd sent him a text to meet her to talk about it.

But there was someone she needed to talk to first.

Once the bedroom door closed behind them, Sarah turned to her and asked, almost eagerly, "Are we going to stay for this funeral, too?"

"Do you want to stay?" River asked.

Sarah nodded.

"Are you turning into a funeral groupie?"

Sarah smiled. "Yeah, I'm thinking of dyeing my hair blue, too. But seriously, she was Gigi and Toby's great-grandmother. Right? It was just the grandfather that was different than they thought. I can't keep track of all the DNA stuff."

DNA didn't necessarily make people family. Noah hadn't been close to his sister, not like Luke was to Jackson. She'd seen the love he had for the child he was raising, the same love the Sebastians had had for Michael and still had for Luke. "Carolyn actually isn't biologically related to Gigi and Toby. Her son wasn't their grandfather. Like I tried to explain earlier, you and Gigi and Toby actually had the same grandfather. My father."

Sarah nodded. "So we're even closer cousins then. I really think we should be here for them anyway since Carolyn was still like their step-grandmother or something."

"We will stay for the funeral," River said. "But after that, do you want to stay?"

Sarah froze for a second as her dark eyes widened with hope. "Are you seriously considering it?"

River nodded. "I've never seen you as happy as you are here. Maybe I should be a little concerned since there have been so many murders and deaths and . . ." She shuddered, but she smiled as she did to let her daughter know that she was just kidding. "I'm actually really proud of how strong you've been."

"This place has made me stronger," Sarah said. And she smiled widely for a moment until the smile turned into a frown, and she shook her head. "But we can't stay."

"Why not?" River asked. "I thought you wanted to."

"I do," Sarah admitted. "But I know this place makes you miserable, Mom. You couldn't wait to run away from it, and you never wanted to come back."

River nodded. "That's true, but maybe I should have stayed. It's like you said, this place makes you stronger." Her mother was certainly stronger than River had ever realized.

But now she didn't have to worry about Fiona's guilt or innocence or her lies or truth. It was all over now. And they could really leave . . . if they wanted.

"I think GG Mabel will stay, too," Sarah said. "She and Dr. Jeffries are really hitting it off."

"Do you think we should have warned him?" River asked, but she was only kidding. Sort of . . .

"Well, he won't have to worry about security," Sarah said. "She'll make sure nobody goes through his trash."

River hugged her daughter. "You are so amazing." And she

was even more amazing here. "I want to stay." She knew it was what was best for her child.

Sarah hugged her back once before pulling away. But she wasn't rejecting River's affection this time like she used to. She was staring up at her, her dark eyes narrowed. "I will only do this if you really want to stay," she said. "I don't want you making any more sacrifices for me."

"What do you mean?"

"You tried to take a bullet for me the other night, Mom," Sarah said.

"You're my baby."

"But I'm not a baby anymore," Sarah said. "And you have to stop living your life like I am."

"What do you mean?" River asked again, and this time she really didn't know.

"You don't date. You barely go out for anything but work and your gross green smoothies," Sarah said. "Your world revolves around me, and I really want you to have a world of your own."

River sucked in a breath, but she had to acknowledge that her daughter was right. "I'm sorry. I didn't realize I'd put that much pressure on you."

Sarah shrugged. "It's okay. I didn't have a world either except the one inside my head. Now I do . . ."

"Here," River finished for her. "We are definitely staying."

Sarah hugged her again. But River was the one who pulled back now as she felt her phone vibrate. She pulled it out and checked the screen. Then she glanced out the window at the light moving through the cemetery.

Sarah ran to the window and peered out. "Is that the grave digger? I thought I saw him once . . ."

"Me too," River admitted. "But that's not the grave digger. That's Luke."

"Ahhhh . . ." Sarah murmured. "Are you meeting him?"

River nodded. "Is that a problem?"

"Because he's my uncle?" Sarah asked. "No. My dad had his chance and let you down. I don't think Luke will."

River was hoping the same thing. "I guess I'll take that chance." Luke Sebastian was worth the risk.

Luke had never been one of the kids who'd hung out in the cemetery trying to catch a glimpse of the grave digger. Or at least using that as an excuse to party here.

Maybe that was why he'd never hung out here because—he knew what excessive partying led to . . .

Accidents.

Disappointment.

Death.

It was all around him. Lying in the graves he passed as he headed toward the grave digger's. And one seemed to happen just about every time he came here.

So he was taking a chance coming back. But when River had sent him that text—**I need to talk to you. Tonight? Our spot?**—he hadn't dared to tell her no because what if she was leaving already? Carolyn wasn't really related to her. She wouldn't have to stay for her funeral.

That family had been through so much that even Luke felt a little sorry for them. At least for Noah and Sarah and River.

But he felt more than pity for River.

"Hey," a soft voice whispered.

And he turned to find her standing behind him. The moonlight slipped through the clouds and shimmered in her hair, making it shine like gold. She was so beautiful.

"Hey . . ." he whispered back, his throat suddenly very dry.

She smiled at him then as if just that word had been a compliment. Then she asked, "What were you going to order me to do?"

"I wasn't going to order you to do anything," he said. She'd already thought of him as a jerk for a long time. Maybe she still did.

She smiled. "I know. But you said that if you could . . . and then Carolyn dropped dead."

"Yeah, you Golds really know how to keep the business going."

She shuddered. "Yeah, a little too well, but you didn't answer my question." She stepped closer to him, close enough that she could touch him. And she ran her fingertips along his jaw.

"Stay . . ." he said. And he lowered his head and kissed her gently, before pulling back and repeating, "Stay . . ."

She giggled. "Does sound a little like you're ordering a dog around, but I guess I have been a bitch to you."

"No," he said. "I was the one who misjudged you. And I swear I'm not ordering you to do anything," he said. "I know that you have every reason to leave."

"But I'm starting to think I have more reasons to stay," she said. And she kissed him back, softly, before pulling away.

His heart was beating fast but it felt lighter. He felt lighter. And he couldn't keep the smile from his mouth. "What are those reasons?"

"Sarah, she's thriving here despite all the tragedies . . ."

"Jackson will love it if she stays," Luke said. "So would I. I'd like to get to know my niece. But is she your only reason?" And now his heart beat even faster, with anticipation.

She shook her head. "No . . ."

He waited, his breath starting to hurt his chest as he held it in.

"I want to find Michael," she said.

He nodded.

"Not because I'm in love with him or anything," she said. "I loved him as a friend, but I'm not sure I was ever in love. But I care about him. And he's Sarah's father and I want to know what happened to him." She tensed though as if dreading what that was.

Luke dreaded finding out what that was, too, because he was pretty certain that nothing good had happened to his brother.

But he nodded and admitted, "I want to find him, too." He'd already started looking but hadn't had any success yet.

"But you're another reason I want to stay," she said. "I want to see what this is between us . . ."

That tightness in his chest eased now, and he smiled. "Good."

"Yeah, I think it might be good," she said.

That wasn't what he meant, but from the twinkle in her eyes, he suspected she knew it. Then he noticed another twinkle. It wasn't a star. Or the moon that suddenly disappeared behind those clouds again. It was a light.

She turned and released a shaky breath. "You see it, too?" she whispered.

"Yes . . ." But he wasn't sure what he was seeing. He refused to believe that it was a ghost.

The grave digger was going to have to be more careful now, or he might become more than a legend. The sheriff was spending entirely too much time around here. Because of her, because she was back.

She was all grown up now. Not the child he'd seen that night all those years ago. The night he'd taken her boyfriend, just as he'd taken other boyfriends of other hapless young girls over the years.

River had been hapless. And it seemed as if her daughter was as well . . . as was that boy who'd come out here with her. Maybe he would be the one who disappeared next . . .

Epilogue

16 years earlier . . .

Lyle McGinty, 1899–1990.

Michael's flashlight beam illuminated the engraving on the tombstone of the grave digger. This was where he and River had agreed to meet. But he was early.

River had told him midnight because she figured everyone would be asleep in the house by then and she could sneak out with her bag without anyone catching her. It was already dark with not even a sliver of moon or a star burning in the black sky that seemed to hang low over the cemetery. The wind whistled, sending leaves rustling across the ground, and the fountains gurgled water out of the concrete swans' mouths. Michael was so damn excited to go, to start their life together, that he hadn't been able to wait any longer. Fear also coursed through him, making his hands shake. Or maybe that was the withdrawals . . .

His mom used to shake like that. That was how she'd probably crashed the car and injured Luke when he was a toddler and Michael was a baby. Either the booze or the drugs or the withdrawals . . .

Michael wasn't going to be like her, though. He wasn't going to be an addict, too. He was going to be a father and a husband. Luke was wrong. Keeping the baby wasn't a mistake. It wasn't selfish . . . though he felt a little sick at the thought that it could be. That the baby might be better off with someone else . . .

Just like River would be better off with someone else. Michael was a mess, just like his mother had been. He hadn't gotten away as early as Luke had. He'd spent too much time with her, was too much like her.

But for River and their baby, he would be a better man. He would be a man instead of the scared little boy he felt like so often. A sound rose above the rush of the wind and the rustle of the leaves and the gurgle of the fountains.

That strange scraping sound he and River sometimes heard when they were out here. Like metal striking a rock.

He swung around, away from the tombstone. The clouds shifted overhead, letting some moonlight streak through to illuminate the silhouette of the person standing behind him. He let out the breath he held with relief. "Oh, it's you . . ."

"Who did you think it was? The grave digger?"

Michael laughed, but without any real humor. This wasn't funny. Scaring someone wasn't funny, and Michael was scared, nerves skittering around in his stomach. "Uh, I'm waiting for someone . . ." But he didn't dare say who that was.

"River." The person stated it with absolute certainty.

Had River sent them here instead to turn Michael away? To tell him that she'd changed her mind? Maybe she'd decided not to keep the baby after all. Hurting, he could only nod in confirmation.

"You found the grave digger instead."

Michael groaned now. "This isn't funny, you know." It was a sick joke, especially since the person held a shovel. "What the hell are you doing?" With that shovel? With gloves, with the

way they were dressed . . . as if they didn't want anyone to rec-
ognize them . . .

Or they wanted people to think they were someone else . . .

Something else. A ghost.

"It's you . . ." He suddenly realized. "Making that noise,
walking around here at night . . ."

That shovel started to rise.

Michael stumbled back, tripped over the tombstone behind
him, and fell onto his back on the grass and the grave. The air
left his lungs for a moment. Or he would have yelled. Or at
least called out for her . . .

River. He couldn't leave her like this. He couldn't leave their
child.

Before he could move, that shovel swung, the blade coming
down hard on his head. Then he could hear and see nothing
else, nothing ever again.

Visit our website at
KensingtonBooks.com
to sign up for our newsletters, read
more from your favorite authors, see
books by series, view reading group
guides, and more!

Become a Part of Our
Between the Chapters Book Club
Community and Join the Conversation

Submit your book review for a chance to win exclusive
Between the Chapters swag you can't get anywhere else!
https://www.kensingtonbooks.com/pages/review/